Also by the author:

<u>Poetry</u>

For Toby, Everything for Toby (1997) Wing & The Wheel Press

Ten Poets (1999) editor, only Wing & The Wheel Press

Piecework (2000) Wing & The Wheel Press

Chin-Chin in Eden (2003) Still Waters Press

Dark on Purpose (2004) Little Poem Press

The Hole in Sleep (2006) Wood Works Press

The Agoraphobe's Pandiculations (2006) Little Poem Press

The Lita Conversation (2006) Southern Hum

The Chloe Poems (2007) Maverick Duck Press

Some Identity Problems (2007) Foothills Publishing

Pictures from Lang and Fellini (2007) Sheltering Pines Press

Grit (2008) Amsterdam Press

The Tense Past (2010) Flutter Press

Before the Great Troubling (2011) Unbound Content

Mitmensch (2011) Folded Word Press

The Heart is Open (2011) Right Hand Pointing

To Writing You (2012) Origami Poems Project

Our Locust Years (2013) Unbound Content

My Father is Still Dying (2013) Flutter Press

Body (2013) Chapbook Journal

The Catastrophe of my Personality (2014) Blue Hour Press

The Sky Needs More Work (2014) Upper Rubber Boot Books

The Medicament Predicament (2015) Redneck Press

Stone (2015) Origami Poems (chapbook)

Opaque Melodies that Would Bug Most People (2015) After the Pause
  Books

Mountain (2015) Fairfield Press

Home (2016) Fairfield Press

Among the Mensans (Iris Press) 2017

River (Fairfield Press) 2018

Madstones (BlazeVOX Books) 2018

Alphabeticon (Staring Problem Press) 2019

Dog (Fairfield Press) 2019

Prose

Talk: A Novel in Dialogue (2002) Livingston Press
We Are Billion-Year-Old Carbon (2005) Livingston Press
Short Story and Other Short Stories (2006) Parallel Press
Following Richard Brautigan (chapbook) (2006) Plan B Press
Publisher (2007) Writers Write Journal Press
Listen: 29 Short Conversations (2009) Brown Paper Press
The Ballad of the Two Tom Mores (2010) Bronx River Press
Following Richard Brautigan (novel) (2010) Livingston Press
Notes toward the Story and Other Stories (2011) Aqueous Books
Gardner Remembers (2011) Pocketful of Scoundrel
I'll Give You Something to Cry About (2011) Queen's Ferry Press
Frank Comma and the Time-Slip (2012) Wapshott Press
The Travels of Cocoa Poem Lorry (2013) Leaf Garden Press
Diddy-Wah-Diddy: A Beale Street Suite (2013) Ampersand Press
As a Child: Stories (2014) MadHat Press
Memphis Movie (2015) Soft Skull Press
Robert Walker (2016) Livingston Press
Camel's Bastard Son (2019) Cabal Books
The Adventures of Camel Jeremy Eros (2020) Cervena Barva Press

The Diminishment
of Charlie Cain

Corey Mesler

Livingston Press
The University of West Alabama

Library of Congress Control Number 2021930435

Typesetting and page layout: Joe Taylor
Proofreading: Hayley Jacobs, Parker Marquez

Cover Layout: Joe Taylor
Cover Artwork: Jeane Umbreit
Author photo: Cheryl Mesler

For my Cheryl, who keeps me here.

As Huck Finn said, "I don't want no better book than what your face is."

"The struggle to exist, to not disappear in this moment, is the advancing root of the struggle to exist throughout the whole passage of time. We need to help each other in this struggle. You by asking, I by struggling to respond. This is the law of love, which rules the universe."
—Jacob Needleman

ONE

"There is, of course, an ordinary medicine, an everyday medicine, humdrum, prosaic, a medicine for stubbed toes, quinsies, bunions and boils; but all of us entertain the idea of another sort of medicine, of a wholly different kind: something deeper, older, extraordinary, almost sacred, which will restore to us our lost health and wholeness and give us a sense of perfect well-being."
—Oliver Sacks

Charlie Cain had a pain. It was in the lower right quadrant of his back. He thought perhaps his kidneys were there. Or gall bladder. Or liver. The truth is that he had no idea what was there. Charlie Cain was not a hypochondriac but he was not *not* a hypochondriac.

The truth also was that Charlie Cain's girlfriend, Amber Dressing, had left him because she had fallen in love with another man, a doctor. Now, thinking about that doctor made Charlie sick. He was sure the doctor was handsome and fit. Amber worked at a fitness center. Charlie had a bit of a belly and he was sure Amber had been turned off by his body.

After a full week of the pain he decided to see a doctor. Charlie had no insurance because Charlie worked for himself. He was a freelance writer and, generally, reviewed anything any newspaper or online zine asked him to. His payments ranged from $35 to $150 per piece but, honestly, the $35 gigs were more frequent. Charlie thought he was whoring out his talent and there is some truth in this. Anyway, Charlie's finances were not that great. He looked back on the days that he worked for UPS and his steady paycheck brought him nice things like food, gas and a beautiful girlfriend: Amber Dressing. Amber was small and willowy and she read books. Heart-whole Charlie loved her the way he'd never loved before.

Charlie lived in a house in a nice neighborhood north of downtown. The house was left to him by his parents, who died in a car accident on Charlie's 22nd birthday. Amber loved Charlie's house because it was so suburban quaint. They made love on Charlie's parents' bed. Charlie never learned whether that was a turn-on or a turn-off. In any event, Charlie was a victim of ghosting. Amber gone. Charlie dead inside.

Our thoughts keep drifting toward Amber. We were talking about Charlie and his undernourished bankbook and his mysterious pain. He called his friend, Meyer.

"Meyer, I have this pain in the lower right quadrant of my back," Charlie said.

"Who is this?" Meyer answered.

"Charlie. Cain. I have this pain."

"Charlie."

"Yes, Amber's boyfriend."

"I heard you broke up."

"What? Yes, technically. You know me though, right?"

"Amber's stuff, isn't she?"

"Yes. Meyer, I need your advice."

"About pain."

"You're a med student, aren't you?"

"Yes. I can't prescribe. I can't even really tell you what to do."

"I have no insurance."

"Ah."

"No money."

"Ah ha."

"Can you help me?"

"What? Like an operation on my kitchen table?"

"Certainly not."

"Don't you have real friends you can call?"

"Ok, yes. Sorry I bothered you."

Charlie hung up in a huff. He could call his friend, Ken, but Ken was usually stoned or drunk or suicidal. Given that, he had scant hope for good medical advice from Ken. Charlie could call his sister, Ruby, but Ruby was a worrier. It was her job. She was the family worrier. She was also the kind of person to whom you had to say, "It was a joke," a lot. He was reaching for the phone to call her anyway. If the conversation went well, maybe, just maybe, he'd ask her about the pain in his back. The phone rang. Charlie, answering the phone, often sounded like an ape who was surprised that there were other apes around.

"It's Meyer," Meyer said.

"Hi Meyer."

"I can help you. You got a pen?"

Charlie found a pen. "Yes."

"Write down this name. Dr. Milton Raphael. Got that?"

"Yes. Yes, Meyer I've got that."

"And here's his address and phone number."

He gave those to Charlie. "Thank you."

"You're welcome. Oh, and Charlie?"

"Yes."

"Don't make an appointment whatever you do. He'll be expecting you."

"But, Meyer—"

Meyer had hung up. It occurred to Charlie that Meyer might be pulling his leg. Charlie could not find a listing for Dr. Raphael in the phonebook or online. There was only one reference to a

Milton Raphael, M.D. online and it was a college newspaper in Oregon. When Charlie clicked on the link he found it was to a page that no longer existed. The doctor's address he had been given was in an area of town Charlie did not know well. He decided the next morning he would drive there and, if it looked fishy, he would turn around and go home.

After a fitful night Charlie woke irritable, and the pain in his back was acute. He dressed gingerly and ate an English muffin with a single soft-boiled egg. At 8:30 a.m. he was in his ancient Volvo heading east toward the office of Dr. Milton Raphael.

As he approached the part of town where the office was he was nonplussed. Surely, there were no active businesses here. He turned onto Vine Street, rolling slowly. He turned down the radio so he could see the address better, and then there it was, a three-story apartment complex as grey and dead as last year's leaves. He stopped, the engine rumbling. The whole street stank of decay. Though it was almost nine in the morning no one was about. Charlie put the car back into gear and that was when he saw a curtain move in a downstairs window. The face peering out seemed to be a small child's, a girl perhaps, with dark eyes.

Charlie turned off the car and the curtain dropped back into place. He made his way carefully up the cracked sidewalk. The office number he was given was printed on a small card which was tacked onto the only door still attached in the bottom story. Above the address: Dr. Milton Raphael, D. P. S. A small, chipped cement platform with three steps and no railing led to the door. Weeds, like unruly whiskers, sprouted from the cracks in the steps.

Charlie knocked and the door was immediately opened by the young girl from the window. She was around 12, Charlie guessed, with dirty blond hair and eyes as black as the ace of spades. She wore a simple white shift. In brief, she was beautiful, in a decidedly ethereal way.

She showed Charlie to what was a sort of waiting room. He was amazed at the warm comfort of the place, as if he had stepped off Skid Row into the Ritz. The dark, plush furniture was handsome, vintage but in excellent condition. The mantle above the large fireplace—in which a cheerful blaze was crackling—looked as if it had been carved for the Knights of the Round Table. The lighting was dim, principally emanating from an ancient, crystal chandelier, in whose center winked the eyes of elves and fays.

"He's expecting you," the young girl said behind Charlie's back, startling him.

"Oh, thank you."

"Through that door," she said. And she smiled. It was as if light had come from a stone. Again, Charlie thought, what a beautiful child.

Dr. Raphael's office was more of the same: dark, luxurious furniture, oak bookcases full of esoteric texts, medical manuals and novels. Heavy drapes and low illumination gave Charlie the impression he had stepped back in time. This was a set from a 1940s Warner Brothers melodrama. And Dr. Raphael completed the picture. Instead of a white coat he wore a smart suit of dark blue with light pinstripes and a collarless black silk undershirt. He had the salt and pepper beard of the older Freud.

"That's Annie," Dr. Raphael said, extending a hand.

Charlie shook the doctor's hand which was soft and cold.

"I'd be lost without Annie. Wise beyond her years, she is."

"Is Annie your daughter?"

Dr. Raphael looked over his hornrims. "I'm told you are having lower back pain."

"Yes," Charlie said, and he reached around to place his hand over the tender spot.

"I see."

"I'm a little flummoxed. Who made the appointment for me?"

"Don't worry about it. Why don't you sit on the table there? Brush the cat off."

A beautiful, brindle-colored cat, somewhere between the size of a house cat and a bobcat, looked at Charlie with dancing blue eyes. Charlie didn't want to try and move it.

"Get down, Metagrobolize."

The cat reluctantly hopped down and disappeared under the desk.

The table was a simple table, again of brunet wood. No white paper. And no medical instruments anywhere in sight. Nevertheless, Charlie took his place on it.

Dr. Raphael came forward and took Charlie's hand. "Just relax," he said.

Dr. Raphael pulled down each of Charlie's eyelids and gave them a good look. He pulled on his ears, and as he did, he sniffed each one.

"Open your mouth, please."

Now the doctor grabbed Charlie's tongue and held it firm between two fingers.

"Mm," the good doctor said, leaning over to smell Charlie's breath.

Charlie didn't know if he was meant to repeat but he said, "Mm."

"Fart much?" the good doctor asked.

"Excuthe me?"

"Sorry." He let go of the tongue. "I asked if you fart much."

"I don't know how much is much. I fart after eating. Sometimes on an empty stomach."

Dr. Raphael nodded and seemed to be thinking.

"Lemme see your hands."

Charlie held out his splayed fingers. The doctor pulled each finger. A couple of them cracked. He put his face up to the half-moons on each fingernail.

"Uh huh," he said.

"Do you want me to take my shirt off?" Charlie asked. He was feeling slightly panicky.

"No, no. Thank you."

Dr. Raphael returned to his desk and sat down. He thought for a moment.

"Much sex?"

Charlie hesitated. "No, not right now."

"But recently?"

"I had a girlfriend. I don't have her anymore."

"Mm hm. Masturbate?"

"Of course."

"Good, good." He thought a minute more. "Here's what I want you to do. Start taking these every morning with your breakfast. Probably best if you take only one and eat something with it until we see what they will do."

Dr. Raphael scribbled a note on a small pad of paper, at the top of which was the logo and name of Redrider Industries.

Charlie looked at the note. It said something like 'Buttonazole.'

"That's all?"

"For now, I think, yes. Thanks for coming in."

Dr. Raphael sat and smiled. It was Charlie's move. He stood up.

"Ok, thank you, Dr. Raphael."

Charlie backed out the door.

"Close that, would you?" the doctor asked.

Charlie did and he looked around the outer room again. Annie was nowhere to be seen. The room was as quiet as a statue.

Charlie shook his head as if he'd awakened from a strange dream. He was pleased his car was still there and, apparently, unmolested. It was 9:30 in the morning so he drove straight to Walgreens. He waited, as usual, in the line at the pharmacy. Walgreens always had a line and, when you reached your destination, there was a surly pharmacist wondering why you were bothering them.

After about 15 minutes Charlie reached the pharmacist, who was a young black woman, as pretty as Halle Berry. She curled her lip. Charlie handed her the piece of paper.

"What is this?" the surly Halle Berry said.

"My prescription."

"Next," she said, pushing Charlie's paper back toward him.

"Wait, wait. I just got this from Dr. Raphael. I assume you have drugs here."

Halle Berry gave him the look she saved for dogs that pee on the carpet.

"Buddy, nice try. You can't scribble a drug on a piece of paper and expect us to give it to you."

"Listen, I swear. This is what he gave me. I know it looks odd but he's a real doctor."

Charlie suddenly didn't know why he believed this.

The pharmacist looked at the note again. She beckoned one of her mates over. The new guy had a face like a dropped cake.

"What's that?"

"I don't know."

"What does it even say?"

"I think it says buttonazole...." Charlie's voice petered off. He was losing hope.

"Get out of here," the guy said.

"Next," Halle Berry said.

Charlie stepped on the foot of the person behind him. The foot was wrapped in a bloody bandage. With an apology thrown over his shoulder he stumbled toward the door. He was shaking by the time he got back behind the wheel of his antediluvian Volvo, and he had to gather himself before he started back for Dr. Raphael's office

He parked and sprinted for the door the note clasp in his sweaty hand. He pounded on the door.

"There you are," Annie said, opening the door. She was dressed in an absurd ball gown and tiara.

"Where's the doctor?" Charlie burst in.

"He's out," Annie said, quietly closing the door.

"Of course he is. What kind of outfit are you running here?"

"I don't understand your question. You ran off without paying this morning."

Charlie realized then that he had. He felt embarrassed. And he paused to catch his breath.

"I'm sorry," he said. "But that doesn't make any difference because this prescription is a fraud."

"I assure you it is not," Annie said. Charlie had the odd feeling that Annie belonged at the Madhatter's Tea Party. She sat down and crossed her thin legs.

"I took it to Walgreens and they said—"

Annie raised her palm and cut Charlie off.

"Walgreens is for the others. You've been sent here because your cure cannot be found at Walgreens."

"Sent here? I'm all muddled."

"I can see that you are. If you had not bolted this morning we could have taken care of everything right here."

"I came out of the office and you were gone. Naturally, I thought—"

"I understand what you thought. You have no patience, impatient patient. I was in the lavatory and, had you waited a moment, I would have taken your payment and given you the nostrum the doctor prescribed."

"I'm sorry. I didn't understand how things work here. This is a very unconventional office."

"For unconventional cures."

"But why do I need an unconventional cure? I only have this pain in my lower right quadrant."

"Is that really all that's bothering you, Charlie?"

She spoke his name as if they had grown up together. She looked at him with gentle appraisal, as if she could peer into his pneuma.

"What do you mean?"

"Are you happy, Charlie?"

"I don't see—"

"Are you in love, Charlie? Are you satisfied with your life currently?"

"Well, no."

"There are you."

"Where am I?"

"Right here with us where you belong. Now if you will just pay I will take the doctor's note and retrieve your medicine."

"I have no insurance."

"Neither do we." And she simpered. "Nor do we take it. Cash only."

"I—I don't have much cash. How much is it?"

"Let me have the note."

Charlie handed her the wadded, retted note.

"I think I can make this out. Of course. That will be ten dollars."

"Ten dollars."

"That's correct."

Annie uncrossed her legs and recrossed them the other way.

"This seems so—"

"I know. Ten dollars and I fetch your meds."

Charlie opened his wallet and took out two fives and laid them softly on the desk.

"Ok," Annie said. She stood and left the room. Charlie waited.

"Here we go," Annie said, returning with a small umber vial with a black squeeze bulb top.

"Drops?"

"That's right. One under the tongue with breakfast. One with lunch. One with dinner."

"And then what?"

"Well, if one day's dosage works—huzzah!" Annie raised both arms like a cheerleader after a score.

"I see. Ok."

"Thank you, Charlie Cain."

"Thank you, um, Annie."

Charlie drove home. He put the vial in the middle of his kitchen table. Should he wait till the morning to start the full day's dosage? He wished he had asked. He was hungry so he made himself a bologna sandwich on white bread, with some corn chips and a coke. Before he ate he lifted the vial and shook it against the light. The liquid was murky as if minute, squirmy things were suspended in it. Without thinking any further he unscrewed the stopper and dropped a tiny globule under his tongue. It was acrid but not unbearable.

He ate his lunch.

Then he began work on a book review due for the daily paper. The writing went well for a while. Phrases appeared on the screen as if by conjuration—conscious thought was not creating but the better angels were. After about ninety minutes Charlie stretched and looked at the screen. He had already completed his approved word count. This felt good. Charlie admitted that he felt good. The pain in his lower back was now only a slight whirr.

With dinner—some light pasta with olive oil, lime juice, and garlic—Charlie took another drop of his medicine. So far, no effects, side or otherwise. He wondered how long before he would feel better. Another question he should have asked.

He watched a little television—TCM was showing a Glenn Ford festival—and about ten the pain in his back had returned. He was also experiencing some slight vertigo. He decided to sleep rather than brood about it. He slept well the entire night, bothered only slightly by strange dreams about animals that no human eye had before discerned, manticores and teratisms. By the time he awoke the sun was coming in around his curtains in honeyed shafts.

Charlie rose, feeling light of limb and heart. The pain in his back was all but gone—a small pebble of pain was all that remained. He shuffled into the bathroom and turned on the shower. Under the water Charlie relished the slight needling of the spray and the heat that steamed the air around him. He shampooed his hair, shook his head like a dog, and opened his eyes. It was then that he saw something anomalous about his hands and forearms. They were—almost transparent. They flickered like an old film and seemed lit by a lemony inner light. He shook one and it was flesh and then not-flesh, flesh and then not-flesh. Charlie's heart constricted. Fear filled him.

He turned off the water and stepped outside the shower. The entire bathroom was filled with fog and Charlie opened the door. In the clearing atmosphere he surveyed his entire body. The flickering filled his whole frame.

"Eek!" Charlie eeked.

He grabbed a towel and wiped the mirror clean. His head—his face—were indistinct. He was transparent. He could see the fleur-de-lis wallpaper behind him through his forehead.

"Eek!" he said again.

He quickly found his robe and wrapped himself in it. His body's shape was there beneath the terrycloth but his hands and head were jars of fireflies. He ran into the next room. What to do? Call 911? What would he say? That he could see through himself? They'd laugh and never come.

He went to the kitchen and started a pot of coffee. He paced while it dripped. When he'd gotten himself a cup he took a bagel from the cabinet and sat at the kitchen table. The coffee felt restorative and he ate the bagel only to keep the coffee from burning a hole in his stomach. He kept looking at his hands—he did not recognize them as part of him. Then he saw the bottle of drops sitting on the table in front of him.

He pondered what to do. Had the drops caused this? Was it because he didn't take three in one day? Did that mean he should take another right away? The dithering was making his globe even lighter. He squeezed another drop onto his tongue and followed it with a bite of bagel and a swallow of coffee. He sat still as if something were going to happen right away. After fifteen minutes he got up and walked around. After another fifteen he decided to get dressed.

He found a pair of jeans and a t-shirt, socks and tennis shoes. When he dropped the robe onto the bed he looked down. Never look down, his incipient brain said. And he wished he hadn't. Everything was gone. Gut, thighs, cock, legs. Charlie was completely invisible. He ran back into the bathroom. Nothing stared back at him from the mirror.

Am I dead, Charlie wondered? Were the drops poison?

He ran his hands down his torso and was relieved that he could still feel himself. He gave his penis a reassuring tug, as if this were a test for nullibiety. He still existed. Unless he was a ghost. A ghost with a penis.

He pulled his jeans on and the effect was horrible. This was worse. He could not go out in clothing. It would appear as if the clothing were floating along by itself. He took the pants off and laid them carefully on the bed.

He called Meyer, who answered after one ring. Except it was only the outgoing message: "It's Meyer. At least it was this morning. Leave me a message or leave me alone."

"Meyer," Charlie said into Meyer's phone. "It's Charlie. Call me back soon please. It's important."

Charlie felt paralyzed. Did he dare go out? How could it get any worse? What if he rematerialized and was naked? Charlie decided to go out on foot and walk around his neighborhood, staying close to home.

He went out his back door and left through the back gate which let onto his neighbor's yard. He crossed the yard and emerged onto the street behind his. He then circled back to Brock Way, his street. He was creeping as if he were perceptible. He was extremely conscious of being naked. His dangly parts felt as vulnerable as baby birds. A little hardball of anxiety sat in his chest. A few folks were out, getting into their cars, retrieving the paper, one fellow already with the sonic roar of his leaf blower going, shattering the early morning air.

To his right was his neighbor Ken's house. Ken was as close

to a friend that Charlie had in the neighborhood. Charlie tended to keep to himself. Ken was married to Christine, a short, shapely woman, whose brown eyes were deep pools.

Charlie peeked in Ken's window. Ken was sitting in front of his TV having a beer for breakfast. Charlie went around to Ken's back door to see if it was locked. It not only wasn't locked it was ajar. From inside the kitchen a black smell emerged. Ken had obviously burnt his breakfast. Charlie slipped inside.

He walked into the den and watched Ken watch TV for about a half hour. That was pretty dull but Charlie's heart was still beating rapidly. It was exciting being in someone else's home without their knowing it. Why? Why should that be exciting?

Charlie went upstairs. Ken's wife, Christine, was nowhere to be seen. Did she work and Ken stay home? Charlie thought this might be the case. Charlie entered the master bedroom where the king-size bed was still unmade. It appeared as if they still slept together. Charlie tried to imagine that kind of commitment and was made sad by the idea. He began quietly sliding drawers open. He paused at Christine's underwear drawer and drew a few pairs of panties out. It was not as exciting as he thought it might be. In the bottom drawer he found a pistol. He lifted it out and checked to see if it was loaded. It was. Why did he care? He couldn't very well carry it out. A floating pistol would gather more attention than a parade of Nazis.

He quietly slipped back downstairs and past Ken and out the back door. There were a few more people milling about. He paused again at the absurdity of walking unclothed through his neighborhood. It was like a dream, not a nightmare exactly, but an inscrutable dream whose import was lost upon waking.

He walked closer to the fellow with the leaf blower. The blare was thunderous. The guy, wearing a sweaty wifebeater, was large and hairy—he resembled the strongmen in old circus movies.

Charlie walked within a yard of him and stood face to face. The blower was raking across Charlie's ankles but the guy was oblivious. Charlie was completely undetectable.

Charlie knocked the leaf blower out of the brute's hands. The man started, looked at his hands, looked at the blower which lay on the ground trembling like a dying animal. He reached down to pick it up and Charlie put his foot on it. The fellow jumped back. He looked around. No one was watching this strange transaction. He bent one more time and this time, by yanking the machine upward, he sent Charlie ass over teakettle.

"Oof," Charlie said like a comic strip gag.

The guy dropped the blower.

"Who?" he said.

Charlie lay still. The giant moved forward. He was standing between Charlie's legs, though since Charlie couldn't see his legs either, Charlie didn't know. Still, he quietly moved backward, the pavement a corrosive on his bare ass. When he had moved sufficiently out of the guy's reach Charlie stood and moved away quickly.

He left the guy still looking around. He was more afraid than Charlie.

It was, perhaps, at this moment that Charlie first understood the power of invisibility. As a child he had once played a game with his cronies called Which Super Power Would You Have? Charlie had chosen invisibility. It was no secret why. If you were invisible you could see ladies undressed.

This childish thought now made Charlie smile. He had gone from despair to amusement in a very short while. And he further thought that, since this condition was assuredly temporary, there was no time like the present to have some invisible fun. Charlie became a horndog, just like that.

He thought then of the young divorcee who lived opposite his house. Charlie had spoken to her a couple of times—he thought her name was Lorraine—but she was too lovely for Charlie to fantasize about. She was a tall blonde with a little spray of freckles on her nose. Charlie made his way toward her house.

Her car was in the driveway. Did she work? He had no idea.

He walked around the house trying to look in windows but they were all covered. So he simply went to the front door and knocked. His heart was again beating fast. What would he do? The answer was easier than he thought. She answered the door still in a bathrobe. She looked around the porch.

"Hello?" she inquired. Charlie slipped by her into her house.

Her house was furnished tastefully if spartanly. He sensed a certain sadness in the room. While he was considering this Lorraine walked past him into the kitchen. There were half-eaten eggs and a cup of coffee at the table where Lorraine sat down. Her bathrobe gapped slightly and Charlie thought he could see the bottom half of one breast. Lorraine sat for a long time sipping her coffee and pushing eggs around on her plate. She was lost in a reverie. Charlie didn't know people sat still and did nothing for such a long time. He was growing bored when she finally stood up and put her dishes in the sink. She went off to a bedroom. Charlie followed a few paces behind. There was an ironing board set up and an iron there, already hot. Lorraine began ironing a skirt. Charlie stood and watched her, his back against the wall. She was especially lovely.

When she finished ironing she lay the skirt on the bed next to a shirt and some pantyhose. Then she shrugged off the robe. She was dressed only in thin, white panties. The panties had a fingertip-sized hole at the top near the elastic.

Charlie exhaled as if punched which caused Lorraine to take a step back and reflexively cover her breasts. She scanned the room and the hall outside. Charlie stood stock still. Lorraine relaxed slowly and lowered her arms. Charlie was in love. Her breasts were great sea swells and her thighs smooth and freckled. He wanted to touch her. He wanted to get her to remove her panties but could think of no way to accomplish this. Charlie could feel the blood engorge his cock. Did he dare touch it? He did.

But he stopped quickly enough. What if he came and the ejaculate was not invisible? He had much to learn about his new condition. Instead he watched Lorraine get dressed and then, after a few quiet moments, he glided back outside and returned home. When he got home he tested his theory, fresh from the memory of Lorraine's immaculate body. He sat on the edge of his bed and masturbated. And, sure enough, the ejaculate was visible, a viscous, silvery puddle at his feet. He got a washcloth and wiped the floor. Then he wondered if blood would also be visible once it left his body. He didn't have the stomach for that test just then.

He didn't have the stomach for anything right then. His invisible head was swimming. Sensory overload was making Charlie a dull boy. He decided to shelve any further plans and eat some food and go to sleep and see what's what in the morning.

He fixed some rice and vegetables and ate them in front of the television. There was a nature program on so he channel-surfed. We allow that if this were a film, he would stop on Turner Classic Movies and *The Invisible Man* would be showing but Turner Classic Movies was showing *Cry of the City*. Still, the old black and white movie brought *The Invisible Man* to mind and Charlie thought about swathing himself in bandages and sunglasses and a hat. Perhaps, at some point, that would be what he would do. For now, he felt safer being unseen.

About halfway through eating, Charlie wondered if could see his own dinner as it passed through his impalpable alimentary canal. This science experiment was a bust: the food disappeared within him. He didn't want to think about peeing and shitting. It *interested* him, but it also made him a little bilious.

Charlie slept naked that night, the first time he'd ever done that. And he slept the night through, only slightly bothered by a dream about a missing dog. Charlie had never owned a dog, not even when he was small. His parents were too busy to care for one.

*I*n the cool light of morning, Charlie knew what he had to do. He had to go back to Dr. Raphael and tell him what had happened. Surely this was not normal, even given the eccentricities of his practice. The problem, Charlie Cain knew, was getting there.

He decided to take a bus.

After determining the buses he needed to get to Vine Street Charlie walked to the bus stop. There was one person waiting. Luck was on his side. When the bus stopped for this rider—an older woman dressed in a muumuu—it was easy for Charlie to sidle around her and into an empty seat.

At the next stop a couple got on the bus. He was a young, chinless chaplain and she a small, reedy brunette with her hair in a bun so tight it looked screwed on. The chaplain sat next to Charlie and his wife sat in Charlie's naked lap.

"Oh!" she said, rising again.

"What is it, Antonia?" the chaplain asked. He looked at her with years of forbidding patience.

"I thought I felt someone sitting there."

Charlie held his breath. He looked around. There were a few seats in the back.

"Sit down, dear," the chaplain said, firmly.

She reseated herself on top of Charlie. Charlie was sure she could feel his breath against her neck. She was trying to sit without actually making contact which made her look ridiculous. Her husband gave her a stern, Protestant glare.

She settled down, moving against Charlie as if he were a beanbag chair. Her slim buttocks kept up a turning motion as she settled around his crotch. She ground and ground, believing that she could find a comfortable seat beneath her. Then something odd occurred. She relaxed. And, as she relaxed, a small, smug grin seamed her thin face.

Charlie tried not to move though her bony butt was uncomfortable scrunching down on him. And she was making small, surreptitious movements with her cheeks. Charlie willed his willy not to rise but a half-erection began to emerge. The chaplain's wife let out an involuntary purr. Her right hand fell along Charlie's thigh and her thin fingers began to knead his skin, like lust's whisper.

"Hmm," she said, almost to herself. Her husband looked at her and she gave him a prim smile.

Her hand grew warm on Charlie's skin. His cock rose. The chaplain's wife's exhalation was louder than she intended. Though Charlie had spermatized late yesterday he accomplished an impressive erection.

"Dear, what is wrong with you? Please remember who you are," her husband said.

Charlie didn't much like the way he talked to his wife. She shrank from his words as if afraid of a blow. Charlie put his hand under one of her buttocks and repositioned her so that her crack lay along Charlie's now completely erect cock. Charlie caressed her narrow buttock and she lay back, resting her head alongside Charlie's chin. Charlie moved gently against her, rising into the material of her dress until he could feel the warmth between her thighs. Now her hand moved up Charlie's thigh seeking his middle point. She found his balls.

"My God," she whispered.

Her husband looked at her threateningly but she did not even turn her head.

"You're luscious," Charlie whispered in her ear.

She sighed and squeezed Charlie's balls.

Now she put her purse over her lap. She was wearing a full-length skirt, but by scrunching up handfuls of the rear of it she managed to open a path at least to her sensible cotton underpants. Charlie maneuvered his cock onto her panties which were already soaked.

"Take me," he whispered.

She grabbed his pole and pushed it past her panties. It sank into her like a lance into a streambed. She moved gingerly but with force, squeezing him. Her husband turned away from her, placing his long legs in the aisle. He was reading a small breviary. The bus kept making its stops but Charlie and the preacher's wife were lost to the world now. And when the preacher's wife came, a prim orgasm achieved by pushing down so hard on Charlie he thought she'd pull a hamstring, she let out a soft hiss like steam escaping and her orgasm triggered Charlie's. He let loose a hot stream inside her tight, Protestant vagina. It was the first simultaneous orgasm of Charlie's life and, assuredly, of the preacher's wife's.

The chaplain and his wife got off a few stops later but, before she rose, she put a hand up to Charlie's cheek and Charlie kissed her neck passionately.

"O Holy Ghost," she exhaled.

Charlie had missed his stop and so got off as soon as he could and doubled back. But, as he walked, something occurred to him. The last 24 hours had been—*interesting*. Did he want to be cured of invisibility? Should he visit the doctor? But his better half adjudicated and suggested that Charlie at least find out if this condition was permanent or a fluke which would eventually wear off.

The last bus stop was still a couple blocks from Vine Street and Charlie had to walk the ravaged streets to get to the office. He had to sidestep broken glass and spilled food and twisted bits of metal because he was barefoot. But he was thankful that the day was warm. He wondered if the winter would be impossible for him if he did not regain his visible body.

He found the building readily enough and, once again, he approached it warily. Surely this was an abandoned piece of property. He was reminded that the office itself was the converse of the exterior, a place of opulent comfort. He found the door but it was locked so he knocked. And waited.

He knocked again. And waited.

Charlie wondered if perhaps they were looking outside and could see no visitor and, hence, were not answering the door. Or maybe they were not answering because they did not expect him. He moved to one of the windows and put his face to the glass. He was standing in damp earth which was sticking to his feet. He could not see the interior very well so he decided to see if the window was open. It slid upwards on a creaky wood track. The room inside was empty save for a broken table, an old hurricane lamp, and shards of glass.

"Damn," Charlie said.

"What?" a startled voice behind him said.

Charlie turned and let the window drop. It fell with a clatter.

"What the effing?" the fellow now standing in front of Charlie said. He was obviously homeless, his clothing a collection of rags and stained castoffs, his face a dirty red color partially covered with sticky dark whiskers.

Charlie slipped sideways as quietly as he could but the fellow still yelped and jumped backward. He was watching the ground where a pair of foot-shaped mud things were moving surreptitiously away. Charlie now began to trot, shaking his feet as he ran, watching out for sharp objects. When he looked back the poor fellow was seated on the concrete steps outside what formerly was the doctor's office, shaking his head from side to side.

Charlie cleaned himself once he was in the clear and found the bus stop again. His mind was a tourbillion. The doctor could not have moved away that quickly. Something even stranger than he had contemplated was going on. He knew he had to get home and call Meyer again.

A beautiful young woman wearing tight black pants and ear buds got on the bus and, for a brief, dirty moment, Charlie thought about sliding underneath her before she sat down, but he did not. He was sexually spent at any rate. And he had other things on his mind.

*W*hen Charlie got back home he retrieved the key from where he had hidden it in the flower bed and let himself in. Once inside his familiar surroundings, he felt a little calmer. He sat down and picked up his cell phone and called Meyer. He got voice mail. Meyer's message said, "You may or may not have gotten Meyer. It's not for me to say."

"Meyer, it's Charlie. Call me as soon as you get this please."

While he waited for the call he fixed some lunch and ate it at the kitchen table. He had no plan. If he could not talk to Meyer he felt stymied, stuck at home. As he sat, he began to think about Amber. It was odd that, with everything that was happening, he had forgotten that his heart was broken. Amber didn't want him anymore. She didn't want him even when he was corporeal, possibly because his corporeal self was not handsome enough for her. He had a bit of a belly.

Charlie thought about wandering the neighborhood some more. The adventures within walking distance were almost irresistible. But Charlie was also hagridden. His mind would not let him enjoy this strange happenstance and, instead, jumped from one fret to the next. If he was never visible again his life would be—what? Not over, certainly. But implausible, ridiculous. Nothing prepares a man for living his life unseen. As far as he knew he was the only invisible man, but, as soon as that thought filtered through, he wondered. Were there others? How would he know?

Charlie watched TV. He read a little. The book he was reading was about a cult in California which believed its preacher was the resurrected Penitent Thief, Dismas. They called themselves the Dismals, apparently without irony. The book bored Charlie now. Just a few days ago he thought it the most compelling thing he'd read in ages.

Charlie ate because he was bored. Another nagging worry: when he needed groceries what was he to do? The only answer that presented itself to Charlie was that he would have to pilfer food, a few items at a time. Perhaps from his neighbors. And, in thinking about that, Charlie gave in to temptation and decided to walk his neighborhood.

He closed his front door and hid the key again. It was a balmy evening, an hour or so before sunset. Only a few neighbors were outside. The brute with the leaf blower was sitting on his porch, seemingly dejected, his abandoned tool lying on the sidewalk in front of him like an executed boa constrictor. Farther down, a young couple Charlie didn't know were standing next to one of their cars arguing. Their heated colloquy seemed worth a closer listen.

They were arguing about some guy the wife worked with. Jealousy is a nasty poison. Soon that subject morphed into a squabble about sex in general, and then, almost inevitably, money. It was boring stuff. Charlie felt mischievous though so he honked the horn of the car, startling both parties.

"Jesus!" the woman said. She was about 30, pretty in an overly made-up way, slim except for her thighs. He was tall with a receding hairline. One got the feeling he liked being taller than her.

"Now what's wrong with the car?" the fellow said, exasperated, as if this too were her fault.

"It's your car," she countered.

They both paused, perhaps at the end of their misused wits.

"Sure, blame me," he said, inanely.

Charlie thought that was enough fun with them but before he left he reached in and turned on the radio.

"What in the name of God?" the man expostulated as Charlie strolled away.

Of course, he wanted to check on Lorraine. Again, he tested the windows and saw nothing so he rang the front doorbell.

After a few moments the door was opened and a guy the size and shape of a silo answered the door. Behind him Lorraine stood, dressed to the nines. She had a cocktail in her hand.

"That happened the other day, no one there," she said.

"Kids," the slab said.

Charlie walked away. He thought he might check back later to see if he could catch them in bed. Then Charlie paused to wonder at how his mind was working. Was he always this roguish, this devilish? He'd become a voluptuary. Perhaps that was a side effect of invisibility. He'd certainly always been interested in women in a physical way but his record of maintaining a relationship was a poor one. He sat down on the curb. Melancholy spread in him like a dose of barium. If he could see his bare feet, he'd see that they were scuffed and red from walking on them. The soles felt inflamed. He sighed and rose and started for home.

A car careened within a foot of him and Charlie fell back on the grass. His heart went wild within its spectral cage. His heart wailed, frightened and frustrated.

"Watch where you're going, asshole!" Charlie yelled.

The car stopped. The heads of the neighbors turned his way. An eerie silence fell over the neighborhood. The driver of the car walked around his car twice. He glared at the distant neighbors. He craned his neck and re-entered his car. He drove away so slowly it was dreamlike.

Charlie went home.

The first thing Charlie did was check his cell phone. Still no return call from Meyer. He tried again and got voice mail again. He checked his email. There were many messages but none that he needed.

He read for a bit and then went to bed. Again, he slept without pajamas and Charlie began to think of himself as a nudist. The thought amused him and he fell asleep without worrying about how his naked body would take colder weather, or rougher terrain, or heat, or nicks and scrapes and rashes and eczema. He slept in dreamless oblivion and when he woke the next morning he decided it was a good day to start his life as a burglar.

Even though he had food in the house he wanted *other* food, someone else's food. He left the house without showering, shaving or even washing his face. It occurred to him that perhaps he would eventually start to smell. Or would he? Does an invisible body sweat?

He eschewed the questions in his quest for breakfast.

He started next door at Harvey and Jane's. Harvey worked

for one of the downtown banks and Jane worked from home, some kind of craft business. Charlie had a vague memory of Jane trying to sell him some handmade yarny thing that was proof against witchcraft or somesuch. He had politely demurred. Now, as he stood in their living room, the evidence of her 'art' was everywhere. The colors, dun and orange and muted purples, were stomach churning. Charlie had never been in their home because he and Harvey did not see eye-to-eye on much, including politics. Harvey was a blowhard and Jane was more like his pet than his wife. He disliked both of them. So, taking their food seemed like a fine idea on his first morning as a thief. The only thing he had to be careful about was carrying food home. For this reason he chose the closest house first. Of course, he could just browse when he was hungry and eat wherever he found the best food.

Now Jane was still standing on the porch. She was sure she heard footsteps when she opened the door and was waiting for some neighborhood scamp to show himself. Harvey walked past Charlie and onto the doorstep.

"What are you doing?" Harvey asked his wife.

"Kids knocking on the door and running. I heard them. They can't be far away."

Harvey looked out over his wife's shoulder.

"Shut the door and come inside. What difference does it make?"

"Lorraine said the same thing happened to her. I'm gonna catch them one of these days."

"Crime spree," Harvey said, dismissively. "Shut the door, Jane."

Harvey was dressed for work in a cheap suit with a tie that was fashionable ten years ago. Maybe it was fashionable again. What did Charlie know of such things? Jane was wearing a faded crafts fair t-shirt and sweat pants. She was plain—her name a curse perhaps—but sweet, in a fading Southern belle sort of way.

Charlie sauntered into the kitchen. The breakfast dishes had not been cleared away. He picked up a pork sausage link and popped it whole into his mouth. It was cold but tasty. He took a sip of orange juice out of a nearly empty glass. On another plate was a smear of egg yolk and half a piece of toast. He sopped the toast in the creamy yolk and behind him Jane screamed.

"What the fuck?" Harvey said, hustling back to where Jane stood in the kitchen doorway. "You're gonna give me a goddamn heart attack."

"Watch," she said. She was pointing a shaky finger right at Charlie, whom, of course, she could not see.

"What?" Harvey said.

"Just watch. The toast was floating in the air."

Harvey stood still for a moment to let that sink in. Charlie was smiling and standing as still as a sword in a stone.

"I'm going to work," Harvey said, turning on his heel.

Jane stood a bit longer in the doorway. She waited…waited. Just as her patience was waning Charlie put his finger in the yolk and slowly wrote the word, "Satan."

"Holy Christ," Jane screamed and ran out the front door in search of her husband.

Charlie fixed himself a cup of coffee and drank it. Then from the fridge he took some cheese, half a roasted chicken, some fresh vegetables, and a macaroni salad. In the freezer he found a bottle of vodka. He wrapped these things in a tea towel and tiptoed out the back door which was only a few paces from his own. The key was at the front door however so he left the food on the back stoop and walked around the house and let himself in. On the way he saw Jane standing a half block down the street, turning quietly this way and that, looking for succor, or sense.

It was in this way that Charlie began his life as a housebreaker. He eschewed doing book reviews though books kept arriving on his doorstep. He ignored the phone calls from his editor at the paper. He ignored all phone calls as he waited in vain for Meyer to call him back. He knew eventually he would have to locate Meyer and try to find, perhaps, the secret behind this dark magical turn his life had taken. But a reluctance—and fear—kept him from seeking Meyer or anyone he might confront while invisible. Amber stayed in the back of his mind. He knew, eventually, he would also have to either confront her or his feelings for her.

*H*e found the afternoons the best time to steal things but the nights held their own special enticements. Perhaps it was juvenile but Charlie relished the idea of watching his neighbors in their beds. He thought it odd that it was rare to catch someone *in flagrante delicto*. People didn't have as much sex as Charlie thought they did. He had never had a relationship last past the honeymoon phase where sex is such an adventure.

A week passed.

One afternoon, in search of something better than lunch meat and soft drinks, Charlie ventured onto the next block. He didn't know as many people there. The first house where he knocked he received no answer but a neighbor across the street whipped his head around at the sound of Charlie's fist on the door. So, at the next house, Charlie rang the bell. He heard footsteps and the door was opened by a middle-aged woman in paint-flecked overalls. She looked around outside and closed the door. Curiosity did not spoil her earnest expression. She seemed preoccupied, as if her mind was sifting grander things. She was about Charlie's height and was quite lovely. Easily ten years Charlie's senior, she was rounder and her face was etched with finely drawn lines. Her full lips were dry and her whole natural face reflected a seriousness that was more attractive than young skin or a slim figure. Her chevelure had silver highlights. Her eyes were a dazzling blue.

Charlie followed her back down the hallway into a large, airy room with high, generous windows. There was an easel set up and a painting begun there. The whole room was a crash of color and chaos. Canvases lined the walls, stacked four or five deep, mostly turned inward. There was a mirror, the kind you mount on a door, leaning horizontally against the wall. The woman went right back to work as if she'd never been disturbed. Charlie quietly sat on an old armchair and watched her paint. There was a radio, also paint-spattered, sitting at the woman's feet, turned to a jazz station. It burbled softly and the woman hummed, often not along with the radio.

Charlie was mesmerized by this fascinating female creature. It was an unlikely *coup de foudre*. It would not be overstating things to say that he fell a little in love with her. He decided to spend the entire afternoon with her. Mostly that meant just sitting and watching her work. She painted carefully but freely, her arm moving in graceful arcs like an athlete's. The canvas was a riot of color and sensation. It drew Charlie in. She painted for over two hours and then sighed heavily and stood back. Charlie wished he could see what she saw, what she was hoping to see. He wished he understood art.

She seemed finished for the day if not satisfied. Perhaps she was also satisfied. As she walked out of the room she was unhooking the straps of her overalls. She disappeared into the bathroom and tossed the spattered overalls into the hall. Charlie got quickly to his feet. He prayed she would not close the bathroom door and, when she did, he felt bereft. It was not kinkiness which drove him to want to see her unclothed—or not entirely—it was *tenderness*. He wanted to know this woman right down to her bones. He waited down the hall till he heard the shower turned off.

When she emerged she was wrapped in two towels, one in her hair and one at her waist. Her eyes seemed sad, almost vacant. Her breasts were full and hung somewhat desultorily down her chest. Her round belly had small hairs around the navel. Charlie wanted to kiss her there. Instead, something proper inside him made him avert his eyes. There are privacies, he thought, there are still privacies. He backed slowly away as she walked nearer. At one point she stopped as if she thought something was amiss. Charlie froze. She was only three feet away.

"La," she said and did a U-turn into the kitchen.

Charlie let himself out the front door and, on his way back home, entered another home and scored a pork tenderloin. He trotted home—his feet had grown tougher and the bottoms were aging like leather—because the piece of meat was so large. Only one small child noticed its impossible flight and she pointed and giggled.

When he reached his own house, he saw that the grass had been cut and the yard tidied, the flower beds weeded, and there were a half-dozen plastic bags at the curb. He had almost forgotten about the lawn service that came with the house. He fretted for a moment about arriving home when they were there. He would worry about that if it happened. Charlie put the tenderloin in the slow cooker with some potatoes and carrots and sat down in front of the television. But he did not turn it on for a while. His mind was full of that woman and her wild canvas. And, for some reason, he could not get that mirror out of his head, the mirror leaning on her wall. It haunted him.

The next morning, he googled her, searching for local female artists.

He discovered her name was Sudie Nimm. She had shown around town for a couple decades but most of her work was currently sold through Nocturna Gallery, a small boutique gallery in a ritzy part of the city. Charlie wrote down the address.

In his new life as a pilferer Charlie had to graduate from foodstuffs to cash. He had bills to pay. He usually took only a little at a time, but at one house, where he also got a nice pasta salad, he found an envelope by the bedside table with hundred-dollar bills in it. The temptation was too great. He took a dozen. He didn't want to alarm the neighborhood watch but he also felt safe. Who would be looking for a ghost as the culprit?

Charlie began to spend a large amount of time at Sudie Nimm's house. Every time he rang the bell he felt a little guilty and a little frightened. It sent a thrum of anxiety through his spine. But she always answered and always he slipped by her. He sensed she was beginning to get irritated by the interruption and he thought perhaps she didn't write it off as kids' pranks the way most of her neighbors did.

The fourth day Charlie visited he tried the door and found it unlocked. Had it always been unlocked and he had been ringing for no reason? Or, more curiously, had she started unlocking it so she didn't have to stop painting? Charlie decided that was absurd. He reasoned that many in the neighborhood left their doors unlocked, or at least they had before the current rash of food thefts.

Charlie was content to sit in her studio and watch Sudie paint. She was so graceful in her movements. She danced with the canvas. Sometimes she would stop and take a step back and assess what she was doing but most of her movements were confident and smooth. Sometimes, when she stepped back, she looked around the room as if searching for the pair of eyes she sensed were there. How could she know that they belonged to a ghostly, see-through, naked man?

Charlie followed Sudie around her elegant house, watched her eat in the kitchen, where sometimes she ate standing up and staring out the window over the sink into her backyard. Charlie also liked to sit in the bathroom while Sudie bathed. Sudie liked long, hot, scented baths and watching her lather her aged but fine-looking body made Charlie happy. Sometimes he wanted to reach over and soap a breast or the sweet small hummocks of her knees. He had to content himself with watching, and carrying the retention of her scent home with him.

Now, Charlie, though invisible, still had to take care of the complications of the human body: eating, cleaning, voiding and sexual desire. This latter was a tad problematic. Charlie had the urge to feel a female body next to his. Of course he did. He was still oh so human. He masturbated nightly to assuage the pain of desire and to try to keep himself in line during his visits to his neighbors. Sometimes he thought of Sudie but mostly he thought of strangers, movie stars and pop singers. He had a great desire to visit Amber and make love to her again but he fully grasped that this was impossible.

Therefore, some days, he did not visit Sudie. He gave in to his animal side and began looking for the houses where women were home alone.

That was how he discovered Patience Spent.

She lived three streets east of Charlie's house. He found her not when he was looking for food but when he was looking for amusement. He was in the mood for a prank when he saw her sunbathing in an inflatable kiddy pool in her backyard; his first thought was to let the air out of the pool. He did not know she had a body like a lingerie model until she stood as the pool deliquesced around her. She was wearing a bikini that was drawn on by a celestial hand. She was as curvy as a vine of ivy.

"Shit," she said as she stood.

Charlie watched the water run off her greased surface in slow motion. He counted every drop. He wanted to be every drop. He wanted to run down her body.

He stepped back as she began to move toward the house and tumbled backwards over the garden hose.

"What in the world?" Patience said, staring at a place in the grass where the shape of a man sat like a shadow.

Charlie scrambled sideways like a crab. He made more noise than he usually did and he was sure he was caught out. Patience's eyes followed the sound of his movement.

"What are you?" she asked. She was not panicked. She was.... *curious*.

Charlie rose quietly and tried to slink away. Patience's eyes followed him.

"Don't wanna talk?" Patience Spent said, narrowing her eyes. She shrugged. "Silent duppy," she muttered.

Charlie didn't know what a duppy was but he was afraid of this woman's powers of perception. His first thought was to run. Except he wanted to be near her electric splendor. As she turned and walked toward her house he breathed a sigh of relief. And saw then that the bottom of her suit was a thong. Charlie's heart ached.

As she reached her back-stoop Patience turned and looked again at the yard, scanning it with genuine interest.

"Come in if you want," she said, matter-of-factly.

Charlie closed the space between them but let her enter the house and close the screen door. After a moment he crept to the stoop and cautiously opened the screen door. Nothing happened so he stepped inside.

She was standing in the kitchen mixing a large pitcher of lemonade. She looked up and smiled. Charlie was inside now and was mesmerized by his surroundings. There was not a clear space on the historiated walls of the living room, nor on any surface, including the floor. The décor was a recherché hodgepodge of photographs, religious objects, and plaques imprinted with maxims, pieces of hoodoo, an eye of god, a dreamcatcher. There were pictures of Gurdjieff, John Dee, Madame Blavatsky, Anton Mesmer, Blake, Sacheen Littlefeather, Alan Watts, Jimi Hendrix, Robert Fludd, Osho, Rasputin, Polyidus, Rod Serling, Yeats, Nostradamus, the Erythraean Sibyl, Donovan, Mr. Rogers, Timothy Leary and Baba Ram Dass.

On every surface sat objects of veneration. Crystals, wands, seeing balls, religious texts, sexual toys, and small carved figures. On every window ledge sat blue bottles of various sizes and shapes. And above it all, suspended from an exceptionally high ceiling, was a hollow, balsawood pyramid.

"I'm Patience," Patience said to the room. Her eyes flashed. "Though my name is, at times, a stumbling block to the erasure of ego and game thinking."

Charlie still could not talk.

"You are welcome," Patience said. "I knew you would come."

Charlie backed into the living room. He sat on the edge of the couch so that his body would not make an imprint. Patience drank some lemonade and then moved into the living room. From a lower desk drawer she drew forth small finger cymbals. She put them on her fingers and closed her eyes. Then, slowly, sinuously, she began to shimmy and undulate, making her own tintinnabulation to accompany what was, in Charlie's eyes, the sexiest dance he'd ever seen. She had no self-consciousness. She almost seemed to be in a trance.

Charlie's cock rose.

She danced for ten minutes while Charlie was rapt and breathless. Then she took her bathing suit off. Her body was the most perfect female body Charlie had ever seen or ever would see. She was muscular, like a belly dancer, and shapely as any movie star. But there was an earthiness present that even movie stars could not limn.

"Come," Patience said. "Rise."

Charlie followed his cock and rose also. He felt entranced.

"Dance with me. Your presence is warm and, ummm, blue, a glowing deep blue."

Charlie took a step forward. Patience's eyes found him though, of course, she could not *actually* see him.

"Come," she said again, and held out her arms.

Charlie shuffled closer and Patience's hands found his shoulders. It seemed as if it had been a long time since he'd been touched.

"What manner of spirit are you?"

Charlie still had not spoken. He did not know the language of gods.

Patience ran her hands down Charlie's chest and onto his hairy belly. Charlie now worried about his pot gut again. But Patience's hands were soft and kind.

"You are shaped like a man," Patience said. "Mm, good. Can you speak?"

Charlie kept quiet. He only wanted her to keep touching him. She obliged and in a second found his erect penis.

"Ah, I thought so. You are Priapus. A tantric lifeforce. Mm."

Her soft hand began to work Charlie's penis, rolling it with slow fervor. She cupped his balls with her other hand.

"May I?" she asked, reverently.

"Ah," Charlie abruptly said.

"You speak," Patience Spent said. "Trust me. I am here for you. Tell me your name."

She continued to work his penis and scrotum and Charlie continued his silence.

"I will take you in," she said.

And Patience Spent went down on her knees to the god and put his holy rod (rood) into her mouth. Charlie tangled a hand in her chocolate hair. Her ministrations were almost religious but she was also practiced at the oral arts. Soon Charlie shot off inside her mouth, almost collapsing over her back. They stayed that way for a long time, an absurd sexual tableau. Then Charlie straightened up, one vertebra at a time, and Patience let his limp member fall from her lips. She then bowed further, touching her forehead to the dark, hardwood floor.

She stood up and found his face with her hands. She brought her mouth up to his in a ritualistic kiss and passed his sperm back to him where it slid down his tongue, and then down his throat like an oyster.

"I am not worthy of your seed. Not yet," she said, humbly. "I will be. I am working on me."

Patience now stepped back and tried to 'see' her visitor. Charlie felt her eyes on him. He was mesmerized and now a bit frightened. When Patience turned back toward the kitchen to get another drink Charlie watched her naked butt move away from him, and, shaking his head, he made his exit. He was stumbling, dizzy as a goose.

As the screen door closed behind him Patience called out, "You are welcome here anytime. You are safe with Patience."

Charlie lurched back home. At one point he stepped off the curb wrong and knocked over a child's bike. From a group of surprised eyes he ran like a wolf. Once home he fell onto the couch. His head was spiraling, outward, inward. But, as he calmed, a smile spread on his face. He felt... formidable. He was a Man.

That night he ate a little tenderloin and rice and watched a Harold Lloyd marathon on TCM. Around eight p.m. there was a knock on the door. Charlie stopped eating, muted the TV and sat stock still. The knock came again. Charlie set his plate on the couch cushion next to him. His mind was skimble-skambled with what-ifs. The first was absurd. What if it was Patience Spent? Then: What if it was Amber? What if it was Sudie? What if it was Dr. Raphael? What if it was Ken? What if it was the police? (How?) What if it was Meyer? (Oh, he wished it were Meyer.) What if...no one was there?

This last thought spooked Charlie.

Charlie tiptoed to the door. He had no eyehole so he just listened. Another knock made him jump like a firecracker. He stepped around to the side and then recognized the car out front. It belonged to the editor of the paper, Ellis Bruce.

There was nothing to do so Charlie did nothing. He returned to the couch and sat quietly until his visitor went away. He was sure Ellis had heard the TV. He was sure that that was not a good thing.

One day, sitting in Sudie's studio, watching her work on a new canvas (she had apparently finished the one she'd been hard at for some time, though Charlie was not art appreciator enough to recognize finished from not-quite), Charlie had the uncontrollable urge to reveal himself to this lovely and soulful woman. And, as the urge went through him like a fever, he contemplated what that might look like. Surely, just by speaking he would upset Sudie, perhaps even send her out of the house afraid to return. Yet, the urge remained. He imagined sitting next to her and talking calmly about what had happened to him, how this new identity manifested itself and how he was feeling about that. He was sure she would understand.

He imagined a conversation like this:

"So, after I found that I was invisible I was terrified."

"Of course."

"I tried, in vain, to find the doctor, to find his assistant, to find the friend who had sent me there but I could not."

"I'm sorry, Charlie. That must have been a rough time." (Perhaps here she would place one of her soft, strong hands against his cheek.)

"It was. And then something curious happened. I discovered that, though fraught with complications, I was enjoying being unseen. I was enjoying being…nobody."

"You're not nobody, Charlie Cain."

"Not to you, Sudie. Oh, how I have longed to talk to you this way."

"What complications are you speaking of, Charlie? What's the hardest part about being invisible?"

"Going out. Yet I must. At first, of course, it hurt my feet. And I was initially flummoxed by not being able to carry anything with me. In a sense it's just me against the world. I have no shield, so to speak. There's no Complete Idiot's Guide to Being Invisible. I am a complete isolato."

"Oh, I see. You cannot take things with you."

"I cannot."

She would think for a moment. "So, Charlie, I guess you're saying that you're naked right now sitting next to me."

"I'm sorry, Sudie. Yes, I am. I should have made that clear. I'll go if you'd like."

"Heavens no! How could I pass this opportunity by? Come here, Charlie Cain."

Charlie's reverie had totally immersed him. He cleared his head and realized that Sudie was no longer in the room. He trotted out to find her. She was in the bath with a flute of wine.

Charlie sat on the toilet and watched her. She seemed almost sad, mopey, but perhaps it was only contemplativeness. Sudie sighed.

Speech gathered in Charlie's throat like a cough. He swallowed it.

Sudie drank some wine.

Charlie put out his hand and let it hover over Sudie's silver-streaked hair. Sudie looked up. Charlie moved quietly away. He was interrupting her pensive time. He let himself out and walked home, a bit pensive himself. On the way he took the opportunity to knock the leaf blower out of his beefy neighbor's hand one more time.

"Fuck," the guy said.

One afternoon he was visiting one of his favorite houses. It was here he often found casseroles and steaks and lambchops and homemade desserts that were taste delights. He also found money lying around on dressers and end tables. They must be pretty well off if money was treated so cavalierly. Sometimes there was a teenage son around and that made pilfering a bit difficult, but today he had the house to himself. In the refrigerator he found some kind of fish wrapped in foil with lemons and herbs. It smelled divine. And, in the back, a jar of homemade dill pickles. He was fishing that out when something brushed his feet. He jumped back, dropping the pickles which shattered on the floor and chased the cat, which had rubbed up against him, out of the room. It all happened so fast Charlie was a little wabbly.

And then he stepped wrong and a piece of glass entered his left foot at a 45-degree angle.

"Shit!" Charlie yelled.

He left the fish. He left the mess on the floor. And trailing blood he limped out of the house. All the way home he worried about the police. They could follow blood. They could DNA it and find Charlie. He began a zigzag pattern, moving between houses, yard after yard, and, every few steps, he wiped blood into the grass. When he emerged onto Brock Way his heart stopped. Not actually, of course. That's just what we say in stories.

There in front of Charlie's house sat Ellis Bruce's car. And leaning against it was Ellis Bruce. He was reading something off his cellphone.

Charlie crept nearer. The bleeding had not entirely stopped. Charlie crouched in the grass about five yards away from his editor, who was now talking into his phone.

"I'm telling you I'm worried about him," Ellis was saying.

"I'm gonna call the police. At the very least they can get him to come to the door."

Charlie was aghast. Charlie was frightened.

The phone conversation lasted a tad longer. Who was Ellis talking to?

"Ok, ok," Ellis said and put his phone away.

Ellis then, in exasperation, went to the front door and knocked in exasperation. Charlie assumed this was not the first time he'd knocked today. Then Ellis sat on the porch.

Meanwhile Charlie was watching blood leach from his body. It was vaguely surreal since Charlie couldn't see his foot, just a small red leak, a floating scarlet line, seeping into the ground. It made Charlie a little nauseated and he thought he might endanger himself further by throwing up. Ellis stayed a long time. Hence, Charlie sat a long time, bilious and fretful and bleeding. He was sure that any moment the police would arrive, or a Sherlock Hawkshaw, having found his bloody trail from pickle jar to here. Also, the grass was making his patoot itch.

Finally, Ellis stood, looked once more around the neighborhood, walked to his car and left. Charlie rose and moved toward his door. He decided it would be better to use the back door and he had secreted house keys by each portal. He let himself in, tracked blood across his kitchen floor, and, in the bathroom, found antiseptic and bandages.

Obviously, he had to stay inside the rest of the day. The bandage looked like a small white and seepy red creature scuttling across the floor. Charlie ate some hamburger helper for dinner—he'd gotten it from the Rojas's house and he cursed them briefly for their poor diet only to discover how absolutely delectable the heavily salted, processed food was. He spent his evening watching a basketball game with the sound on low.

The next day Charlie's foot had healed enough for him to take off the bandage and venture out in search of food and/or adventure, with perhaps a much-needed visit to Sudie's. He was becoming obsessed with Sudie. Was it love? Well, it wasn't *not* love. She fascinated him, especially by her contented solitude. Did she live just for her art? She never seemed to be out or have visitors. There didn't seem to be a male presence in her life. (To his shame, Charlie went through her desk while she was in the bath one day. There were no letters, no diary, nothing that would count as a life outside her home.) He'd also made a study of her bookshelves which contained high-brow novels, art books of course, some esoteric spiritual texts and a whole shelf of psychology and self-help books with titles like, *Feel the Fear and Do it Anyway*, and *Coping with my Disorders*.

The day was temperate and there were few people about. Charlie walked a little farther than usual and stopped when he saw a man kissing his wife goodbye at their car. Charlie sidled into the house and the wife followed after she finished kissing her husband, which took inordinately long. Ah, love, Charlie thought.

It was a beautifully designed house and Charlie guessed one of them was an interior decorator. Charlie had an impulse to mess everything up and, simultaneously, an impulse to tread lightly so as not to disturb the Feng shui.

The woman, young, pretty, athletic, with the yellow ponytail of a teenager, went off to the rear of the house so Charlie checked out the kitchen. There were gourmet foods in the pantry, wines and other spirits, and a refrigerator stocked with necessary food-stuffs, all neatly arranged. No boxed foods here. These young lovers cooked from scratch. Charlie stopped to consider the comfort of such a life and he was envious. Would he ever have that? Would he ever have any kind of relationship again that didn't involve fortean sex? As he imagined this couple's perfect life, he ate some foie gras terrine with black truffles. It was only slightly better than hamburger helper. He just had time to swallow and let the refrigerator door shut when the young woman entered the kitchen. She was wearing running shoes and gym shorts and a t-shirt that said, *Why Don't We Do It in the Road?*

She sat down at the island in the middle of her spacious kitchen and pulled out her cellphone. She speed-dialed someone.

"Hello there," she said. Her voice was surprisingly husky.

"Ha ha," she said. "No, I'm about to go for a run."

Her smile was a thing of beauty.

"Yes, he's gone…Not till tomorrow night…I know...Ha, yes, yes…I want that, too….I want it now even. Isn't that wicked?... Ok, yes, ok…I love you, too…Wait, I will…I will…I'll wear that if you'd like…Ok, 6 then. Use the back door."

Charlie was appalled. And titillated. And intrigued. This was certainly food for thought. It emboldened him for some reason. He moved closer to her. He could smell her shampoo, feel the heat rise from her perfect body. She jumped.

He'd gotten too close. She pushed back from the island and stood up, turning a complete circle. Charlie did not move away. He could have touched her.

Then he did touch her. He licked the end of his finger and set it, gently, against her lips.

She screamed.

Charlie went out through the front door quickly. She did not follow. He was a little sorry he frightened her, but not that sorry. He had half a mind to return to her house to ruin her tryst and made a mental note of the address just in case.

As Charlie was thinking about picking up some more food before returning home the sky grew plumbeous and then darker still. A storm was coming up fast, like a wild animal uncaged. This was not good news for Charlie. He was going to be caught outside wet and, hence, visible. He began to trot home. Drops the size of grapes began to pelt him. His body started to hold the moisture and his shape was quickly discernible. Up ahead he could see two guys working on a car at the curb. Charlie got off the street and began to jog across the lawns. This was worse because now his shape *and* his footprints were visible.

"Look at that," one of the mechanics said.

"What?"

"I don't know. That—moving—movement."

"Moving movement?"

"That—shape." He was pointing with a car tool.

"I don't see anything. Gimme that."

As he rounded the corner of his street Charlie sped up and,

sliding on the sidewalk in front of his door, he snatched up the key and quickly let himself in. A boom of thundered chased his tail inside. As he was closing the door he saw Ken's wife, Christine, standing by the curb. Her face was a twist of distress and astonishment.

*T*he first time Charlie visited Nocturna Gallery he found himself standing outside for a few minutes waiting to follow another guest in. After a while he gave up and opened the glass door himself and walked in. The woman at the front desk, just to the left of the door, looked up and, momentarily her face wore a querulous curl. Then she went back to the book she was reading.

Charlie felt good in the well-lit, mostly white space, with art all around him and, save for the bibliophile receptionist, no other people. The gallery was small and the space divided into thirds, in other words space for three separate artists. Charlie eschewed the other two and stood a long while in front of Sudie Nimm's work. There were a dozen canvases, all the same size, all done in related colors: greys, light blues, streaks of livid black. She was given the most space, possibly because she was so well thought-of. Charlie, having never given art much thought in his previous and visible life, was taken with her work but he didn't now know why. Though not exactly abstracts—there were pieces of modernity and faces and limbs in her work—they seemed a wild chaos, held together by some elemental force: earthquake, hurricane, flood. Images swirled and collided. Elements crashed up against each other, sometimes melding into strange, otherworldly constructions. There was violence here but also something else, something mitigating, something spiritual. Was it love? Was it religion? Charlie was rapt.

A few days later he returned to the gallery. He had not been able to get Sudie's images out of his head. Rather than visit her he wanted to steep himself in her finished work. This time he followed an elderly couple into the gallery. They went first to the receptionist (who turned out to be the owner of the gallery, an older woman with a face that was both sweet and stern) and Charlie, of course, went and stood in front of Sudie Nimm's wall. Again, he was moved, and again he did not know why.

Then he heard her name. The couple who had preceded him were asking about her work and, apparently, discussing price. They were going to take some of her art away.

"We'd like to talk to the artist before we decide which pieces," the woman was saying.

"I'm afraid that's not possible," the owner said.

"Is that gallery policy?"

"Not exactly a policy but some artists wish their private lives protected."

"And this Sudie Nimm is one such artist."

"Let's say she wants me to handle all sales. Hence, the gallery." The owner gave a wry smile, as if she'd won a debating point.

"Does she ever visit the gallery?"

The owner hesitated. "Sudie Nimm is agoraphobic," she let out.

"She's afraid of—what? Closed spaces?"

"She stays at home," the answer came. "Sudie Nimm does not leave her house."

Charlie's heart began to beat in an almost painful fashion. He had to leave the gallery. He went to the bus stop and waited. He felt hurried, flushed. He wanted to see Sudie, to make sure she was alright. On the bus there was the usual mix of business folks, hipsters and blue-collar workers. Charlie sat at the rear. A young couple entered and started in his direction. He was so distracted by the storm in his head that they almost sat on him before he could move.

Once back in his neighborhood he went straight to Sudie's. The door was unlocked but she was not in her studio. Her bedroom door was open and, as Charlie tiptoed past, he saw her asleep on her bed, on top of the covers. She was wearing an old white slip, which was slightly yellowed and wrinkled and had slipped up her legs, exposing her large, veined thighs. She was snoring softly, little exhalations which sounded a bit like a dog's.

Charlie watched her sleep for a few moments and then went to the studio. Quietly, somewhat guiltily, he began to look at the stacks of canvases that lined the walls. For the first time he allowed himself to view work that he had not been given permission to view. There were many styles represented, some wildly different from the work at Nocturna, some in a similar vein, but with different colors and patterns. Charlie was smitten with them all. For some reason, he took her work personally. He felt *possessive*.

Charlie did not hear her come in. When he turned she was standing in the doorway staring straight at where he was and where some of the paintings had been moved away from the wall and spread out on the floor. Sudie stood there, barefoot, her hair a wild nest, her face inscrutable. She was not afraid, but she was troubled. Charlie scooted away on his butt. He watched her stillness, as if she were a deer and he an interloper.

Sudie turned her head slowly, this way and that. She looked back to where Charlie had just been. And then she whispered, "Jack?"

Who is Jack? Charlie wondered.

Then a few tears rolled down Sudie Nimm's beautiful cheeks.

Charlie was heartsick. Somehow, he had caused this. And when Sudie sank down to the floor in the doorway and sat there quietly weeping Charlie slipped around her and ran.

Back home he was too upset to know what to do. What had happened? What had he witnessed? Eventually, he settled down and got online. He ignored the 600 email messages that he'd been ignoring for weeks. And he googled.

Jack Nimm had been an administrator with the local symphony orchestra. Three years ago he died from pulmonary disease. Was this why Sudie was a recluse? Or had she always been? Charlie googled 'agoraphobia,' but bogged down reading about it. The topic seemed too large, too diffuse. He didn't understand, and he wondered if he could.

But, Charlie's heart filled with love. Sudie Nimm occupied a place in his heart now that had formerly been only a black hole. What did he want from Sudie Nimm? Nothing, he wanted nothing from her. He only wanted the chance to be near her sometimes, to watch her, to learn from her about art, and life. About art. And life.

Charlie the Thief. This is what he was now. A thief and, perhaps, a sexual predator. He stole food and money out of necessity. And he observed women in their private moments out of a necessity, too. This is what he told himself. In his present condition the only sexual release he could find was observational. He saw a lot of naked women. He watched them do things few men get to witness. He watched them make love to their husbands and lovers. Then he went home and masturbated. Thinking himself beyond the pale of humankind, he was restrained by no conscience and he used his extraordinary condition to prey upon his compatriots.

Poor Charlie, ghost-lover. A man, thin of substance as the air.

He had not forgotten Patience Spent. He was a little afraid to return to her. But, of course, he needed to. Her sirenic presence on this plane was, surely, a blessing for him.

One evening he returned to the home of the young, athletic blond who was cheating on her husband. He had had a bad day and had spent most of it indoors trying to set up an online payment system that would allow him to convert his cash and stolen goods into money in his various accounts. It was almost more than he could handle. So, he rewarded himself with a little voyeurism.

But, on this night, the lover was not there. The husband was.

Once inside, Charlie found the couple watching television. They were already in their pajamas and he was nodding off next to her, his legs across her lap. This did not seem promising. Charlie decided to see if he could goose things along.

He moved behind the couch and stood over them. They were watching—or not watching—some inane reality show. Trailer Park Gigolos. If only Charlie could find a more sexually stimulating show than this drowsy couple. He thought about that for a while and decided it was improbable.

He had another idea and, though it had its risk, he was delighted with it. The husband was spread out on the couch, his eyes opening and closing slowly. She seemed to be watching the television but she also seemed a million miles away. She was thinking about *him*, Charlie thought. The guy on the phone. Her sweetback.

Charlie reached over and touched the husband's inner thigh with a fingertip. Nothing happened. He used more fingers, raking upward, gently, toward his crotch. The husband fluttered his eyes but the shades went back down as if they weighed too much. Charlie went all in. He found the fellow's penis through his thin pajama bottoms. Charlie began to rub it in earnest. It thickened quickly. It was a pretty substantial cock, thicker than Charlie's own, but about the same length. Now the man kept his eyes closed but he began to smile. Charlie squeezed. He gently pumped him. It felt strange jerking another man off, but oddly stimulating. It was kind of a turn-on, Charlie admitted to himself. The penis poked its stiff head through the gap in the pajama bottoms. Charlie straightened up.

The man opened his eyes. He blinked a few times. He looked at his own hard pecker. He looked at his wife with a devilish smile.

"Lover," he whispered.

His wife turned. "What?" she asked. She seemed surprised. His cock was out!

"My lover," he repeated.

"What is it?" She was wary but, perhaps, titillated.

"Look what you do to me."

He pulled aside his pajamas.

"Oh ho," she said.

"You want this."

"I just might," she said. "What brought this on?"

He was momentarily mizzled. "I was going to ask you that?"

Charlie feared he was about to lose them.

"No matter," she said. And she went down on him.

Charlie thought it was about the best show he'd ever seen. They never left the couch but they managed 4 ½ different positions. It was so hot Charlie could not wait to get home to perform his paw-paw tricks so he did it while watching them. Later, while straightening up before bed, the wife found the small, glutinous puddle behind the couch and looked at her husband admiringly.

"How many times did you come?" she asked.

"I lost count," he said, smiling.

"Well, you've got some range, Tiger."

One morning Charlie found a single, printed page stuck under his door. It was from the Neighborhood Watch. Apparently, someone had been stealing food and small amounts of cash and there was a meeting at Henry and Katy Ford's house to discuss options. A representative from the police would be there to guide the discussion.

Charlie's initial response was distress. But his invisibility, if it had done nothing else, had emboldened him. How could he be caught? No one would believe that an invisible man was responsible for the pilfering. Charlie decided to attend the meeting.

The Ford's house was on Charlie's street, two blocks east, on the corner of Brock Way and Regulator. Charlie walked down in the gloaming and joined a number of couples who were gliding into the Ford's open front door. Inside there was a table of food and about twenty chairs jammed into the small living room. The interior of the house was nondescript: it could have been anyone's house in this neighborhood at this time in human history. Henry and Katy Ford seemed like dull, well-meaning folks.

The police officer who attended was named Peter Natural. He was a large, Aryan fellow, as handsome as a coat of mail. His leather gleamed. His revolver looked as big as canned ham. Charlie observed him at close range. This fellow smelled like trouble to Charlie, though, honestly, Charlie had been cowed by authority his whole life.

Henry Ford opened the proceedings. "Thank you all for coming. Sorry there aren't more chairs. Honestly, we didn't know how well this would go over. But Katy and I welcome you to our home. We have been victims of the sneak thief, as most of you have been, and, well, I'm no speaker, I just thought we should talk about what we can do."

Charlie was sure he'd never visited the Ford's house. What was their game?

"This thief is wily," a large red-haired man said. "No one has seen evidence of his presence. It's as if things just started—evaporating."

"We lost an entire pork tenderloin," an asthenic guy said.

"We lost money."

"Casseroles."

"Sandwich meat. And wine."

The litany went on and on. In a way it made Charlie proud. He'd made an impressive haul with little evidence left behind.

"He cut himself in our house and the police now have his DNA. He left bloody footprints through our house and out onto the lawn. The police sent for their dogs but it rained before they got there and the dogs lost the scent quickly."

"He cut his foot?" a middle-aged school teacher asked.

"Apparently."

"Well, for goodness' sake. Why was he barefoot?"

Charlie now fretted. Could the DNA thing come back to bite him on the ass? He had no idea how that worked but he was fearful. Surely there was no way to match that blood to any criminal record since Charlie had never been arrested.

The meeting went on and on. Charlie grew bored. Before he left he visited the Ford's bedroom and found a small diamond ring in a jewelry box. He took it because it was small. He took it because thievery was becoming irresistible to him.

Days passed. Weeks passed.

Charlie spent a lot of time at home. He was still dodging visits from his editor, still stealing from neighbors, still sending his bank cash to deposit (the jewelry he'd taken he ended up dropping in a Salvation Army deposit box), still finding his invisibility preferable to his old life.

When he went out he usually visited Sudie. Some days he spent an hour there; somedays he stayed through supper and into the evening.

One day he entered Sudie's home by the unlocked front door. Sudie was not in the studio. She was sitting in the living room watching the front door. She had seen it open and close by itself. She held herself very upright, very steady.

She waited.

Charlie waited also. He stood just inside the door in the foyer that opened onto the living room. The tiled floor was cold under his feet. He studied Sudie and the queer expression on her face. It was grim and determined and as full of sadness as a jail is full of company. She was dressed in a clean full-length dress of shimmering blue. She was not dressed for painting. Charlie found her uncommonly beautiful and his heart reached out to her. He cautiously moved toward her.

When he was within a couple yards he stopped and studied her face further. She now wore awareness like a herding dog.

Sudie whispered a single word which escaped her mouth like a short exhalation, "Jack?'

Charlie did not know what to do. Did he dare speak?

He did not wish to speak. Instead he moved toward Sudie and stooped down. He took one of her hands in his. She sighed.

"It is you," she said. "I knew it was. Who else would it be? You told me you would return."

Charlie squeezed her hand as if answering.

"I miss you," Sudie said. "I love you, Jack."

Charlie leaned forward and placed his lips lightly on Sudie's. She kissed back eagerly.

Charlie broke the kiss but kept hold of her hand.

"Jack, my love. You still have your body?"

She reached out and put her other hand against Charlie's chest. Then she ran her hand down his chest and over his arms and, finally, up to his face. She felt Charlie's face and a quizzical look ran across her face.

"Is it you, Jack? I feel you. I feel you, but it is different. Death does this. Sweet death. I am ready, Jack. May I follow you?"

Charlie shook his head back and forth so hard that Sudie felt it.

"My Jack," she said and tears rolled down her cheeks.

Charlie kissed her again. He let go of her hand and wiped the tears away. He wanted to speak but he did not want to ruin Sudie's reverie.

"Kiss me again, Jack," Sudie said.

Charlie did. This time Sudie's kiss was fierce, pressing her face hard against his.

"Jack, Jack, make love with me, please. I will undress for you right here."

Sudie reached for the zipper at the back of her dress but Charlie stopped her hand. He brought the hand back between them and he held it gently and played with her fingers. He had wanted Sudie from the very first moment he saw her. She was a goddess. But he did not want to make love with her in the guise of her deceased husband.

He let go her hand and moved back a few feet. Sudie looked pained and querulous.

Charlie chanced a whisper as he moved a few more steps back. "Sudie. Paint," he said.

Sudie's tears now flowed freely.

"Jack," she said.

Charlie was drifting toward the door like smoke.

"Paint, my love," he whispered. And he was gone.

Charlie left Sudie with a mad consmatteration of thoughts caroming around in his pate. He loved her. He also desired her. Selfishly, he thought of returning and taking her to the bedroom. It would only further break her heart. And she would certainly recognize that the man making love with her was not her late husband.

Charlie thought of Patience Spent.

Night was coming on and a chill was in the air. Charlie's skin was pebbled with goosebumps. He found Patience's house and the front door was locked. Charlie thought she might be out and this made him sad. He did not want another lonely night of handjive and fantasy. He wanted flesh.

He knocked lightly.

After a moment he heard footsteps coming toward the door. Patience was suddenly before him. She stood in the doorway and looked out onto the seemingly empty porch and the purply gloaming.

"Is it you?" she spoke, after a few heartbeats.

Charlie put a hand out. She found it immediately.

"I knew you would return. Come."

Charlie followed her into her jazzy, eccentric den. Candles burned on every surface. Did she always keep them lit? Or did she somehow know that this was the night Charlie would return?

She was wearing a full-length, green satin robe decorated with alchemical symbols.

"Sit," she said.

She sat cross-legged amid a bunch of large, colorful pillows. Charlie sat opposite her. The pong off her body was heady, a very human redolence. Patience closed her eyes and seemed to be lost in her own version of imploration. She opened her eyes after a few moments.

"Tell me who you are," she said.

Charlie's mind swam.

"Are you Eros?"

"I am who you need," Charlie whispered. He did not know where that came from.

Patience smiled like one receiving godhead. "Mm," she said. "You speak."

"I can," Charlie whispered.

"I understand. Words can be bridges but they can also be loose footway stones. I only seek the bliss of the Clear Light."

Charlie smiled. This witchy, wily, wiry woman intrigued him. He also remembered how unearthly sexy her body was when she danced for him.

"I have oils," Patience said. "Shall I anoint your body with them?"

Charlie thought about this. That could be fun. But he wanted to get to the good part. He was impatient with Patience. He wanted her to touch him again.

64

"I want nothing between our skins," he said.

"Ahh," Patience answered. "My skin is yours."

She stood. The satiny dress had a side zipper which she now unzipped. She was wearing nothing underneath. She returned opposite him and took up her cross-legged position again. Charlie's eyes ran over her body. Her full breasts—one with a vein as blue as campfire smoke snaking across it like a stream, her taut stomach, her dark and tangled sex. Her furze bush was black as sloe and thick like a thicket.

"Shall I undress you?" Patience asked.

Charlie took one of her hands and placed it against his chest.

"Ah, yes," Patience said. "I was raised Catholic but quit when my overly eager interest in the phallic saints gave my priest the vapors and he chucked me out."

Patience's hand circled Charlie's breasts, clockwise then widdershins. She found a nipple and pinched it. She ran her hand down his chest slowly. When it came to his belly Charlie tried to suck it in some but to no avail.

"Buddha belly," she said. "Buddha with a wang." Patience giggled.

Her hand had found Charlie's cock which was as hard as the devil's dam.

"Damn," she said, wrapping her hand around it. "Your chakras must be magnificently aligned."

Charlie said, "Huh."

"Mm, my spirit being. I am so happy you like Patience's sex. I want only to please you. Shall I drink your essence again?"

"For starters," Charlie said, a bit too loud, a bit too enthusiastically. It certainly didn't sound like a god's voice.

Patience's hand hesitated a moment. Then she took control again. "Lie back."

Charlie did. There were pillows everywhere. He felt as if he were in his own private harem.

Patience began to lick his Buddha belly and then down around the tops of his thighs. Her long-nailed fingers tickled his scrotum. Charlie thought he might burst prematurely. He was usually not quick to come but Patience Spent was expert in the ways of physical love.

She took him in her mouth and, while she worked him, she hummed with pleasure. Her little Pooh tune was such a turn-on. She also placed the tip of a fingernail at the entrance to Charlie's anus. It felt like sex with a hummingbird.

Charlie put a hand on each of her shoulders. "Rise," he whispered.

Patience lifted her mouth reluctantly off Charlie's holy member. Her face was rapt. She looked as if she were part of a religious ceremony that might take her to the next bardo.

"Now fuck me," Charlie whispered.

"Oh, Oh!" Patience said, and she began to cry. Charlie wondered if he were destined only to make women cry. A shudder ran through her delicious body.

Slowly, reverently, Patience rose and moved forward. Charlie was mesmerized watching her perfect body rise above him. She put her hands out and found each of Charlie's hips and she then placed a knee on either side of him. Slowly, slowly, she lowered her wet sex onto Charlie's taut manhelper.

"You are so large, my divinity. You fill Patience."

Charlie could not believe how good she felt. She squeezed him with her vaginal muscles. He'd never been made love to this way. And she looked so beautiful, almost...*beatific*.

While she began to move on him, grinding her ass down, closing her eyes and moving like she did when she danced, Charlie put a hand on each of her full breasts. She moaned and that was all it took. Charlie emptied himself into her.

"Ommmmmmmm," Patience said, her face twisted with pleasure. "Aummmmm," she said again. "All peaceful. All light." And then, "Wait, wait...wait...I am re-entering my body. I am flesh AND spirit."

Charlie was still shuddering into her. Patience closed her eyes and pushed her pudendum forward with muscular exactitude.

"Oh My Fucking God!" she screamed as she orgasmed on Charlie's consecrated cock.

She lowered herself slowly onto Charlie's chest. They sighed together. Her hair smelled good. Charlie put his arms around her and they lay there for a good while, like all young lovers from across the great wash of time. Charlie kissed her hair and petted her back, relishing the silkiness of her skin.

Patience made little mewing sounds and planted small kisses on his chest. She seemed blissed out, like a child after too much sugar.

"I have reached nirvana, egolessness, the immutable light, Buddha Amitabha," she said, after a while. "I did not think I ever would, or at least not this young. I've been studying hard for years, though. All in preparation for you."

Charlie answered by putting a finger under her chin and kissing her.

"That is nice," Patience said.

They lay quietly for a while longer.

"Shall we go again?" she said, looking where Charlie's face would be if he were visible. "How many times can a god come?"

Charlie shrugged.

Patience put her head back down. "We have all the time in the world," she said. And then added, "Beyond that even!"

Charlie smiled. He stroked her hair.

"I want to please you in every way," Patience said.

Charlie kissed her again.

"I know every position in the Kama Sutra," Patience said. "Amun and Tawaret guide me."

Charlie felt his member filling again.

"Oh yes," Patience said, feeling it beneath her. "Again and again. As above so below."

She rose and, reaching back with her hand she positioned Charlie's cock inside her vagina.

"Mm," she said.

"Mm," Charlie said.

When they began to move again Patience closed her eyes. She was communing with the infinite. Then her eyes popped open.

"Oh! What shall I call you?" she asked, her face full of pious fervor.

"Charlie," Charlie said.

TWO

"It is only shallow people who do not judge by appearances. The true mystery of the world is the visible, not the invisible."
—Oscar Wilde

More and more people were ringing Charlie's doorbell and knocking on his door. Ellis Bruce came about once a week. He sometimes shouted through the door, threatening to call the police because he feared something dire had occurred. If he only knew.

Ken and/or Christine came by. Sometimes Christine left baked goods on the porch. If they were staking out the house to see Charlie emerge and pick up the food they were disappointed. He got the food alright but usually at night when his vagility was less complicated, when his invisible movements were further cloaked by darkness.

More troublesome: Charlie's sister Ruby had gotten wind of Charlie's unavailability. Charlie was ignoring her phone calls and emails until she showed up on his doorstep. After that he called her and the relief in her voice was gooey and melodramatic.

"Charlie, thank God," she said.

"Hey, Ruby, what's up?" Charlie disingenuously answered.

"Charlie, Charlie, you're not answering the phone or emails or your doorbell. What the hell is going on? If Mom and Dad were alive this would kill them. Are you alright? Do you need me to come over? Are you hurt? I talked to Ellis and he said he'd heard the TV numerous times and he didn't understand why you weren't reviewing or answering or what all. He was going to call the cops, did you know that? He was going to break down your door, Charlie. You can thank me for stopping him because I assured him that I would contact you and, thank God, I did, right? Charlie, what's going on?"

"Sis, this is too much. I'm fine. I'm a little ashamed to admit what's going on."

"Tell me, Charlie. We could always talk."

This was not true.

"Well, Sis, please don't talk about this much because I'm full of self-doubt and my confidence wavers."

"Charlie, is this a sex thing? Did you fail with some cold-hearted woman? Because, if so, Charlie, I'll have a thing—"

"Sis, Sis, let me finish."

"I'm sorry, Charlie, it's just that—"

"Sis!"

"What Charlie, what?"

"I'm writing a novel." This reason made no sense, of course. Charlie was inanely adlibbing.

There was a silence that stretched around the world. Charlie thought perhaps he had killed his sister with this astounding news.

"You're writing a novel," she finally said, in halting tones.

"I know. It's absurd. How dare I presume I can."

"No, no, Charlie, that's great. But, what are you, you know, living on?"

"I had some money saved. And with the house paid for I have little overhead. So to speak. Have I thanked you for being so generous about the house?"

"Yes, Charlie. Well, ok. Thank God you're ok. Do you want to have dinner some night?"

"That would be lovely."

It wouldn't.

"What night is good for you?"

"Will Grace be there?"

Grace is Ruby's wife. She is a large woman with beautiful white hair and a heart that is too open. The world has stepped on her. Charlie likes Grace very much.

"Of course. Though, you know, we have our rough patches."

"Of course," Charlie said, as if he knew a lot about relationships.

"So, what night, Charlie?"

"Let me call you."

"Charlie, you can't be writing 24 hours a day. Surely you can give me a night."

"Well, the thing about that is, Ruby darling. I'm sorta seeing someone new."

But they aren't seeing me, Charlie thought.

"Charlie, that's wonderful! Bring her!"

"Oh, it's too soon for the meet-the-family thing. But, who knows?"

"That's wonderful, Charlie. And Charlie?"

Ruby was one of those people who made you answer conversational speed bumps like this.

"Yes, Ruby?"

"Just between me and you. I never cared much for Amber."

Amber, Charlie thought. Amber.

He had almost forgotten her. Almost.

Then she appeared on Charlie's front porch one evening. Charlie's front porch was becoming a very popular local stop.

Amber's knock was light and tentative, as if a fairy were seeking admittance.

"Charlie," she whispered.

It was easy to ignore her at this point.

"Charlie," she spoke a little louder.

Charlie crept to the door. He was inches from her. Yet he would never hold her again.

"Charlie, Ellis called me. He's worried about you."

Charlie put his hand to the door. Amber's voice. That voice. Once it had whispered endearments sweet as Tupelo honey into his ear.

They stood there on opposite sides of the door for a few minutes. Charlie imagined that Amber had put her hand on her side of the door and, in this way, they were communicating.

Then he heard her walking away. He almost cried.

He hung his head. And, in hanging his head, he saw the note she had slipped under the door.

Charlie, the note began. It was written on a check deposit slip.

Ellis called me to ask about you. I explained to him that you and I were no longer together. He told me that you had just about dropped off the face of the earth. I allowed as to how I didn't think I could be any help but that I would check on you. So, I came by. I have a queer feeling that you're inside the house right now and purposely ignoring me. I understand if that is the case. But, Charlie, I do still care about you. Please call and tell me you're ok.
With affection,
Amber.

With affection, Charlie read again. He put an intangible thumb over those two words. *With affection* was nice, Charlie thought. Maybe only polite. She didn't say, *Love*, for instance. Because she no longer loves Charlie. He already knew that.

To call or not to call.

Charlie called.

"Charlie, very good," Amber answered the phone. "You're alright, then."

It sounded like Amber, but a reserved Amber. Not the same woman who laughed at his jokes. Who shared his bed.

"Hello, Amber," Charlie said. "I'm fine. Tell Ellis to stop worrying. Tell everyone to stop worrying."

"That sounds like a Sisyphean task," Amber said.

"Right," Charlie said. Now he was the straight man.

"Why are you hiding out?"

"I'm not hiding out," Charlie said with some indignation. Of course, he was though.

"You're not answering your phone or emails and you're not answering your front door when you're home."

"I answer my front door," Charlie said, defensively, as if this accusation was going too far.

"Ok, Charlie. I'm glad to hear your voice. I'll tell Ellis you're ok and to stop bothering you."

Charlie hesitated. There seemed more to say but what it was was beyond him.

"Goodbye, Amber," Charlie said.

"Goodbye," Amber said.

Was she disappointed?

So, this was how Charlie decided to visit Amber at home, even if her doctor boyfriend were there. Or especially if he were there.

Charlie went at night. The buses were less crowded. And most people were home and not wandering around so he felt even more invisible, though he realized invisible was like pregnant. There was no less or more.

He walked from the bus stop to Amber's apartment. Her apartment complex was ritzy, complete with a doorman and a lobby that looked like a set from *The Maltese Falcon*. It required some patience for Charlie to wait till someone else arrived so he could enter. He waited about fifteen minutes and a woman with a small dog in her purse walked by him.

"Hello, Charles," the woman said in a plummy voice.

Charlie was startled. Then he realized the doorman's name was Charles. Had it always been and he'd forgotten? How many times had Amber entertained him at her place? She always said she preferred Charlie's house because no one could hear them. In bed Amber was a bit of a screamer. She was also one of those people, who, in sex's afterglow, feels embarrassed about everything that had just happened.

Charlie reached Amber's door. He could think of no other ploy than knocking and slipping in. He knocked.

Charlie heard footsteps and saw a shadow fall over the peephole.

"Who is it?" Amber's voice said.

Charlie stood still. He was flummoxed.

A bad moment passed. Amber started to move away from the door. Charlie rapped lightly again. Amber's eye returned to the peephole.

"Who is it, please?" Amber said, with an edge.

"Amber," Charlie whispered.

74

The eye moved quickly away from the peephole. Now the air was fraught with tension. Charlie felt as if he were watching a melodrama. What would happen next?

He heard the chain being slid back. There was a second's pause and then Amber opened the door. She looked down the short corridor. She stepped outside to look closer and Charlie entered her apartment.

When Amber closed the door and relocked it Charlie found a chair at the opposite end of the room and sat quickly in it. The television was on. Amber had been watching CNN and eating what looked like eggplant parmesan. Where was her beau, the good doctor?

Charlie spent the evening in the chair. He watched Amber eat. He watched her watch TV. He watched her take her dishes to the sink and clean the kitchen. It was a long night and a little boring. Except that Amber looked so beautiful. She'd lost a little weight and there seemed to be sadness around her eyes—though Charlie admitted he might be imagining this, or wishing it were so—but she was still the woman of Charlie's dreams.

Around ten Amber turned off the TV and began to turn off the lights in the living room. Charlie followed her with his eyes. When she moved toward the bedroom he followed with his invisible body.

He watched Amber brush her teeth. He watched her pee.

Then he watched her change from her work clothes into her pajamas. Charlie suppressed a gasp when she was clad only in panties. It didn't last long enough. She was into her nightclothes before Charlie could savor the moment. She didn't wear sexy, filmy nighties like a movie star. She preferred matching tops and bottoms with cartoon animals on them. Tonight she was wearing Yogi and Booboo.

Amber got under the covers and leaned against her bed pillows and read her book. Charlie moved closer to get the title. Amber was reading a novel that Charlie had reviewed a couple months ago. This touched him. He moved back toward a corner of the room where there was a chair with a slip lying across it. Charlie sat there and watched Amber read. He loved her. Still, he loved her.

After thirty minutes or so, Amber put her book aside and turned off the bedside lamp. She lay on her back. As Charlie's eyes adjusted to the dark he could see that Amber's eyes were open. She seemed to be contemplating something weighty. Then Charlie watched as she snaked an arm underneath the covers. She closed her eyes and, in a moment, began to breathe deeply.

When she started to pant Charlie felt his cock stiffen. O Amber, his heart sang.

Amber was biting her lower lip and moving like a piston, the covers rising and falling. Charlie knew some vocalizing was coming. Did she still scream?

"Nnnnnn," Amber said, bearing down.

Charlie's eyes were wide. His erection hurt.

"Ngngng," Amber said. Then: "Oh God, Oh Rich, Rich, yes, yes, YES YES!!"

She fell back.

Charlie exited quickly. He stopped in the bathroom and relieved himself into the toilet.

On the way home Charlie was a mixed stew of emotions. His heart hurt worse than his erection had. Fucking Rich. I'll kill the bastard. Why wasn't he home with his paramour, treating her like the wonderful woman she was? Was he making rounds, seeing patients, pulling twelve-hour shifts?

Then Charlie remembered something. The doctor Amber left Charlie for. His name was Frank.

Where was Frank? And who was Rich?

Charlie began visiting Amber often. Not every night but most nights. And every night she was alone. He didn't get a repeat performance of Madame Fist and her Five Daughters for another week and the repeat performance was better for Charlie. It was similar to the first time but for one significant change. Amber said his name when she came. She said *Charlie*.

Charlie went home that night with plans for a little five-on-one himself, to enjoy the idea that Amber was thinking about him. Instead he lay wide-eyed and cried. He would never have her again even if the use of his name meant she longed for him. He would never have another woman because he was invisible. His mind snagged on Patience again. It was erotic but it was empty. Still, what else did he have?

One night Amber was not home. Charlie, poor mooncalf, hoped she wasn't out with Rich. He still was clinging to the scant hope that Amber thought of him *that* way.

So, Charlie took the bus back to his neighborhood. On the bus there were a couple of punks with a lot of attitude. They entered and walked down the aisle as if their very presence put fear in the hearts of all in attendance. One of them was smoking a handmade cigarette. The bus driver asked him to put it out. He ignored him.

They sat a few feet behind Charlie. There was an elderly couple cowering in their seats, squeezed together against the window. This was an invitation, apparently, to these fellows.

"Hey, Mom," one of them said, the wit of the two.

The other guffawed and spat. He'd learned this from watching bad TV.

"Mom, I'm sorry I didn't come home for dinner. I was at the

whorehouse again."

"Har har har," his partner said. He blew smoke toward the old man.

"Look," the old-timer said.

"We are looking, Pops. It's what we do best. We look. We survey. We make our own rules. Got any questions?"

Others on the bus stared straight ahead. They only had to make their own stops.

Charlie rose and plucked the cigarette out of the smoker's mouth. He turned it around and placed it gently against the young gentleman's cheek.

"Jesus Christ!" the punk yelled.

"What are you doing?" his partner said.

"I'm burning, that's what I'm fucking doing. Look at my cheek!"

His friend began to laugh. "You forget which end goes in your mouth again?"

A couple passengers tittered. Now the wit played to them. He belittled his own friend.

"Sorry, folks. Sometimes I have to teach junior the simple things. Just yesterday he ate solid food for the first time."

Big laugh.

His friend was fuming. "I'll slit you," he sputtered to his entertaining pal.

"Watch it now, Brucie. Do watch yourself."

"I'll slit you!" Brucie repeated.

The bus stopped.

"Meet me outside."

Brucie followed him out. Once they were outside the driver shut the doors and the entire bus watched while they beat on each other. Smiles all around. And, when the bus started moving again they all applauded. They didn't know what they were applauding.

Charlie de-bussed in his neighborhood. He walked to Sudie Nimm's house. The house was dark and the door locked. Charlie sat on her stoop. Despite his triumph on the bus he felt bereft and desolate. What was he longing for?

Amber. He loved her and would never have her. He admitted that even if visible he probably would never have her.

He walked to Patience Spent's. She was home. He had a good time.

Charlie didn't return to Amber's again for a while. Instead he satisfied himself with stealing food, watching his neighbors in their private moments, and irritating the people who had always irritated him.

Chip and Aya Steele were the only Black people in Charlie's neighborhood. He was fascinated with them because he didn't know many Black people. They were still a minority where Charlie lived.

Chip Steele worked at an accounting firm. Aya was a fabric artist whose etsy shop was very popular. They had one child, a girl eleven years old, named Billie. Billie was a track star at the local elementary school. Once Charlie saw Billie outrun the neighborhood's fastest dog, a border collie yclept Saskia. Billie won a bet with that race and the loser, a raggedy White kid named

Whitey, who had to carry Billie's backpack at school for a week. Charlie had no idea if the bet's outcome was enforceable but he was charmed by the leggy young girl.

Once Charlie followed Billie into her home and he watched while they prepared a dinner and sat down together and ate it. Charlie was ravishingly hungry—he'd forgotten to eat because he had walked again to Sudie's house, only to find it locked and dark again—and, as Chip brought out a meatloaf he had prepared, Charlie's mouth began to water. As the family ate Charlie walked quietly behind them, around the table twice. They were so lovely. Charlie found no way to sneak a bite of food. He returned to a chair in the living room from which he could watch them eat. They were animated and chatty and they laughed often. Charlie was captivated by their easygoing familial banter.

After dinner Billie went to the kitchen to clean up and her parents went to separate rooms. Charlie thought he could sneak some food while Billie cleared the dishes. She was rinsing off plates when Charlie plucked a brussels sprout from its bath of butter on one plate. Unfortunately, it was a plate that Billie was about to pick up. She jumped back as if burned. She whirled, her face a mask of terror. Now Charlie felt terrible. The last thing he wanted to do was scare Billie Steele.

Billie kept her back to the sink and the kitchen cabinets as she moved crabwise out of the room. Charlie followed her. They found Aya Steele in the library reading a book.

"Billie, what is it?" Aya greeted her daughter, whose face looked stricken.

"Mom," Billie said. "I think this house is haunted."

"Billie, what in the world? We've lived here for five years. Have you ever seen a ghost?"

"Ghosts are invisible."

"Ok, Dear, have you ever seen evidence of a ghost?"

"Just now."

"In the kitchen. A ghost? What was it doing?"

"Eating a brussels sprout."

They both gaped for a moment. Then they burst into guffaws.

"Eating a brussels sprout?" Aya sputtered. "Billie, you have the best imagination."

Billie laughed too and the laughter cured her of the idea that she had witnessed some kind of paranormal episode.

"I guess I was thinking about something else," Billie said, as her laughing subsided. "I guess I imagined it."

"Ok, Dear. Do you want me to finish cleaning the kitchen?"

"No, I'm ok," Billie said and she padded off to the kitchen.

Charlie stayed a while in the library watching Aya Steele read. She was reading John Cooper Powys' *A Glastonbury Romance*. It was a book Charlie had abandoned a third of the way in. He was impressed.

After a few more minutes of watching Aya he found Chip Steele in his bedroom working on some kind of drudgery that Charlie assumed was boring as hell. He left the Steeles and went home where he made himself a large pot of black-eyed peas, which he ate in front of the television. He didn't notice the new note that had been slipped under his door sometime during his dinner.

It was from Amber again.

"Dear Charlie," it began. *"I find that I have been thinking about you. If you get a chance please call me. Or come by some-time. Yours, Amber."*

Not 'your Amber' but close enough. Charlie's heart beat fast. He called Amber.

"Hello, Charlie."

"I got your note. Why didn't you call?"

"Oh, I don't know," Amber said so softly Charlie could barely hear her. "I thought maybe you'd be home and I could see you."

You'll never see me, Charlie thought.

"Did you knock?

"No, I didn't." There was a long pause.

"Amber?"

"I didn't knock because it was silly of me to come."

"Not at all. What's going on?" He wanted to ask about her doctor. Or about Rick? Was it Rick? No, Rich. The name she'd said while masturbating.

"I guess I wanted to see you. I'm sorry."

"I'm sorry I missed you." Charlie didn't know where to go with this.

"Charlie," Amber said.

Charlie waited. Then said, "Yes, Amber?"

"Do you want to come over?"

A sob almost escaped Charlie's chest. He had nothing prepared to say. What could he say?

"I wish I could, Darling," was what he came up with.

"Oh. Why can't you?"

"I just, well, I can't right now. I do want to."

"Charlie, did you call me Darling?"

"I guess I did." Charlie chanced a laugh.

"You've never called me Darling. What does it mean? Don't tease me, Charlie. I'm going through a rough time. You can't imagine."

Charlie wanted to say, "YOU can't imagine mine." Instead he said, "I'm sorry, Amber. I'll try to come soon, ok?"

"You don't mean it," Amber said.

"I do," Charlie said, but she had already hung up.

*T*he next night Charlie visited Amber again. He went early so he could follow her in and not rely on the trick of knocking on the door. While he waited for her he watched a group of kids in a nearby park playing frisbee golf. They were so young and strong and agile and—*present*. Charlie yearned. Charlie felt severely diminished.

When Amber came walking up the sidewalk Charlie's tenderness for her spread through his shriveled soul, until he saw her face which was drawn and sad. He followed behind her. She greeted the doorman. At her apartment door he got too close and Amber heard him breathing. She whipped her head around. The corridor was empty. It was even empty of Charlie who had already entered her apartment.

Charlie stationed himself in the same chair he sat in before. It afforded him a view of the kitchen and the entire living room. Amber, after changing out of her work clothes—Charlie stayed where he was—returned to the living room, where she picked up the *TV Guide*. She was planning another lonely evening. She was wearing pajama shorts with Gumby on them and a tank top. Her willowy body made Charlie hurt in his invisible heart.

In the kitchen she heated a frozen pizza. While it cooked she returned to the *TV Guide* and studied it. Charlie watched her read as if she were as interesting as Jane Goodall's apes. Her legs, as shapely as plaster saints, drew Charlie like a lamentation.

While she ate she watched *Murder, She Wrote*, a show Charlie had never seen. It was of passing interest. After the pizza she put her plate in the sink and returned to the show. After *Murder, She Wrote*, she watched another show and then another. Charlie grew restless and bored. He wanted to inject some excitement into the evening for his beloved, Amber. She seemed as sad as organ music.

Finally, she went to bed.

Charlie followed into the bedroom. Amber read for a bit. Then she set her book down and leaned her head back against the pillow. She was thinking hard about something. Charlie wanted to soothe her brow.

Then she undid her pajama top, closed her eyes, and began to flutter her hands over her own breasts. Charlie marveled anew at the thick nipples which he used to trace with his finger as if they were ON buttons. Amber pulled her nipples and they rose accordingly--and so did Charlie's cock. When Amber's hand went below the covers, apparently into the top of her pajama shorts Charlie wanted to cry. She was so beautiful. Beautiful and sad and as sexy as a tangle of cats.

When she started to breathe heavily and make little muttering sounds, Charlie crept closer. He just wanted to watch. He cautiously drew the cover down. He could now see where her hand disappeared into her pajamas. It was driving him crazy. He forgot caution and began to stroke himself.

Then something stopped him. Amber said his name. Charlie's eyes grew wide. She said his name again.

Now, Charlie can be forgiven. He was crazed. He slipped onto the bed beside her. Then—then—he leaned over and took one perfect nipple into his mouth.

"Oh Charlie," Amber sighed.

How far could he go and she stay in her fantasy?

He snaked a hand down her stomach. Parallel to her own arm Charlie entered the sacred chamber of her pajamas. The heat from her body warmed his hand.

"Oh, mm," Amber said.

Charlie gently pushed Amber's hand aside and began to finger her himself. Amber took her hand out of her pants and scrunched further down into the pillow. Her breathing was ragged. Charlie scooted closer until his hard cock met her sweet, smooth thigh.

"Charlie," she said, and grabbed his cock.

She was getting frantic now. She pumped him while he had two fingers inside her.

"Oh Charlie, Charlie, fuck me now. Fuck. Me. Now."

Charlie didn't need to be told twice. He rose above her and swiftly but gently entered her.

"God," she said. "Oh God, Charlie."

"Amber," Charlie said, between breaths. "How. I. Love. You."

"Oh Charlie, just keep fucking me."

He did. She came and then a minute later Charlie came. It was quite an orgasm. He was emptied of everything save his love for her. That increased tenfold.

Charlie lay on top of her, drowsing. She might also have been asleep.

Then she screamed.

Charlie leapt off her and off the bed. Amber's eyes were wide open. She was terrified.

"Who's here?" she yelled. "Oh God, oh God."

Then she reached for her phone. She called 911.

This began, for Charlie, a period of abnegation, of being a homebody. Occasionally he talked on the phone to his sister or his editor, but he felt sick at heart about what had happened at Amber's. The sublime joy of making love with her was replaced with fear and guilt and self-loathing. He was sick of being invisible. He was sick of Charlie Cain.

Then, as if his own life took possession of him, Charlie did something remarkable. He really did start writing a novel. He called it, tentatively, *Memoirs of an Invisible Man.* What else did Charlie have to write about? Write what you know served Charlie well. Who else could write the great Invisible Man novel? He thought of a better title: *I'm Off to See the Piss-Cutter.* He would tell the story of the mysterious doctor Milton Raphael. He could call him something else. No good having a witch doctor mad at you.

And then Charlie wondered if indeed he were the only invisible man. Did the mad doctor make invisible people willy-nilly? Were there scores of them, hundreds, thousands? And what if Charlie could find an invisible woman to be his mate?

All these cracked, crazed ideas were pingponging around in Charlie's invisible cranium. He made extensive notes on a legal pad. He put these sheets in a folder and on the folder he wrote, "NOVEL, begun 5/8/--. Charlie Cain."

And, on his laptop the novel began to grow like dough rising. With all this free time it wasn't too long before Charlie had written 30,000 words. And he was far from through. What a tale he had to tell! Fictionalizing his own bizarre state came easy to Charlie. He added more zest to his concupiscent adventures. He bedded every housewife on his block. It was insane how easy it was to make love to a woman while being invisible (he wrote) because most women, most people, would rather live in a sexual fantasy than seek actual partners. They couldn't know that the ghost was an actual partner even as he came inside them.

And, in writing and fantasizing, Charlie began a chapter about the conquest of an African-American neighbor he called Maya. Charlie was especially turned on while writing this chapter. He decided to pay his Black neighbor a visit, *for research* he told himself. He also was low on food and money.

So, he slipped into the Steele's home and found Aya there alone. Charlie had a semi-erection already. He'd already written this scene, which ended with his character, Maya, screaming with abandon as his protagonist pumped into her.

Now, Aya looked around suspiciously as Charlie moved around her, avoiding direct contact. It was a dance Charlie had gotten good at. What should Charlie do next? He needed some food, so he went toward the kitchen while Aya moved off toward the back of the house. Charlie found some small items he thought he could sneak out with, a little tin of sardines, some cream cheese, some shaved turkey, a jar of olives. He collected these things and put them on the counter. Then he heard the rumble of pipes in the wall. Aya was taking a shower.

Charlie quietly moved toward the bathroom. The door was open. He could see Aya's dark, curvy shape behind the semi-opaque doors. She was softly singing a Kate Bush song. Charlie stood in the doorway transfixed. Her voice was lovely and her movements a graceful dance.

She turned the shower off and opened the door. She stepped out.

And there she was, as beautiful as Charlie's fantasy. Her chocolate skin shone like dark light. Charlie watched as she dried herself. When she walked toward him Charlie was tempted to take her in his arms right there but, instead, he stepped aside and then followed her into the bedroom.

He was thinking about the scene as he had written it. It seemed inevitable. She would give in to his soft caresses. She would lie back and spread her perfect legs. Charlie would soon have her frantic with pleasure.

Before she could step into her panties Charlie approached. He put a hand out. He moved that hand toward her buttocks. He hesitated as she raised her leg to put her panties on. Then he cupped one perfect cheek.

Aya Steele screamed so loud that the windows shook. She screamed and screamed and screamed.

Charlie ran. He did not scoop up his foodstuffs. He ran all the way home and, once inside, he vowed never, never again to use his visibility to make love to a woman.

And he let his novel lie doggo.

This was the beginning of a dark and fallow period in Charlie's life.

Charlie did not leave his home, except for food or money, for months. He stayed home and ate and watched TV. He grew fat—though he could only tell when he showered—and his protuberant stomach grew more protuberant.

He could not bring himself to read the novel he'd started writing. How dare he presume he could create anything as refined as a novel? He was *other*. He was despicable.

Charlie took stock of himself and he found himself morally wanting. He was ashamed of what he had done with his invisibility, whether it was a curse or a benison. He examined his life. The stealing would have to continue for now. He could not think of another way to make money or get food. So, how could he enrich his life in a more mature and honorable way.

He started with his neighbor, whose name was John, Charlie thought, though it could be Tom. John owned a small chain of chicken restaurants, but in the neighborhood, he was mostly known for his cars. He owned two, though he was a bachelor and lived alone. One was an Audi, tricked out with all the latest gizmos. The other was an antique Mustang from the 60s. This latter car John was rebuilding himself and weekends that was all he did. Charlie decided to observe him. In this way Charlie might learn how to repair cars, something that had seemed beyond his ken up until this time. Every weekend Charlie sat on an uncomfortable stool and watched John work. Sometimes Charlie had to get down on the pavement with John so he could peer underneath the car and watch the precision work the mechanic was doing. It was difficult for Charlie to grasp—having started from point zero he felt as if he'd begun too late—but he persevered and after a few weeks, Charlie began to understand what did what on a car.

Also, during the same week, Charlie began auditing classes at the State College. He had picked up a list of classes from one of his neighbor's house, whose hoodlum son was set to attend. Charlie gravitated toward English classes, of course. He decided he could do two a day and began with Medieval Literature, under Dr. Grymme, and The American Novel, with Dr. Helen Randall.

One of the ways Charlie tried to be a better person, a more chaste person, was that he began dressing when at home. He thought his nakedness was too liberating, made him indeed feel like a libertine. How many of us could walk naked into a woman's home and not think about sex? So, when at home—obviously he couldn't do it when he went out unless he was dressed like Wells' invisible man—he wore either pajamas and slippers, or a t-shirt and jeans and slip-on tennis shoes. He also started working out a bit with hand weights and simple exercise. He was improving his nonexistent flesh. He felt like a better man.

And he only thought about Amber when he wasn't busy doing homework or writing his novel. He'd gone back to the novel, inspired by his English professors.

*T*he novel was now entitled *I'm Looking Through You*. It was not about a man who suddenly finds himself invisible. It was about a man who lives, his entire life, on the fringes of existence. He's rarely seen, never talked to, never touched. The reason for this— and here Charlie was a bit murky in his thinking—was that the man, whose name was Frank Comma, was unattractive, boring and shy. Charlie thought this a deadly cocktail and he wrote in a fever now that he had stopped his own sins of the flesh. In his writing he could be wild. In his writing he could be the libertine he dreamed of being. Truth was Charlie had better sex while invisible than before and this made his chasteness more difficult and also something more admirable.

Frank Comma hesitated, the novel began.

After that sentence Charlie wrote 15,000 words and that was when he once again abandoned the novel as a foolish, egotistic enterprise. A week passed. He did schoolwork most evenings. When he picked up the novel again and reread those opening words he saw that they were ok, not great, but sturdy enough to build on. He wrote now like a house afire.

After a week he had completed 50,000 words. He knew this to be long enough to be called a novel and part of him (a fragile, emaciated part of his ego) congratulated himself on reaching this length. But the story was far from over and Charlie far from spent. He saw the story up ahead of him, a rainbow, a suspension bridge, and he knew he had to follow it.

During this time the doorbell rang numerous times. Often it was Ken and Christine. He had talked to Ken once on the phone to reassure him that he was alright, but had burned his face in a freak grilling accident and he preferred not to see people for a while. This prompted a visit from Christine about a week later.

"Charlie," Christine said through the door. "Your real friends don't care how you look."

Rather than talk through the door Charlie remained quiet.

"You let us know when you're ready to see people and we'll be back," she said.

Charlie waited. The screen from his laptop glowed like a light calling him back.

"You will, won't you, Charlie? You'll let me know and I'll be back like a shot."

The switch to singular from plural bothered Charlie a bit but he put it out of his mind. He had a book to write.

Sometimes Charlie thought beyond the end of the book. What would he do then? Try to have it published? He would have to insist on no author photos, no interviews, no contact whatsoever. He would out-Pynchon Pynchon.

These were idle dreams, of course. Charlie had no idea whether his novel would be good enough to be published. Even as a critic he sometimes couldn't say why a novel didn't work, or why one did.

And, then like a satori flash, Charlie saw that, even if his novel wasn't good he could write another one that was. Charlie's thinking was new to him. Charlie's thinking was . . . writerly.

Charlie's classes went well. He was learning a lot. Reading for his Medieval lit class was a bit of a bore but The American Novel inspired Charlie to write, and to read better books. (Swiping the books from the local chain bookstore was a bit of a challenge but he developed a method of moving them outdoors, during the day, and hiding them in the giant planters near the entrance of the store and then retrieving them by night.) He had never read John Dos Passos, or Kate Chopin, or Nathanael West, or E. L. Doctorow. Reading *The Book of Daniel* was a rush. Charlie tried to picture Doctorow writing it, tried to imagine he understood his scheme, how his story reached toward the universal by fictionalizing actual events. This last aspect particularly encouraged Charlie. He wanted to write The Great American Autobiographical Novel Which May or May Not Have Anything to do with Autobiography.

He was kept busy with school work and going to classes for a good long while. Eventually he stopped writing the papers required since he couldn't actually turn them in. And going to classes was a hassle, especially on inclement days. He did enjoy the classes once he got there. There were a lot of pretty, young women and that was both a turn-on and a distraction. There was one woman in his American Novel class who was smart as Professor Randall and so pretty Charlie had to turn away sometimes. She was brunette and freckled. Charlie loved freckles. He also loved women who could talk about Hemingway, Zora Neale Hurston and Joseph Heller.

As he let some of the schoolwork go he began to review novels again. Ellis had kept up the practice of mailing books to Charlie's house. It wasn't uncommon for Charlie to find 4 or 5 mailers with ARCs in them on his doorstep. Charlie began to get interested in new fiction again and he emailed Ellis and told him he'd be sending reviews again. This pleased his old editor and friend and it kept him from showing up at Charlie's house. It had been a while since anyone knocked on his door. Ken came once, knocked and walked away. He was as high as a boiled owl.

And Ken's wife, Christine, came once more. She knocked and just stood there. Through the peephole Charlie could see she was weeping, and she kept wiping her red eyes with the back of one hand. Charlie didn't want to talk about whatever was making her sad.

He wanted to see Amber again. He wanted to make love with her again. This physical need was troublesome. He masturbated so he could write without the distraction of his seemingly unquenchable lust. But, often, after masturbating, or even during, he was made sad and he would mump about and curse his malady for locking him in his home.

One night, late, Charlie ventured out again. There was a nip in the air and it gave him horripilation and shivers. He hurried to the nearest house with a lit window. He wanted to catch a couple in bed, or a woman undressing. He was flesh-lonely, even if his own flesh was transpicuous. At the Steeles' the bedroom window was lit with an orangey glow. O, to see Aya naked again, that would be delightful, Charlie thought.

There was only a sliver of space between the curtains and Charlie pressed an eye to it. He was faced with good old human nakedness within seconds. But it was not Aya, it was Chip. He was sitting on the edge of his bed and his schlong was in his hand. Where was Aya? The answer to that never came. Charlie did not really want to see Chip fax the pope, though it was interesting at a squiz.

At another home he saw a bedroom window's fuscous light and was able to peer inside. It was a couple Charlie had seen around but he did not know their names—Blackburn? Blackbird?—and he caught them in their nightly ritual, reading side by side before sleep. A few other houses, further from Charlie's, yielded even less stimulating views.

Charlie gave in. He hiked over to Patience Spent's. By the

time he got there he was freezing.

He didn't expect the back door to be unlocked but it was and, for a moment, Charlie worried about Patience's safety. The house was dark. Charlie banged a shin against the kitchen island. He stepped in something soft on the floor. He was trying to remember the layout of the house. He was sure Patience was in her bed asleep and he had not previously made it that far into her home.

He found the room and she was indeed asleep under a massif of scarves and throws and eiderdowns. The room was lit by a glowing Himalayan Salt Lamp. Patience made a soft susurrus while she slept, not exactly a snore but a sweet exhalation in 4/4 time.

Should Charlie wake her?

The hillock of blankets looked warm. Charlie lifted one side of the covers and slithered beneath them. Patience was curled like an S, with her backside toward him. The warmth underneath the covers was otherworldly lovely. Charlie chanced scooting closer and he gently draped an arm over the sleeping woman's jutting hip. Patience sighed but stayed asleep.

Charlie moved his whole body against her. There was a moment of stillness. Charlie could almost hear her eyes click open. She began to hyperventilate.

Charlie put his hand over her mouth but Patience was wiggling like an animal caught in a trap.

"Patience," Charlie whispered. And again, "Patience."

She had almost made it out of bed when she stopped. She lay still.

After a moment she said, "Is it you?"

"It is I," Charlie said.

"O my God," Patience said.

She reentered the dark tent of blankets and brought her body up against Charlie's. Charlie pulled her closer and put his mouth over hers. It was the kiss of human passion and need. When it was over there was silence and stillness from Patience. She seemed to be mulling something over.

"You kiss like a man," she said.

Charlie was stymied.

"Turn off your mind, relax and float downstream," he said.

It was chancy using such a quote but Charlie was still unpracticed at being a god.

"Yes," Patience said. "Yes. Take my yoni now."

Eventually Charlie and Patience fell asleep with Charlie's flaggy dingdong still inside her. In the morning Patience was surprised to find her god still asleep in her bed. She ran a hand down the length of him as if measuring him for a suit. Charlie opened his eyes and briefly panicked. He certainly hadn't meant to spend the night.

He put his arm around her again and they kissed again.

"Morning breath just like a man, also," Patience noted. Charlie held his breath, morning and all. "Tell me," she said. "Do you like scrambled eggs?"

They sat together at the breakfast table like an old married couple, though one of them was undiscernible to the human eye. Charlie was nervous. He had not eaten in front of anyone for ages.

Patience kept up a solid patter. It felt like decades of occult study had brought her to this moment and she was giddy with the power of it.

"I guess I never expected you to eat like a man," she was saying as her pretty, naked hips swiveled with the stirring of the eggs in the cast iron skillet. "Though it makes sense when I think about it. Didn't Jesus come as a man? Didn't Buddha?"

"Do not overestimate me," Charlie said. He was pretty much using his regular voice now. It seemed he had captured this poor dingbat and anything he did was blessed in her eyes.

"Of course, of course," Patience said. She brought two plates of eggs and thick brown bread toast to the table.

Charlie had not been cooked for since his limpid life began. It seemed the sweetest of treats. He dug in. The eggs were buttery and lightly salted and tasted like manna from heaven.

For a moment Patience was transfixed by the hovering fork and disappearing bite of food. As the forkfuls disappeared into Charlie's gullet she smiled in appreciation and began to eat herself. This did not slow her babble.

"The Egyptians, though polytheistic, did have a hierarchy of sorts, Amun and Isis were top of the pyramid, so to speak. And they also had humans who became gods. Imhotep comes to mind. Do you know Imhotep? I don't mean, do you actually, like, hang out with him, I mean, do you know the importance of Imhotep? Or perhaps you do hang out with him. I am only shone glimpses through rends in the veil. I do not know the afterlife except through trance study and visions brought on through the use of certain herbs and psychedelics. Once, under peyote, I was convinced I was having intercourse with Anzu, you know, the Mesopotamian bird-god. I imagine it was a dream-vision, at the very least, but for weeks afterward I had the distinct impression that I could fly if it wanted to. Can you fly, um, Charlie?"

Charlie shook his head no. Then he realized he had to speak. "Not in the sense you mean," he said.

Patience thought about this for a moment.

"I understand," she said. "Anyway, back to Imhotep. He was a priest of peace, the way Gandhi was perhaps. Or Leonard Cohen."

Charlie let her prattle on. The eggs and toast were delicious and the coffee hot and strong. He did not remember feeling so good.

"Oh, you've finished!" Patience said. "Would you like more food? Or would you like to have a meditation session? I have a new joss stick I'd like to try. Or we could make love again, of course."

Charlie loved her 'of course.'

"Come to me, my child," he said.

*P*atience walked around the table and felt her way toward Charlie's lap. He kissed her tenderly. Soon she was squirming against his erection.

"Do all gods have insatiable lust?" she asked.

Charlie answered the only way he knew how.

Charlie stayed with Patience for one, then two, then three days. He could not think of a good reason to go back home.

One the fourth day, over breakfast they talked some more.

"Charlie, can you tell me anything about the afterlife? I don't mean to press you. You've certainly given me enough already. Just your presence—whoosh—is so inspiring to me. And the lovemaking brings me to peaks of ecstasy I did not think I would find on the earthly plane. But, after we die, I mean, obviously the body carries on, because yours has. And what a body it is. (If Charlie had flesh here it would blush.) I love your body and how your body loves me. It's a perfect fit, isn't it? Yin and Yang."

"Laurel and Hardy," Charlie said, without thinking.

Patience's pretty face crinkled for a moment. "You—You made a joke! Wow, that's like a mind-fucker. I didn't know jokes were part of the holy experience, though the Maharishi had a potent sense of humor and, like you, a potent pecker, from what I hear. But, Charlie, tell me a little about the afterlife, if you can. Is it against the rules to vouchsafe such to humans?"

"Patience, my Patience," Charlie said. He let silence speak for a while.

"What you call the afterlife we call the gaudery. There are elements of it you wouldn't understand but I can tell you this. You still have a body and it's the best your body's ever been and there is a lot of sex. I mean a lot. And it's all loving and guilt free. Love is everywhere and there is no jealousy or proprietorship."

"Charlie, wow, that's heaven. That sounds like satyaloka."

"It is."

"Oh, Charlie, I feel so powerful now, just knowing that. Can we make love again? I want to do it now while I'm still feeling the vibrations of what you just said."

Charlie's wang was a bit tired but, somehow, Patience stirred him to herculean feats of concupiscence.

"First, daughter," Charlie spoke, solemnly, "You must kneel and take me in your mouth."

Patience closed her reverent eyes and crawled beneath the breakfast table. She took his flaccid member, worshipfully, into her mouth. Soon Charlie was ready for more profound positions.

They finished on the yoga mat with Patience bent around him like an inner tube. Charlie didn't even know he was inside her pussy until he came.

They lay in each other's arms in sweet afterglow. An hour of silence passed though neither slept or desired to speak.

Finally, Patience broke the hushed concord. "I think that last one took," Patience said, with a kittycat grin.

"What do you mean?" Charlie asked.

"I think we just made a little deity," Patience said. "Listen to this."

Patience rose and began a frantic, naked search of her shelves, both book and knickknack, and returned with a colorful paperback. She sat down and thumbed through, humming to herself. "Here!" she said.

She said, "Listen. 'The dancing, playful flow of life is, in the most reverent sense, sexual. Forms merging, spinning together, reproducing.' Isn't that vast, Charlie? Isn't that cosmically what's going on here? That's Old Tim Leary. Huh? Isn't that just perfect, Charlie?"

*H*ad Charlie not been convinced that Patience was as flaky as a blizzard he might have panicked a bit at the thought of her pregnant by their actions. Now that he thought about it he realized that he hadn't been practicing safe sex while invisible. Could invisible sperm make babies? Charlie suddenly felt horrible. But, what was the alternative? A glowing condom, floating into a partner's inner core? No. He had to trust that the woman was taking care of things, except with Patience. With Patience he should have asked.

"Are you not on the pill?" Charlie asked.

"Oh no, Charlie. The pill is soul-death. I practice my own form of birth control. It has to do with Vedic principles and mind control. As we say in class: Mind control is Birth control."

"So, why—um, why do you think we might have started something?"

"Oh, I could never use mind control on you, Charlie. I love you too much. I revere you too much. I want you to fill me up with Holy Light and Holy Love."

"I see," Charlie said.

"Is that alright, Charlie?"

"It's alright, my dove. I will withhold the impregnating part of my ejaculate from now on."

Patience giggled. "I think that cow has already sailed," she said.

Despite the twisted metaphor Charlie understood what she meant. But he doubted she could control her body to that degree.

"Patience," Charlie said. "Tonight, I must leave you for a bit."

Patience's face dropped. "Have I displeased you?"

"No, no. I have other matters to attend to. I shall return."

"Ok, Charlie. I trust you'll be back. I will readjust my aura and when you return I'll have something special cooked up. You'll see."

Charlie kissed her deeply and left. Did he truly intend on returning? He thought about it. What else have I got? he asked himself.

Before he left he said, "Patience, perhaps now you should start locking your door. I want you safe. Especially since you wear so little clothing. You know there are bad men out there."

"Oh, Charlie, I know you're only saying what you think I want to hear. I'll be safe as long as I have you."

Charlie worried all the way home.

Later at home he wrote the first poem he'd written in years. It was called, "With Patience I am a God."

The mail in Charlie's mail box was overflowing. He should have returned once or twice to clean things up. What if people had been coming by and they saw no evidence of occupancy? The lawn service had been by and his yard looked immaculate, almost phony, as if laid by someone who worked for Putt-Putt Golf.

Once inside Charlie found his phone first thing. It was loaded with messages. He scrolled through the usual suspects and found a voicemail from Amber.

Amber said, "Um, Charlie. I thought I'd get you. Uh, can we talk face to face? I had this weird thing happen. I can't really talk about it here. How about lunch if you're not busy or something? Um, I guess that's all. Call me back."

This was two days ago.

Charlie called back.

"Charlie, oh good," Amber answered her phone. "Thanks for calling."

"What's wrong, Honey?"

"Honey. That's nice. Thank you. Charlie, can we have lunch together?"

"What's up, Amber? Are you in trouble?"

"Trouble. Oh, I don't know. Can we talk face to face? Do you not want to have lunch with me? Are you still mad at me?"

"I've never been mad at you."

"Charlie, you're not answering me."

"Amber," Charlie said. A long pause ensued because Charlie didn't know what to say. "I'd love to see you but I don't want you to see me."

"That's a cryptic statement. What the hell, Charlie?"

"I mean, I, um, don't look so good right now."

"Charlie, is it your weight? You were always so self-conscious about something that doesn't matter a damn. You really thought I left you because you had a pot gut? Give me some credit, Charlie."

"It's not my weight," Charlie said.

"What then?"

"I—I've got something wrong with my face."

This gave Amber pause. "Something…wrong with your face."

"Yes."

"Charlie, what is it? You have a stroke or something?"

Charlie thought about this. That was going too far. "No, not a stroke."

"Is this a guessing game?"

"No, I'm sorry, Amber. I just don't know how to describe it."

"Wait. Wait. Bell's palsy. Do you have Bell's palsy, Charlie? I've seen that. It sorta makes half your face melt. It's not permanent, you know?"

"Bell's palsy. Yes. That's what it is."

"Oh, Charlie. Come on. It's Amber. Like I would care if your face looked weird."

"Amber, especially you. I don't feel so good about you and me, you know? You dumped me. That doesn't help my confidence."

Amber thought about that. "Oh, yes. I understand. I do, Charlie."

"So, I can't see you right now. Can you tell me what this is about?"

"Hm, I don't know. It's embarrassing, Charlie. I think I'm cracking up."

"Not seriously."

"I don't know. I've been so—so down lately."

"Why down, Amber? Is your doctor not propping you up?"

It was the right moment for a blunt question.

"No, Charlie. He's gone. He was a mistake. I make a lot of mistakes."

"That's not the Amber I know. You're a formidable woman, Amber."

"You're sweet to say that, Charlie. I just—just can't get it together. And I think, perhaps, because of my—*depression*—I'm hallucinating or something."

"What? What kind of hallucinating?"

"Charlie. Charlie, I wish you were here. I can't. Well, it's sort of about you. I don't know—I can't tell anyone else."

"It's about me?" Charlie was about to grok.

"Charlie, ok I'm just gonna say it."

Except she didn't. Charlie waited for what he thought was a long time.

"Say it, Amber," he coaxed. "It's Charlie."

"Yes. Charlie, it's just that, um. Charlie, you know, when I, um, masturbate."

Another pregnant pause. "Yes?"

"I often think of you."

Only often, Charlie thought. I am part of the cast of her fantasies. He held his tongue.

"I do. Anyway. I have fond memories of us, you know, in bed. And I use that. I use—us, that way."

"I understand, Amber. I do, too."

"Really, Charlie? Tell me what you remember best."

"Amber, this isn't about me, right? You were telling me about a problem."

"Charlie. This is hard. I feel so alone."

"You're not alone, Honey."

"Ok."

Charlie was left again to break a long silence. "Ok, most often, I guess, I think about caressing your butt."

"Mm," Amber said. "My Charlie. You always loved my ass."

"Yes. I did. I do."

"Thank you, Charlie."

"So, the problem is—"

"Charlie, one night I was fantasizing about you and touching myself and, I swear to God, don't think I'm crazy, but you entered me. You—you fucked me right there in my bed."

"Except I wasn't actually there."

'Yes! That's right. I mean, I felt it all, Charlie. There was cum in me! Charlie, actual cum. Please don't tell me it was a dream."

"I wasn't going to." Actually, this is exactly what Charlie was about to say.

"So, what was that, Charlie? Am I going crazy?"

"Has it happened again?"

"No. No, Charlie. But—here's the thing. I stopped masturbating. I stopped because that scared me so much."

"I see," Charlie said.

"So, Charlie, anyway. Now. I mean, now. I can't stop thinking about you. And I was wondering if you'd like to have sex with me again."

"Oh. Oh my," Charlie said.

"It took great courage for me to say this to you, Charlie."

"I understand. And the short answer is, of course, yes, yes, I'd love to have sex with you again."

"And the long answer?"

"Amber, my confidence is at an all-time low. The palsy is really ugly…and, it's just been so long."

"Charlie. You haven't been dating?"

"No, Amber. I think I'll never get it up again."

Actually, of course, Charlie's sexual confidence had never been higher. His experiences with Patience had made him more priapic than he'd ever been.

"See, Charlie, we can help each other," Amber said. Her voice was like sweet wine.

"Amber, Oh, Amber. I do want you. I want you right now."

"Charlie, let's do it now. I'm at work but I'll stop and meet you at your house. Oh, please Charlie. I'm—I'm sopping wet."

Charlie groaned. What was he to do?

"Amber," he said. "Come over tonight. It has to be dark. It has to be pitch black."

"Oh, silly Charlie. I'll come. Do you want dinner? I'll bring—"

"No, Amber. Later, long after sundown."

"Ok, Charlie, I'll be there. I can't wait."

"Me either, Honey."

Charlie hung up. Now he had a task. He had to make his bedroom as black as Pluto's palace.

Charlie hung black-out curtains (old bedclothes) on the windows. He took the bulbs out of all the nightlights. He frantically but methodically went around the house looking for any sources of light, even the smallest glow. After a few hours he thought he had the bedroom blacked out but could not trust any other room. She would have to come straight to the bedroom.

That night, long after dusk, the obscurity ticking like a bomb, Amber found a small hand-lettered envelope taped to the front door. The note was to the point: *The door is unlocked. Come straight to the bedroom.*

Amber opened the heavy, carved wood door onto a darkened living room. She could not help but whisper Charlie's name into the murk. There was no reply so she made her way to the bedroom, shuffling to make sure she did not trip. There was faint light coming through the windows. Not so when she reached the bedroom.

"Charlie, are you in here?" she whispered.

"I am. Shut the door once you're inside."

"Charlie, this feels silly."

"Please, Amber."

She did as instructed. Now she stood just inside the door, her eyesight gone. The room was as black as remorse.

"Charlie, where are you?"

"Under the covers."

"What am I to do?" Now Amber felt shy. On the phone she felt emboldened by her lust and her, apparent, sexual phantasm.

"What do you want to do, Amber?"

"Charlie, this feels like a silly game. I'm going to turn the light on."

"NO!" Charlie barked. Amber jumped at his vehemence.

"Ok, Charlie, ok."

"I thought you wanted to see—to be with me. If not, just let yourself out."

"Charlie, you seem so cold toward me."

"Amber, the opposite is true, believe me. I have longed for you."

"Then why this—this charade?

"I've explained it to you, Amber."

"I see. I remember. Your confidence is low because I dumped you and—and your palsy."

"Amber, I'm so glad you're here."

"Me too, Charlie. What should I do?"

"Undress," Charlie said, simply.

"Oh. Ok, Charlie. Um, are you—you undressed?"

"As naked as the day I was born."

"Ok, Charlie."

Amber took off her shoes and set them gently aside. Her feet recalled for her the plush, synthetic carpet in Charlie's bedroom. Next, she pulled down her tights and, since she could see no chair to lay them on, let them flutter out of her hand. She undid her skirt and let it fall and then unbuttoned her blouse. Now, in her bra and panties she hesitated.

"Should I take it all off, Charlie? You used to like to take my underwear off yourself."

Did he? "Yes, Amber, come to me." Charlie's voice sounded deeper, more mysterious.

Amber shuffled forward until her shins hit the end of the low bed.

"Ow, ok," she said. "Make room for me, Charlie."

Charlie held the insubstantial blanket open and Amber slid into bed next to him. The contact of their bodies made them both gasp. Such cellular memory. Such fantasy fulfilled. They both held close without speaking.

Finally, Charlie said, "Amber. Amber, I have missed you so badly. You feel—you feel just like you." He buried his face in her hair. He kissed her ear, and cheek, and neck.

"Oh, Charlie."

She brought his mouth to hers. They kissed.

"Charlie, Charlie. You feel wonderful. You've lost weight."

Charlie chuckled. "You have no idea."

"Undress me, Charlie," Amber said.

Charlie unsnapped her bra with one hand.

"Nice trick," she said.

He put his mouth to one breast and sucked there.

"Oh, Charlie. My Charlie. I feel like a virgin again."

"We'll soon get rid of that impression," Charlie said, reaching a hand into her panties to caress her ass.

"Oh, that first class ass," Charlie said. "Grab my dick now, Amber."

Amber was taken aback—and titillated. Charlie had never talked this way in bed before. He was never so bold. Charlie had a tuffet of hair spreading from his navel to his pubes. Amber ran a hand through that, saying, "Charlie, I've always loved that little hairy path."

Then Amber did as directed and found his member adamantine.

"Jesus, Charlie, have you been working out? Is it possible to make your—your *dick* in better shape?"

"It is. I have," Charlie said. "I got to be good looking cuz I'm so hard to see. Now I'm going to tear your panties."

And he did.

"God!" Amber said.

"You're so wet, my love," Charlie said, as he put a finger to her slit.

"Charlie! Right on—right on my clit! God, that feels good."

Amber was working Charlie's cock. They both were primed for intercourse.

"Charlie, I mean, Jesus. You're so hard and, I swear, you're bigger than you used to be."

"Oh, Amber. I want to make love to you in a way we never did."

"Oh, Charlie."

"What have you fantasized about?"

"Well, Charlie we only used to do it two ways. Anything— anything else would be great. Or even that!"

"I want to fuck you from behind."

"Charlie, my Charlie. Where have you been? Who are you now? I'm overwhelmed. Say it again."

"What, my love?"

"Fuck you from behind."

"I want to fuck you from behind. I want to feel your first-class ass against me."

And so, they did that. They both came. Then they did it another way and Amber came twice. Then one more way and they both came again.

In the morning Amber awoke sore between her legs and in her muscles. She felt as if she'd run a marathon. She was smiling before she opened her eyes.

"Charlie?" she whispered.

There was no answer. She opened her eyes to find she was alone. There was a note. Again, for a writer Charlie was stingy with his words. It said. "Good morning. I love you. Help yourself to breakfast."

Amber was alone. She started to pout until she remembered the night that they had and that Charlie said he loved her. She got up, found her shirt and put it on. Clad only that way she went to the kitchen and began pulling out stuff to make pancakes. While she cooked she sang to herself a Cat Stevens song. Charlie always loved Cat Stevens. Soon she had flour on her nose and between her perky breasts.

Charlie also loved watching his nearly naked girlfriend cook pancakes, in his sunlit kitchen, with a smile on her lovely face.

Charlie called Amber after she got to work.

"Good morning," Charlie said. He felt timid.

"Good morning, Lover," Amber said, her voice like warm honey. Charlie's timidity dissipated like dew.

"Thank you for the sweet note," Charlie said.

Amber had left Charlie a love note wrapped in her torn panties.

"Thank you for sending me home to get new panties."

"Ha. Sweet."

"But, listen, Charlie. Your Volvo is still in your driveway. Where did you go?"

"Oh, the car is dead. I don't know what's wrong with it."

"Do you need money to get it fixed?"

"Oh no, no. Thank you, though."

"So, where did you go? I wanted my morning-breath snuggles."

"My face. I went to the doctor about my face."

"Oh, good. What did he say?"

"She."

"You have a lady doctor?"

Why not? "Yes, Dr. Mari Darling."

"You're making this up."

"I'm not. Pinkie swear."

"Stupid. What did the doctor, Dr. Darling, say?"

"She said I had the hardest cock she'd ever felt."

Amber burst out laughing.

"I'm at work, dumbass. And I said that. I said that about your," her voice dropped, "cock."

"I remember."

"Mmm, me too. Charlie?"

"Yes, Honey?"

"Can I see you tonight?"

Charlie started to say, You can't see me ever again. Instead he said, "Amber, it's difficult."

"Because of your face?"

"Yes, partly."

"Charlie, I love you. Do you think a little facial muscle problem would change that?"

"You love me?" Charlie's heart beat faster.

"I love you, Lunkhead. I want to see you. I wish I was seeing you right now."

"Me too," Charlie said.

"Tonight then? I'll cook dinner at my place."

Charlie took the phone away from his ear. He stared at the screen as if it were Amber's face.

"How about after dinner, in the dark, in my bed?" Charlie

asked.

Amber hesitated. "Ok, Charlie. I'll indulge you. It was kind of—mysterious. It added a dirty little buzz to it, you know? It was a sexual—*adventure*. For you too, Charlie?"

"You have no idea," Charlie said.

After he hung up Charlie lay on the floor and smiled like a deposed king whose kingdom had been returned to him. If only Amber would accept him as an invisible man, Charlie mused. But he knew that could never happen. Charlie had entered freakdom. No one, no one on God's green earth, would understand.

*I*n bed that night they held each other and talked slowly and sleepily of the past and the future. The present existed without comment.

"I'm so happy I found you again," Amber said. "I'm so lucky you didn't go to another woman."

Charlie thought about Patience Spent. "Who would have me?"

"Stop that, Charlie. You're being silly. You're a lovely man. Here, let me feel your face."

Before he could protest she was rubbing his face with one hand as if running a wash cloth over it.

"It doesn't feel droopy," she said.

"You can't feel it," Charlie said. "It looks horrible. I can't wink or smile."

"I don't believe you."

"Let's not talk of it."

"Ok, Charlie."

Charlie pulled Amber on top of him. She straddled him as if

he were a barrel. Her thighs squeezed his hips.

"Charlie, you're so strong, so assertive. I love you."

"I love you, Amber. Was I such a milquetoast before?"

"No, not exactly. I don't know what it was. I am sorry if I hurt you."

"It's over now," Charlie said.

"Charlie?"

"Yes, Love?"

"Will you fuck me now?"

Charlie laughed a short laugh. "Anything you want, Amber."

"Anything?"

"What is it, Minx? What do you want?"

"I want to see your cock."

Charlie laughed despite himself. "Now, now," he said.

"I can use the flashlight on my phone. I don't have to see your face."

"This is silly, Amber. Just take it."

"It's—it's bigger than it was. Is that possible? I want to see."

"It's not bigger," Charlie said, though he too thought it possible.

"It's harder."

"More confidence, I guess."

"Why are you more confidant, Charlie?"

"I don't know. I guess I thought about you a lot while you were gone and I decided to be a better person if I ever encountered you again."

Charlie didn't think she'd buy such hornswoggle.

"I love that, Charlie, thank you. You're such a good lover now. I want to get to that part of the evening now. I've fantasized about it all day."

Charlie said, "When they asked Casanova what made him

such a good lover he replied, 'The tenderness afterwards.'"

"Will you be tender with me afterwards?"

"After, before and during."

"Oh, Charlie, Sweet Man. If I can't see it I believe I'll suck it."

"Well, that would be lovely."

"Come in my mouth, Charlie."

"Really, Amber?"

"I know I never let you before. This is a new us."

"It is a new us. I like the new us."

"Me too. Going down now. Bye-bye, Charlie."

Charlie wished he could see her. She was as invisible as he. But he felt her. The warm swirl of her bazoo, the little kitten sounds of joyance she made.

Later they fell asleep in each other's arms.

In the morning Amber was intent on waking before Charlie but when she opened her eyes he was gone. She could still feel the imprint of his body on hers. She padded naked out to the kitchen to make coffee.

Meanwhile Charlie was still lying next to the bed where he had slowly slid off to avoid her hands. That was too close and Charlie vowed to come up with a way to avoid the morning close shaves. While he was cogitating about this his phone rang. He picked it up off the bedside table. It was Amber calling from the kitchen.

Amber skipped into the bedroom. She was sure she heard Charlie's phone ring. Would he not have taken it with him? He didn't answer so maybe it's here. She began to go through the bedclothes. Charlie had scooted into the corner of the room, squatting on his haunches. He had silenced his phone and slid it under the dresser.

Amber's search for it was perfunctory. Charlie watched her sweet, bare bottom as she left the room. He sighed with love. And then sadness entered him like a flu. He would never have her the way he wanted her. He wanted to be visible again like never before. It was an ache in his intangible heart, an actual, somatic pain.

Later that day, when Amber called again Charlie opted not to answer. He didn't know if he could continue the charade in the darkness. His love for Amber had grown thistles. That entire day Charlie sat in his living room, sometimes reading, sometimes watching TV, sometimes looking at the pages of his novel on his laptop. It was insipid. He was no writer. Everything seemed as bleak as a paper bag full of sour milk.

Amber called numerous times. Charlie just stared at his phone screen, her name like a sockdolager to his kidneys.

She finally left a message: "Charlie, where are you? Did you lose your phone? I hope you're ok, maybe just busy writing your novel? Anyway, I'll be there tonight. In the dark. Leave the door unlocked, please. I love you."

Charlie's chest pain returned like a ghost unlaid.

Did he dare lock Amber out? Does he leave it unlocked and go through the whole thing again? Either choice seemed sad-making. If he locked the door she would be hurt. She may even surmise that he didn't truly love her. That was a thought Charlie could not entertain. He unlocked the door.

"Charlie, where was your phone today?" Amber asked after they broke their impatient kiss.

"I don't know. I can't find it," Charlie said.

"Do you want me to ring it?"

"No, not right now."

Amber laughed. "Not right now, Silly. Right now I want to make love like teenagers."

"Like teenagers on the couch with their parents asleep in the next room."

"Haha! Yes, like that," Amber said.

"Be quiet. My mom is a light sleeper," Charlie said.

"I'm not sure how quiet I can be. You drive me wild."

"Shh. Here," Charlie said, sliding a finger into Amber's wet pussy.

"Oh, Charlie. That feels good. You won't tell the other boys we do this, will you?"

"I'm no braggart. What about you?"

"I told Cindy. She's still a virgin. She'll keep our secret. I just had to tell someone."

"Cindy is no virgin."

"What are you saying? Did you have her? Heh—heh—don't stop fingering me."

"I didn't, but Chuck did. Underneath the bleachers. During the game."

"Wow. That little slut."

"I know. She was a walk-up fuck."

"Do you want to do her or me?"

"Only you, my consort."

"I might do her."

"That I would like to see."

"I bet you would. Sometimes we soap each other in the showers."

"Jesus."

"She's got those sloppy lips."

"On her pussy?"

Amber laughed. "I meant her mouth but, yes, when I soap her there she gets wild."

"Can we invite her over for a threesome?"

"I don't think your parents would approve."

"They're going out of town next weekend."

"Great. I'm sure she'll come. What fun we'll have."

"Cindy, of the sloppy lips, naked. Now my mind is revving."

"Charlie, your mind is so sexy."

"Are you getting as horny as me?"

"Charlie, heh-heh, do you like when I do that?"

"Oh, Amber. Your handjobs are expert."

"How about when I do this? What if your parents saw me do this?"

"Oh, God, yes. And I'll do this."

Amber squealed.

"Shh. You'll have my mom in here in a minute."

"Charlie, where did you learn to do that?"

"I am just experimenting."

"Well, I'll experiment too. Here."

Charlie kyoodled.

"Uh oh, I hear your mom."

"I don't care. Take it. Put it in you. Quick!"

"Oh yes, Charlie. God! You're so big!"

"Like that, yes, move like that."

"Oh, Charlie, I'm gonna come."

"Oh God!"

"Charlie!"

116

"Amber!"

"GOD!!!"

"GOD!!"

"You are a god, Charlie."

"Oh jeez. Oh, uh, hi, Mom."

"Charlie! Ha ha ha ha ha."

Some nights, post coitus, they would talk, holding each other like delicate essentials.

"You know," Amber said. "I'm ashamed to admit that I don't know if you're religious."

"I just converted to Shintoism."

"I don't even know what that is."

"Neither do I."

"Goofball."

"Love bunny."

"You are goofy, funny. I missed how funny you are. Doc isn't funny."

"No, Doc is the serious dwarf."

"He's not a dwarf."

"But Doc was the leader of the dwarfs. I think so."

"Making it ok for my ex to be a dwarf."

"You call him Doc?"

"I did."

"Before he died."

"He's very much alive."

"He's still part of your life."

Amber paused. The silence in the room was like a gray chill.

"No, not really."

"Ok. You don't want to talk about it."

"I don't mind. I don't mind talking. I'll tell you anything."

"Do you know what happens after we die?"

"I do."

"Let me guess. We all become invisible."

"That's a crazy conjecture. What made you think of that?"

"I don't know. Just spitballing."

"Save the spit. Keep the balling."

"I love it when you talk that way."

"Bawdy?"

"Yes, bawdy. My bawd. Talk some more that way."

"I'm not good at that."

"I know."

"I'll get better."

"Ok. You're still a screamer."

Amber slapped him playfully on the chest. "You make me scream."

"I missed your screaming."

"Kiss me, Charlie."

"I can do that."

Charlie kissed her a long time. Her mouth was warm and wet. Charlie loved Amber the way men do sometimes. All the way in.

*T*his routine lasted for a while. The nights were spectacular. Charlie was deeply in love with Amber again. And Amber, while impatient with the shadowy coupling, was more passionate than he had ever known her to be.

But, during the day, Charlie sulked. He worked on some book reviews but his prose was still-born. He could not get his head together; there were bugs there. It was inevitable that this physical change in his body would precipitate a mental change and one that would be spooky and perilous. Perhaps, Charlie thought, the next inevitable step, was madness.

To stave off madness he kept making love with Amber.

One night as he waited in his blackout bedroom Charlie heard the door open. He took a deep breath, for he was always a little nervous right before they made love, emotional detritus from being rejected. Now, waiting, his chest fluttering, he heard, not the sweet footfalls of his paramour, but the soft clank of metal against metal. He was about to call out to Amber to ask what was happening when he heard a soft, male whisper. And then he saw the buttery beam of a flashlight in his living room.

Charlie quietly got out of bed and crept to his door.

There were two of them, bulky men in dark clothes. One was gently unhooking his stereo equipment, while the other was working on the DVR/DVD. Charlie's fear receptor's needle went into the red. He did not know what to do.

Then he realized the advantage he had over them. As a sneak thief himself he began to appreciate their method, their professional mien, their economic movement. He watched for a moment and then he strolled past them into the kitchen, which adjoined the living room and was visible from it.

Charlie first slowly opened the refrigerator door. The light from within did what he expected it to do. It struck fear in his banditti. They stood stock still, staring at the open fridge and then at each other. One of them, the smaller of the two, walked carefully into the kitchen. He stood in front of the open door, two steps from Charlie, and stared at the food as if the answer were there. He turned to his partner and shrugged.

He closed the refrigerator door and returned to the living room. They stood like dogs hoping for a scent, and then, slowly, went back to work.

Charlie pulled the utensil drawer out. It made a soft creak and both men stood straight up and shone their lights into the kitchen. At first all they saw was the drawer open. Poltergeist, perhaps they were thinking. Then Charlie lifted one of the sharper knives from the drawer and flung it at one of the thieves. It stuck in the wall next to him. Quick as a flash he flung another at the other thief who was not so lucky. The knife stuck in his upper arm and hung there like a shop sign.

"Fuck," he yelled.

His partner looked at him and then back toward the kitchen from whence came another knife which hit him in the sternum. It did not stick there but made a lovely gash before falling at his feet.

"Bloody hell!" he said, dropping his flashlight and clutching his chest as if he were Romeo suiciding. While he was doing that the other fellow made for the door and was outside before he could pick up his flashlight and follow.

Charlie enjoyed their crazed, animated speech as they ran for their car. They were pulling away, tires spinning, when Amber arrived.

Charlie didn't have time to close the door. He barely made it back into bed.

"Charlie," Amber shouted upon entering. "Are you ok? The door's open."

"Come to me," Charlie called. "Please close the door."

Amber stood at the end of the bed, her voice shaky.

"Who were those men? Charlie, I think they were robbing you."

"They were," Charlie said.

"Did you call the police?"

"No, I took care of it. I reasoned with them and they left."

"There's blood on the stoop, Charlie," Amber said. Her voice was wee.

"Ok. I did a little more than reason with them."

"You hurt them, Charlie? Did they hurt you?"

"It's all ok, Amber. Come to bed." Charlie's heart was still running like Jesse Owen.

"Charlie, are you hurt? Answer me."

"I'm not. I cut one of them with a kitchen knife and then, well, they rethought their lives in crime."

Amber was quiet for a second and then she burst out laughing. "Charlie, did you really cut one of them?"

"I had to, Amber. They would not see sense."

Amber laughed again. "Charlie, you're, well, you're something else."

"And you are due to be under the covers with me."

When Amber had disrobed and snuggled up to Charlie's chest she again asked what happened.

"It's ok, Amber. There have been break-ins in the neighborhood. I guess I was prepared."

"Oh, Charlie. I'm glad you're not hurt. My Charlie." Amber sighed.

"Yours all the way."

"Can we turn the light on tonight, Charlie?"

"Amber."

"Ok, Charlie. This would be irksome if I didn't love you so much."

"I know, Baby. It's only for a little longer."

"Ok, Charlie."

After Amber had fallen asleep Charlie fretted some more. It was not only for a little longer. It was for all time. Charlie would never again have a body. His thinking went meandering down madding lanes.

"Charlie, last night I woke up in the middle of the night because I had to pee. And when I came back I left the bathroom door open. It was just a little light shining in here, Charlie, so I could see to walk."

Charlie held himself still. His hand was sweating around his phone.

"You weren't in the bed."

"What time was it?" Charlie stalled.

"I don't know, Charlie. When I woke up you were there because your arm was over me but by the time I got back to bed you were gone."

"If you were concerned you should have come looking for me. I must have been in the living room. I woke up at one point and suddenly thought of something I wanted to add to the novel."

This was a story as flimsy as a chewed rag.

"I lay awake for a while waiting for you to come back but I guess I fell asleep."

"And I was gone again in the morning."

"And you were gone again in the morning. Why are you always gone in the morning, Charlie? Are you still afraid of being with me in the light? Haven't we gotten past that?"

Charlie knew it had to come to this.

"Amber, the truth is, I guess this has to end."

"What? What, Charlie? You mean, us?"

"Yes, Amber. I'm not in a good place."

Amber's pretty face was crumbling inward like a wax mask. Her voice had a small catch.

"But—but we're so happy."

"In bed we are."

"That's only because of your restrictions."

"I know that, Amber. I love you. I think I've loved you all my life. But I don't deserve you. I duck you because I don't deserve you. I fear that if you see me you'll leave me again."

Amber was quiet. She was biting a lip. "Oh, Charlie. I didn't understand I had done that to you. I'm sorry. I love you now. You have to believe me."

"I have to go away for a while, Amber. It was coming anyway and maybe it's for the best."

"Go away where, Charlie?"

"To—to a sanitarium."

"What? What are you talking about?" Amber sobbed.

"It's drugs, Amber. I've been using and I can't kick it. I can't kick it without help."

Charlie was adlibbing and he was doing it badly.

"Oh, Charlie," Amber said, and she let loose a fresh torrent of tears.

"I'm sorry, Amber. I will miss you when I'm away."

"Ch-Charlie, when are you going?"

"Today, Amber. I was supposed to go the end of the week but I called them and moved the date up."

"Oh, Charlie. Where is this place? Can I talk to you while you're there?"

"No, Amber. That's against the rules."

"Charlie, listen to me. I'll wait for you. You believe me? I'll wait no matter how long it takes."

"You shouldn't, Amber."

"But I will."

"It could be a very long time."

"I'll be here, Charlie. I love you."

"I—I love you, too, Amber. Goodbye."

Now, for a spell, Charlie went back into hiding. He only went out at night to steal food and money. Some nights he wished he could see Sudie but he was afraid he'd done damage there. He was tempted to see Patience again, and he felt bad for the way he'd left her, but his better self knew that it was kinder to just let Patience go. Who knows what she's thinking? She's not like other women. Yet, he missed her, not for the worship, but for the honey-fuck and for the companionship. She was the only person with whom he could be invisible.

He toyed with the idea of calling Amber and telling her the truth. But, what could she say, faced with that? Of course, she would want and deserve a man who was—*all there*.

He kept the lights off in his house in case she came by. He didn't watch TV but, instead, worked on the novel again, the only light his laptop screen. If he got restless he visited a neighbor's home and listened to their intimate conversations, or sat by them as bored as they were, watching TV, reading books, not even looking at each other. Was marriage always like this? Charlie wondered. Yet, he thought of Amber. He could live with her. She was the right stuff. She was a great companion.

After a while Charlie went to town. He could do this in the daytime if the weather was nice. The crowded sidewalks and the busy stores both energized him and depressed him. This was the world he had lost, the bustling world of multicolored people, all with business on their minds, or a lunch with friends, or a new dress, or vacation plans. Did Charlie fit in with this world, even when he had a visible body? It had been so long he couldn't re-member. Part of him wanted to conceive a version of himself that was gregarious and adventurous and happy.

Weeks went by and then months. The days grew cool, then warm again. Charlie grew despondent. He did not write anymore. He did not seek out his neighbors for titillation. He stole food only when he was hungry.

He dreamed of Amber. He missed her as if a vital part of him had dropped off. Sometimes she called. He didn't pick up. Friends called. He didn't pick up. His editor called and he didn't pick up. *Where is your review?* the message would say. And Charlie would erase it.

He was bluer than the sky. He knew only that he must suffer this for all time. He wanted to be philosophic about it, to submit to fate, but he was not of a philosophic bent.

Then something miraculous happened. On a now rare visit downtown Charlie saw a young girl's face flash by him in a crowd. He tried to remember from where he knew that face. And it came to him like a nightmare returning, like a sickness. Like something frightening…like Hope itself.

The face belonged to Annie, the young assistant to Dr. Milton Raphael. She was going into a jewelry store. Charlie followed her in.

Annie was browsing absentmindedly; she fingered a few items, seemed to linger longest over a garish, ornate necklace. Her eyes shone with desire. What is she doing here? Charlie wondered. Perhaps her plan was to steal something. Why would a young girl browse a jewelry store?

She left without buying anything. Charlie shadowed her. She was wearing a simple, yellow summer dress with small blue flowers on it and on her feet ridiculous high heels, the kind super models wear on the runway. Charlie found he was suddenly very angry with this leggy chit who was partly to blame for his predicament.

As Annie passed an alleyway between two tall buildings

Charlie slipped his hand under her arm and pulled her off the sidewalk into the damp, dank alley. Large garbage bins lined each dark brick wall. The walls were sweating. There was food somewhere that had already turned into non-food. It smelled like motor oil and old oranges.

"What the fuck?" Annie said, staring down at her own arm where nothing had a hold of her.

"Don't scream," Charlie said. "No one will believe you."

"Don't hurt me," Annie said.

"I'm not going to hurt you. I'm going to talk to you calmly and you're going to answer my questions."

"Ok, let go of my arm then. You're gripping it too tight."

"Sorry," Charlie said and let go of her arm.

She bolted. Charlie made a quick grab and came up with hair. He pulled her back against a wall.

"Ow, shit," Annie said. "Let go!"

"Such language for a young lady," Charlie said.

"Ow, let go of my hair!"

Charlie let go of her hair but put an invisible hand on each slender, bony shoulder and pushed her against the wall. A rat skittered out from its hidey-hole.

"You don't remember me," Charlie said.

Annie's little face squinched up. Her look was older than she.

"Doesn't matter," she said. "I get the drift."

"The drift? You're used to being accosted by invisible men."

Annie laughed a short laugh. "I don't remember who you are but you must have been given one of the doc's nostrums."

Charlie was perplexed. He found he was breathing heavily and he willed himself to calm down. "This happens a lot? There are armies of invisible people out there? What kind of evil magic is this?"

"Not many invisibles," Annie said. "I don't think. But, well, the good doctor is quite an alchemist. He's goddamn John Dee."

"John D? John D. MacDonald, the mystery writer?"

Annie giggled. "He creates mysteries, yes. John Dee. Queen Elizabeth's astrologer."

"I don't understand."

"Forget it. Listen, I get it that you're perplexed and lost. You were not prepared for so precipitous a change. I, for one, understand."

"What—Why? Why does he do this?"

"He's a conjureman. Don't ask why."

"I only had a back ache."

"Cured that, didn't he?" Annie burst out laughing. It was a cackle like the sound of tearing burlap.

"I'm not finding this even remotely funny."

"I know, I know. I'm sorry. Listen, what's your name?"

"Charlie."

"Listen, Charlie. How old would you say I am?"

"I don't know. I'm not good at guessing ages. 13?"

"Close enough. I'm 72."

"Shut up. That's ridiculous."

"Said the invisible man."

"Wait. You mean—you mean he made you young?"

"As young as Eve with nature's daybreak on her face."

"That's—that's *incredible*. Are you perpetually 13?"

"Oh, I guess I'm aging, but it's slow."

"Good for you, I guess. I'd take eternal youth over invisibility. This is my curse."

"You don't know enough to see it as a gift. You are still learning."

"I don't need your philosophy. Listen, to me. Is this reversible?"

A shadow passed over Annie's features. "Uh," she said.

"Is it or not?" Charlie's anger was coming back.

"I would have to ask Dr. Raphael."

"You know where he is?"

"Of course. He's in his office, as per usual. I still work for him."

"Then take me there. Now."

"Charlie, are you sure?"

"Yes, I'm very sure."

"Ok, bucko. Let's ride."

To Charlie's surprise they walked to an old Pontiac which was parked on the street. He didn't think Annie would be able to see over the steering wheel but, once inside, the car seemed made for her. Charlie sat in the passenger seat. The car smelled of sweat and a sickly, sweet perfume. The seat was split like a lip and a pout of stuffing hung out.

"You know, I went back to his office once," Charlie said, as the car eased into traffic.

"And it wasn't there."

"That's right. Does he move a lot?"

"You didn't have an appointment."

"No, I know. But I went to the same place."

"Ok," Annie said. She smiled like Merlin, as if she had seen it all and it all was absurd.

Charlie recognized the rundown neighborhood as soon as they cruised into it. The car stopped with a judder and its heavy body shook on its springs.

"You're gonna tell me he's in there now? That the office is

just the way it was?"

Annie gave with a tight-lipped smirk.

"Hop out," she said.

She watched the car door seem to open and close itself. She shook her head and smiled. The magic never got old.

As they gingerly walked up the broken concrete steps Annie pulled a small key from the pocket of her dress. It looked too small to fit the door, the kind of key you might have for a jewelry box. But the door swung inward and Annie gestured toward where she thought Charlie was standing, sweeping her arm like a carnival barker.

"Right this way," she said.

Charlie was agog. The office was intact, just the way he remembered it. Returning to it was like returning to a dream from childhood which you were never sure was not a dream but a memory. As they entered the inner door opened and there stood Dr. Milton Raphael, looking rumpled and elfin. He was smiling. The cat, Metagrobolize, wound between his legs like a brindle-colored shadow.

"What have we here, Annie?" he asked, twinkling. It was as if he knew.

"Charlie—Somebody," Annie said. "He's invisible."

"That would be Charlie Cain. How's the back, young man?"

"Doc, cut the crap. I'm invisible! You can't possibly think I wanted to be invisible. It's been a curse. A fucking curse."

"Oh my," Dr. Raphael said. "Come sit down."

They went into his office. For some reason, entering that well-appointed room and sitting in a comfortable chair felt peaceful to Charlie. His ire went from boil to simmer.

"So, the invisibility was not to your liking? All of it, or just some of the time?"

"Dr. Raphael, you can't do this. You can't make people invisible when they have a sore back. It's—it's unethical."

"Hm, yes. Unethical. I've always stumbled on that one. One does want to be ethical, of course. But the ways of magic, well, they are of greater importance than our human ethical structure. At least, that's the way I've always found it to be. Perhaps it is different for you. Peppermint?" He held out a small, wrapped candy.

"But—but," Charlie sputtered. "You should have told me of the side effects!"

"No effects without side effects, Charlie. How is the back?"

"The back is not important. I did not want to be invisible. Why didn't you tell me that would happen?"

"Because I didn't know, Charlie. Sometimes I'm in complete control and sometimes I am not. I accept that so that I can use the gifts the universe offers through me."

"You should meet my friend, Patience," Charlie muttered.

"Take Annie for instance. She wanted to be younger so her potion worked in spades. I think she meant more perhaps like 21 but, still, she is quite happy. I am sorry you are not as happy."

"Doc, I am as sorrowful as a thousand sighs."

"Well, you look alright, hale and hearty."

"I've been exer—you can see me?"

"A little joke, sorry."

"Right."

"What's been the worst part of being invisible, Mr. Cain? I don't, very often, get to question my patients."

"The loneliness. I am one of a kind."

"Yes. I see. That's an interesting take. I hadn't thought of that. Your friends, your wife. They don't understand."

"I haven't told anyone!"

"Oh, of course. A wise choice perhaps. Did you want to talk about it with someone?"

"Not necessarily. I just want to be flesh again."

"This is genuine? This is what you want?"

"Of course."

"Well, we can help you there."

"Truly? There's an antidote?"

"Mr. Cain. Charlie. There is always an antidote." The doctor paused, opened a drawer, shut it. "Except for stupidity. There is no antidote for stupidity."

"There's no catch? Like in fables, where you get three wishes and, somehow, you never really get what you want?"

"No catch."

Dr. Raphael pushed the intercom button on his desk. "Yes?" Annie said.

"Would you bring Mr. Cain the antidote?"

"Seriously? He is giving up his gift?"

"Just the antidote, Annie."

"Yes, Doctor."

Charlie and the doctor sat across from each other in silence. The doctor was smiling. Charlie wore an expression something like the one Gestas wore, one cross over from Christ. After a while the doctor spoke.

"Won't be a minute. Didn't like being invisible," the doctor said. The last bit was a sort of aside, almost a mumble.

"I did not," Charlie said, with some dignity.

"Tell me. Did you get to see any naked people?"

Charlie blushed, raddled. "There was that. At first. That was fun for a while."

"Uh huh," the doctor was fishing for more.

"I saw my neighbors in ways that would make them blanch if they knew."

"Really. Huh. You went in their homes?"

"Yes. I did. I took food from them, too."

"Yes, yes. I can understand that. Heh heh."

"Doc, if you think it might be a gas to be invisible why not make yourself invisible?"

"Doesn't work that way, Mr. Cain. I can do many things but I cannot always predict the outcome of my work. Once I concocted a roborant to give myself superhuman strength. I wanted to impress a woman. It's always that, isn't it?"

Charlie nodded.

"I was a jackrabbit for three days. It was interesting, but, like you, I wanted back."

Annie entered.

"Sorry, it took me so long. These were at the back of the drawer in a box labeled 'Argo Gloss Laundry Starch.' "

"Thank you, Annie."

"How many? You didn't specify?"

"Oh, only one. One will do the trick nicely."

Annie fished her thin hand into the cardboard box and two fingers came out holding up a small black pill, the shape of an egg, the size of a grape.

"There you go, Mr. Cain," the doctor said, as Annie handed him the pill.

"That's a big pill," Charlie said.

"Yes, but don't break it. Swallow it whole. Once a patient broke his pill and there was a basilisk inside."

"What?" Charlie expostulated. "Are you serious?"

"No. Sorry to joke. But, really, don't break the pill."

"Can I have a glass of water?" Charlie asked.

"Mr. Cain. You don't want to take it here."

"I do. If it doesn't work I want you here."

"I'm sure Annie would love to see you naked, Mr. Cain, but, really, it will be better if you take it right before bed tonight. While you sleep the pill will work its deviltry."

"Ok," Charlie said. "How much do I owe you?"

"Oh, there's no charge for going back, Mr. Cain."

"Oh, thanks. I mean, thank you. What if I need you again?"

"Annie will tell you how to get in touch. Annie, you will drive Mr. Cain home?"

"Yes, Doctor."

Charlie shook hands with Dr. Raphael, whose eyes still twinkled with merriment. In the car Annie seemed thoughtful.

"I wish I had asked to be invisible instead of younger," she said.

"I didn't ask to be invisible."

"Oh, right."

"You don't like being younger?"

"Oh, it's better than waking up with sore joints, but, it's not—you know—*sexy*."

"I see. You miss sex. I do, too."

"No, sexy, as in, you know, sporty and fun. I still have sex."

"Oh," Charlie said. He was embarrassed.

"But, what the doctor said back there isn't true. I did not want to see you naked."

"Ok," Charlie said.

"No offense. I'm gay is all."

"Oh, I see."

They were quiet for the rest of the ride. Charlie told her how to get to his neighborhood and she told Charlie how to get in touch with the doctor if he needed to.

"You click your heels three times," Annie said.

"Very funny," Charlie said.

"Sorry. The doctor's silliness rubs off on me sometimes. Open the glove compartment. There's a card in there."

Charlie punched the glove compartment open. It looked like everyone's glove compartment, that is, a mad jumble.

"One of the red ones," Annie said.

"The only red I see is a playing card," Charlie said.

"That's it, yes. The ace of diamonds. That's the doctor's card."

"Another joke."

"No, no. It's really his card. Put it someplace safe."

"Ok," Charlie said. He was weary of this smart-alecky magic. He did not speak again until they pulled up in front of his house.

"Thank you, Annie," Charlie said, opening his creaky door.

"Don't be mad, Charlie."

"I'm not. Thanks."

He walked toward his house. His neighbor, the leaf blower, watched a playing card float from the car's open door, up to Charlie's porch where it hung in the air until the door opened itself and it floated in. That night he tried to tell his wife what he saw and, when she laughed at him, he hit her.

Charlie spent a restless afternoon and evening and ended up going to bed at an ungodly early hour. He wanted to take the pill and go to sleep. He had faith. He prayed for his deliverance from invisibility. He got the pill down without gagging.

He lay in bed and thought perhaps he should have taken a sleeping pill. He was all keyed up. But he soon fell asleep and into a dream about being the only man left in the world. But, it turned out, he wasn't the only man left in the world. It was just that everyone else was invisible.

When he woke the next morning, after a surprisingly restful sleep, Charlie gave thanks to the arcane powers of the universe. There was his body, flesh and blood. Slimmed since the last time he saw it, Charlie knew body pride for the first time in his life. He practically leapt out of bed to go stand in front of the full-length mirror. There was Charlie. There were his limbs and torso and penis. There his face, a few more whiskers than normal but his face.

Charlie pumped his fist. He danced a full tittup. Then he stopped.

He had a small pain in the lower right quadrant of his back.

THREE

"See me. Feel me. Touch me. Heal me."
—Pete Townshend

We're pleased to have Charlie back in the flesh.

The first phone call Charlie made was to Ellis Bruce. He wanted to have lunch and talk about a new idea he had. Ellis was delighted to hear the fresh confidence in Charlie's voice. Then Charlie called his sister and left a voice message, "Sis, just checking in."

He was postponing calling Amber because he was overwhelmed with a desire to see her—*and to have her see him*. It was a need unlike any Charlie had ever before experienced. His mind created a new world: they would marry, honeymoon in the Caymans, move into his house because it was nicer than her apartment, have two children, grow old together until their children had children at which point they would retire and live off the proceeds from Charlie's novels, all of which had been sold to the movies.

Charlie ran into one of Amber's friends outside a bookstore. They chatted amiably but Charlie was anxious to talk about Amber. When he steered the conversation that way he found out that Amber no longer lived in an apartment but had rented a house in a middle-class suburb on the outskirts of the city. Charlie punched the new address into his phone.

He couldn't put it off any longer. He sat in his recliner and dialed her number. He got a message that said the number was no longer in service. He dialed again and got the message again. This gave Charlie pause. He knitted his brow. He then took a shower, dressed in nice clothes (which were now slightly large on him), and left the house, locking the door and, now, taking the keys with him.

The car, of course, wouldn't start.

He opened the hood. He knew squat about cars, other than waht he'd learned from his neighbor, which wasn't all that much. The engine looked like an engine. He touched some wires. He jiggled a couple hoses. He said, Fuck.

Then his neighbor, the beefy fellow with the leaf blower, with whom he'd never had a conversation, was suddenly beside him.

"Won't start?" he asked. Charlie held his sarcasm in check.

"No, it's cold. It's been a long time since I cranked it."

Charlie was trying to sound like he knew something that he didn't know.

"Probably the battery if you haven't run it in a while. Why haven't you been using it? I couldn't help but notice."

"Oh, I don't know. Trying to save a little money. Using the bus mostly." Charlie had not prepared for this conversation.

"Uh huh. Let's jump it and see if it's the battery. I'll pull my car next to yours. If it's not the battery you could have water in your fuel line. Most likely the battery though. You say you've been taking the bus?"

Charlie was grateful for the help but he didn't want to talk.

"Yes. Thanks for the jump," he said.

While the guy went and got his car Charlie took out his phone and tried Amber one more time. He got the same message.

"Just hook these to your battery," the fellow said, handing Charlie one end of the cables. Charlie looked at them. He was sure he'd seen this done, perhaps even done it himself.

"Negative to negative…"

"Yes, of course," Charlie said. He spotted the little signs. He connected the clamps with trepidation as if the battery were a bomb and he an inexperienced sapper.

When his neighbor started his car he waved a hand out the window. Charlie supposed this meant, Try yours.

He did and the car sluggishly turned over.

"Let it run a minute," the guy said.

Charlie was smiling like a ninny. He was already picturing Amber naked.

"Jim," the guy said, holding out a meaty hand. "Valvis."

"Oh, yes. Charlie," Charlie shook hands, expecting his to be crushed. Instead the guy had soft hands like a woman's.

"We don't talk much," Jim said.

"Yes. Sorry. My fault," Charlie told him. "I'm a writer. You know, introverted, farouche."

"Writer?" Jim said it the way someone might say, *Faggot?*

"Yeah. Book reviews. Essays. I'm working on a novel."

"Uh huh," Jim said.

"Think it's ready to go?"

"Hell, I don't know," Jim said. "I don't even read em."

"Oh, ha. I meant the car."

"Yeah, probably." Jim unhooked the cables. He seemed saddened at the suddenness of the end of their conversation. Perhaps he's lonely, Charlie thought.

"Hey, thanks, Jim. You're great. Let's get together soon. The wives and us, you know."

"Sure," Jim Valvis said.

Charlie was backing out of the driveway when Jim yelled after him. "Hey, are you married?"

Amber's car was in the driveway of her new house. Charlie wondered why she was not at work. He parked and sprinted to the front door. He expected her to jump into his arms.

He rang the bell. He waited. He rang the bell. He waited. He knocked.

No one was home. Perhaps Amber was having car trouble and found another way to get to work. Should Charlie show up at the fitness center? He'd never been there, partly because he was intimidated by all the buff folks with their perfect bodies and perfect beads of sweat, towels elegantly draped over their shoulders, always a little winded, but *only a little* winded.

Charlie decided not to go there but, instead, to return to Amber's that evening.

So, Charlie drove to Sudie Nimm's house. He had not seen the painter for a long time and he missed her. She was a calming presence, which seemed odd since she, herself, had anxiety problems. Perhaps it was her art though Charlie knew nothing about art. One thing was sure. She'd be home. Then, with an inexplicable shudder, Charlie remembered that the last time he tried to visit Sudie the house had been locked and was dark as a tomb.

As a tomb. Surely, Sudie had not died. There would have been an obituary. But Charlie didn't read the paper every day, instead relying on online news sources.

Charlie gently knocked on Sudie's door. The house did not seem as dead as his last visit. Charlie heard feet shuffling toward the door. It opened.

"Yes?" Sudie said, eyeing the stranger suspiciously.

"Sudie," Charlie started. He didn't know what he wanted to say. He twisted his face into a smile. Sudie involuntarily closed the door a half-inch.

"Sorry, Sudie. My name is Charlie and I'm a big fan."

"Thank you," Sudie said.

"Yes, a big fan," Charlie continued, haltingly. "I especially love your—." Here Charlie's mind went blank. He smiled harder.

"What can I do for you?" Sudie asked, not unkindly, but still wary.

"That's all I wanted to say," Charlie said, though his heart was full.

"Ok, thank you. Really, I appreciate it." Sudie was closing the door.

"I wonder," Charlie said just to make the door open again "I wonder if—if you'd like to have dinner with me."

Sudie's laugh was half snort.

"Thank you, but I don't think so."

She couldn't go out to dinner. What was Charlie thinking?

"I could bring the dinner to you."

Sudie's face showed more wariness, coupled with curiosity. She feared her privacy had been breached.

"I know about your condition," Charlie said.

"My condition?"

"Your debility."

Sudie waited.

"I understand you're agoraphobic."

"Ok. Thank you. Sincerely. But, I don't think dinner is a good idea."

And here she finally shut the door. Charlie waited until her footsteps moved away from the door. He walked to his car and sat inside, not starting it, just thinking, sitting still.

Charlie thought about visiting Ellis. He wanted someone to see his physical body, someone who could acknowledge that Charlie was Charlie. He thought of all the people he had slighted during his invisibility. Then, unbidden, he thought of his sexy neighbor, Lorraine. Why not visit Lorraine? Amber, that's why. But, surely, he could just pop in. They were friends, weren't they?

And, thinking about Lorraine and what she represented for him, led Charlie to thinking about Patience Spent. That bridge was probably burnt. She would not accept a corporeal man who was not half-god. He drove to Lorraine's.

Charlie knocked on her door. He had not forgotten the man-mountain who answered last time. He prayed Lorraine was home alone.

She opened the door. She was dressed like Laura Petrie. She was as sexy as a bubbling spring.

"Yes?" she said.

"Lorraine. Hi. It's Charlie. Charlie Cain from over on Brock Way."

"Oh….uh, yes. Yes, I remember you."

She obviously didn't.

"I was just driving by and realized we'd never really talked to each other. I'm trying to be more outgoing."

Lorraine looked him up and down. It's not just an expression. She looked at him from his shoes to his hair.

"Good luck with that," she said, closing the door.

Charlie drove to Patience's.

He knocked. He knocked again. The door was locked.

"Dammit," Charlie said, under his breath. He couldn't have explained why he felt so frustrated, after feeling so joyous about having a body again.

Charlie walked around to the back yard. There was the miniature pool, gone scummy. He tried the back door. He walked around the windows until he found one with a good view inside. He cupped his hands and could see her bed, amid her usual disarray. Memory made an erection.

"Turn around slowly," a male voice said behind him. Charlie

jumped and turned at the same time.

It was a policeman. Charlie thought he was looking at his trouser bulge.

"Officer, you scared the shit out of me." Charlie attempted a laugh.

"You got ID?"

"Yes, yes." Charlie fumbled his wallet out and opened it. He handed it to the policeman. As he did a female officer came around the side of the house.

"What have we got?" she asked the other officer.

"Peeper. Charlie Cain. That you?"

"Y-yes," Charlie said. "I'm not a peeping Tom. This is a friend's house."

"That right? What's your friend's name?"

"Patience," Charlie said.

"Patience," the cop echoed.

"Yes, Patience. Funny name, I know, but."

"Last name."

"Cain."

"She has the last name as you?"

"Oh, sorry, no. We're not related. She's not my wife or anything. Just a good friend."

"And her last name is?"

Charlie had no idea. Had he heard it before? Was he merely forgetting under pressure?

"You don't know your friend's last name?"

"I do. No. Wait. No, I don't."

"Turn around and give me your hands," the officer said.

The female cop approached with twist ties.

"What's going on?" Patience stepped from her back door. "What are you doing?"

She was talking to the cops.

"This man was peeping in your windows. He claims he's your friend."

"That's right. Let him go."

"You know this man?"

"I do. Let him go."

Patience stood like a statue of Justice. She was wearing a full-length muumuu decorated with alchemical symbols: air, earth, fire, water, salt, sulfur. Both police officers stopped what they were doing. They looked at each other.

"Ok," the man said. "Sorry, ma'am."

Patience did not crack a smile. She did not move until they were out of her yard.

"Ok, then," Patience said. "Who the fuck are you?"

Charlie started to say his name. No, he couldn't do that. There was too much to think about wherever he went. Would Patience recognize his voice? She certainly wouldn't accept a god dressed in a man's white shirt with frayed cuffs and jeans a size too large. Charlie was afraid, still shaken by almost being arrested. And his frustration was about to boil over.

"Thanks for getting me out of that," Charlie said.

"You're welcome. Why were you looking in my windows?"

"I wasn't. Well, I was. But not for the reason you think."

"What's the reason I think?" Patience's voice was not mean or ornery. Some of her softness was returning.

"I-I don't know."

"Oh, I thought you knew why I thought you were looking in my windows."

Charlie laughed a nervous laugh.

"You did not want to see me naked. That's the reason you were thinking I thought you were peeping."

"No. I mean, yes."

"You do want to see me naked."

"No."

"Well, that's flattering."

"No, I mean, that's not what I was doing. I mean, you're fetching. You're very fetching."

Patience laughed. "Would you like some lemonade?" she asked.

"I surely would."

Charlie and Patience sat at her kitchen table drinking lemonade and smiling. There was not much conversation for a while. Charlie was nervous as hell.

"You remind me of someone," Patience said.

Uh-oh, Charlie thought.

"Don't you want to know who? Or whom? Is it whom?"

"Whom is it?" Charlie said. He tried a smile. Patience smiled back. Her smile was like music from a music box.

"John Lennon. In his short hair phase. When he was making that war movie, that anti-war movie."

"*How I Won the War.*"

"Exactly! Yes, that's the time period."

"I don't look a thing like John Lennon. But, thank you."

"It's not your face so much. Maybe your voice. Or your aura. I think you have the same aura. He was a beautiful cat."

"He was. Thanks again."

"What's your name, friend? Can you tell me now?"

Charlie thought quick. "What would you like to call me?"

Patience closed one eye. "I like you, Mister." She now looked his face over. "Hmm. Yes. A new name for my new friend."

Charlie was grinning. This was the goofy Patience he loved.

"Quentin," she said, finally. "That's it. Quentin."

"After Walter Scott?"

"You're a reader! I knew it, Quentin. I knew you'd be a reader. But I was thinking more of Compson, you know, Faulkner."

"*Sound and the Fury*."

"Yes! You're beautiful, Quentin, really beautiful."

"Thank you. Doesn't Quentin kill himself."

"Well, yes, technically he does. But he was groovy, dig? He was—driven to make that final choice. We all have to make that choice, Quentin. Who said it's the only question that matters?"

And, so they sat and talked for most of the day. As the sun was going down Patience offered to cook them some food but Charlie demurred. He was sure he was going to have dinner with Amber. His mind had already laid the whole evening out.

"Well, you come back anytime, Quentin. I mean that," Patience said at the door.

Charlie leaned over and kissed her cheek. Together they stepped out into the night air.

"So chivalrous. That's Quentin Durward. My Quentin kisses like this."

Patience kissed Charlie full on the mouth. Her tongue entered and it was all Charlie could do to not grab her ass and pull her to him. His libidinous mind was flooded with memories of the sinuous Patience Spent. He did not grab her ass but he did not break the kiss, which lasted exactly 82 seconds.

"Whoa," Charlie said, when they finally broke. "You're a helluva kisser. I will come back."

Now Patience was looking at him in an odd way. Her head was tilted like a curious hound.

"Something. Something just happened, Quentin. I—I'm moved."

"It was just a kiss," Charlie said.

"Hm, yes. Quentin, before you go would you like to see me naked? We've come full circle," Patience said and laughed.

"Maybe—" Charlie got out before Patience had pulled the muumuu over her head. There was her beautiful body, the body Charlie knew and revered. Here nipples were darker and her aureoles wider spread. And in her center a small mound like a little planet. Patience was pregnant.

"You're expecting a child," Charlie said. His brain felt an overload.

"I am," Patience said. "A new world, Quentin. A whole new world. You know? Babies are microcosms of the macrocosm."

"Uh huh," Charlie said.

"Don't look so stricken. Haven't you seen a naked pregnant woman before?"

"I haven't," Charlie said. He knew he was talking like a robot.

"It's beautiful, baby."

"I. I mean, yes. I know. You're beautiful. Who's the father?"

"Ah," Patience said. "The father is the universe."

Charlie had no answer to that. There was no answer to that.

"Listen, Patience. I better go now. But I will come back and see you."

"Quentin," she said, softly, and placed her palm on Charlie's chest. It was balm. Then she turned and went inside. Charlie listened as she turned the lock.

Charlie drove back to Amber's. He tried her one more time on the cellphone but got the same result. Visions of Patience's stomach wrestled with his Amber fantasy in the part of the brain where such things wrestle.

Amber's house was dark. Charlie sat in his car at the curb and stared at the windows as if he expected them to open like waking eyes. Then he decided that Amber was on vacation. He drove slowly back to his own home. He was sad and frustrated.

As he got out of the car a voice hailed him out of the dusk.

"Charlie Cain, I can't believe I'm seeing you. Are you real?"

It was Ken calling. Standing behind him was his wife Christine. Christine seemed shy for some reason, embarrassed at finding Charlie home. They were both dressed in running shorts and tank tops. Christine had a running bra underneath her top. Both were glittery with perspiration.

"Hey Ken, Christine," Charlie said.

"Man, it's good to see you," Ken said. "Christine, isn't it good to see Charlie?"

"Always," Christine said.

"We've been out for a run. Hey, have you eaten?"

"I have," Charlie lied. He was famished and he had no idea what food he had in his refrigerator.

"Come sit with us anyway. Watch us eat, huh? How about it?"

Charlie saw no reason to say no so he walked along beside them to their house.

"What's new, Charlie?" Christine asked. Her voice was a brunette purr.

I'm visible again, Charlie thought. "Nothing much, Christine. Working on a novel, you know, reviewing books."

"A novel!" Ken said too loudly.

"Trying," Charlie said.

At Ken and Christine's, Charlie sat in the kitchen while Christine started making their dinner. Ken went to take a shower.

"That looks good," Charlie said to say something.

"Roasted eggplant salad," Christine said. "I'll make enough if you want some."

"You know I think I would," Charlie said.

Christine turned around and looked at him. There were depths to her eyes that shook Charlie a bit. Something was on her mind. So Charlie smiled.

"I'm glad," Christine said. "I'm glad you'll eat with us."

This didn't sound like what Christine wanted to say.

"Thank you," Charlie said. "You look great," he added, stupidly. He was fishing and it was inappropriate. Christine was still dressed in her running clothes, sweat-stained and sticking to her womanly figure.

"Charlie Cain, don't flirt with me," she said, obviously delighted to speak this way.

"Ok," Charlie said, stupidly. He couldn't talk except stupidly. What was wrong with him?

"You give up easy," Christine said.

"Christine, you know. We've always been friends. If Ken wasn't—" Charlie stopped himself. His antigodlin momentum wobbled like a gorbellied sheep.

"If he wasn't in the shower? What, Charlie? Tell me. The water's still running. Tell me what we'd do."

This went careening out of control too quickly.

"No, I meant, if Ken wasn't on the scene." This was going badly. "If you weren't his husband. Wife."

Christine worked her way up beside Charlie. Charlie was sitting on a tall stool. She put one fingernail on his thigh. "Next time he's gone I'll call you," she said. And then she kissed him quickly on the lips and turned back to her salad.

Ken walked in.

"Ha, what's going on here? Plans behind my back?"

"No!" they both said, in unison.

*T*he next day he had lunch with Ellis Bruce. They ate at a Midtown eatery that was a hangout for writers and newspaper employees. The place did a nice gumbo, which both men ordered.

"I want a regular column," Charlie said, around a mouthful.

"Of course you do," Ellis said, grinning. "You deserve one."

"Thank you. I have some proposals."

"I'm here to listen. This is a new Charlie."

"You have no idea."

"I'm glad to see you out and looking so fit. Tell, what's the big change in you?"

"Sequestered myself away and cleansed my body and spirit."

Both men were used to speaking fluent sarcasm so Ellis took this as if it were meant ironically. He snorted.

"You certainly were a mystery to a lot of people. Myself I couldn't care less whether you were living in a straw-filled garret or a room at the Y. As long as you send your reviews in and as long as I am convinced that you are living a healthy life."

"I didn't know you cared, Ellis," Charlie said, dipping a sippet of hard, porous bread into his gumbo.

"I care about my writers. I care about my friends. And I care about Kerr and the Warriors."

"How's the wife and kids?"

"Ha. Right. And family, above all. That goes without saying."

"Too often."

"Don't tell me you've become a moralist in your sequestration."

"Not a moralist. But an appreciator. Of life, of books, of writing. Of ways we sustain ourselves."

"Amen, Charlie. I've never heard you so earnest."

"Ellis, I want to get married and I need a steady job. I want a column and my name in the masthead."

"Uh huh," Ellis said. He thought for a beat. "Print and online, I assume."

"Whatever you're doing these days."

"I can probably convince the publisher. He thinks everything is going to be online in ten years and he doesn't give a fuck about print."

"Maybe we can change his mind."

Ellis put his spoon down and looked into Charlie's eyes. He wore a bemused expression but his scrutiny was serious.

"You have come to save us," he said, sardonically.

"I can't save anyone, Ellis. But what I'd like my column to be about is literature, ethics, and the new science."

"New science?"

"That part you'll just have to trust me to deliver. I believe there is a great change afoot, a vast, universal flower that is about to open. I know, it sounds like new age crap. But I've got the goods, Ellis. I can write this. I'll send you an example tonight."

"Charlie, you're making me a happy man. I look forward to your first treatise and I will talk to the big cats tomorrow, Friday at the latest."

"Thanks, Ellis. It will be good to have a steady job again."

As the two men left the restaurant they embraced on the sidewalk.

"Charlie, we should do this more often. I feel like I never see you."

"I'm hearing that a lot," Charlie said.

Charlie emailed Ellis what he hoped would be his first column that night. It was, in short, a statement of purpose. He felt good about it.

The next morning Charlie actually went back to his novel. He didn't know what else to do. He had just reread the last pages he had written—there was something good there, an energy, *something*—when the phone rang. He had never been one of those writers who shut out the world when he worked.

It was Christine. He thought about not answering.

"Hi Christine," he said.

"Charlie, Ken's at work," Christine said.

"Oh," Charlie said. This was bad.

"Ask me what I'm wearing."

"Christine."

"Ask me, schmuck."

"What are you wearing, Christine?"

"Just a smile," Christine said.

There was silence. Christine sighed. "Actually I'm wearing this little frilly lilac thing underneath my raincoat."

This was weird. "Christine, I'm in the middle of something."

"Charlie Cain. Dammit. Let me in before someone sees me."

Christine was on Charlie's front porch. She had called from his front porch. She actually was wearing a raincoat.

"Hello, Charlie," she said, saucily, and walked past him.

"Hi Christine," Charlie said. "It's good to see you, but—"

Christine dropped the raincoat. She was standing in Charlie's living room dressed in one of the pieces of lingerie he had fingered in her drawer. Life plays funny tricks. Maybe this is karma—*good or bad*? Which reminded him that Christine also had a gun in that drawer.

"Jesus," Charlie said.

"Do you like this?" Christine pirouetted.

"Jesus," Charlie said.

"Come here, hunk," Christine said. She was playacting. But it still worked. Charlie was aroused.

"Christine—I—"

"Did you put that on just for me?"

Charlie looked down. He was only wearing a t-shirt and boxers. Being visible had not quite caught up with him.

"Well, no, I—listen, Christine. You look like a million dollars."

"Charlie—do not put a *but* on the end of that. You're gonna make me cry if you don't put your arms around me right now."

Christine's voice cracked. She was timorous. Charlie's heart broke for her and he moved in and put his arms around her. She was as plush as slumbering ardor. Charlie began to kiss her neck.

"Oh, Charlie," Christine said and shuddered. "It's been so long."

"Me too," Charlie said.

"Oh, Charlie, I knew you were lonely. I just felt it."

They kissed. And when they kissed Christine reached down the front of Charlie's boxers and took his cock out. She sighed inside their kiss.

"Oh, oh," Charlie said, breaking the kiss.

He pulled the ridiculous underwear off her breasts so he could suck there and the whole diaphanous thing fell at their feet. Christine's nipples were too large, almost sharp. Christine's body was like a foreshortened centerfold.

"God, you're beautiful," Charlie said.

"Can we go someplace and lie down?" Christine said.

They were still standing in the middle of the living room.

"Of course. The bed?"

In bed they made love hungrily. It was sexy and embarrassing. Some of their feigned passion was clumsy. Some things didn't work as well as they do in fantasy. But, in the end, they both orgasmed, and lay together afterward in a sticky knot.

Christine began to cry.

"No, now," Charlie said.

"Charlie," Christine said, hiccupping like a child. "Ken is—"

"No!" Charlie said, quickly. "This can't be about anything but us. I can't listen to anything else."

Christine pulled back and, with her sad, brown eyes, looked Charlie full in the face. She was thinking.

"Charlie Cain. I think you're practically a saint."

So began a period where Christine called often. Sometimes they got together and perfected their new sybaritic exercise. Sometimes Christine just called and said, "I love you," and hung up. Charlie never returned the sentiment. He did not love Christine. He loved Amber.

Amber, who was seriously MIA.

Charlie had repeatedly called and repeatedly driven by her house. One afternoon he chanced upon a real estate agent hammering her sign into Amber's yard. The agent looked up as Charlie slowed down so he had to brake and park.

As he got out of the car, the agent, hippy with poofed-up blond hair, greeted him cheerily, "You're just in time," she said. She was striding toward Charlie like a hound that's got the scent.

"Am I?" Charlie said, accepting the agent's hand, which was

thick and rough.

"You're not my 3:30?" she asked, letting the hand drop but keeping the smile high.

"I'm not anyone's 3:30," Charlie said with a laugh.

The agent laughed too.

"Are you house shopping?"

"Possibly," Charlie said.

"Can I show you this one? It's a steal. Seller very motivated."

"Ah," Charlie said.

He followed the agent who used a key box to open the front door.

"As I say, very motivated. As you can see the renter's things are still here. But she is gone and this will be cleared away soon. Imagine the room empty if you can. Note the high ceilings in the front room."

Charlie was feeling a little bilious and it was putting him on edge.

"Can I see the bedrooms?"

"Of course. Are you married, uh…" She was waiting for his name.

"Dr. Bennell," Charlie said. "Single but sometimes I have threesomes over."

The agent was waiting for Charlie to laugh.

"Right through here is one bedroom, the larger of the two."

It was Amber's room, with the bed where Charlie had last made love with her. The bed was stripped. It looked obscene, like a body waiting for the coroner.

"Hmm, yes," Charlie said. "I can put the mirror on the ceiling. Nice high ceiling. Plenty of room, right?"

"Of course," the agent said. Her smile was slipping.

"Why is the owner motivated, as you say?"

"Oh, well, I believe, and you didn't hear it from me, the renter got married. We're not supposed to, you know, gossip, but I heard tell she married a rich doctor. The same doctor who owned the house. Apparently the renter fell in love with the owner."

Charlie suddenly felt ill.

"Are you ok, Dr. Bennell?"

"Bathroom," Charlie said.

"Right through—" she said but Charlie was already there and closing the door. Inside the bathroom, which still had some of Amber's cosmetics on the sink, Charlie did not upchuck the way he thought he was going to. He sat down on the toilet and breathed deeply.

"Are you ok, Dr. Bennell?"

"Yes, yes. Bad lobster for lunch. Give me a moment."

"I do have a 3:30," the voice came back.

Fuck your 3:30, Charlie thought, but instead let silence answer. He waited longer than was necessary and then brushed by the agent on his way out.

"I'll have my receptionist call you," Charlie said.

On the front lawn a young couple was approaching the house. The man was tall and angular, as if he were made from pipe cleaners, and his short, brunette bride was about 8 months pregnant. They smiled at Charlie before spotting the real estate agent following him out.

"Black mold," Charlie whispered to the string bean husband as he passed him.

Charlie called Ellis when he got home. He asked him point blank.

"I know nothing," Ellis said. "I haven't seen or thought about Amber in ages."

"Ellis," Charlie's voice broke.

"Aw, Jesus, man. You want me to come over?"

"No. Thanks."

Charlie hung up and got online. He was afraid to do it. It only took two false starts before he found their wedding announcement as it had run in the newspaper. The picture of Amber was one Charlie had taken a year ago.

She went back to her fucking doctor, Charlie thought. She went for the gold. Now Charlie remembered Amber telling him that she would wait for him no matter how long his (phony) loony bin stay lasted. Some resolve. She must have run straight back to him. Little liar. Little phony. Little crappy little bitchy bitch.

Now she was Amber Slip. She married Dr. Bernard Slip, who Charlie used to call Dr. Sleep because he used hypnosis on his patients to get them to relax. He was cutting edge. Now his cutting edge had cut Charlie's life in half.

Perhaps he hypnotized her into marrying him. Charlie's mind cast about for any explanation except the most obvious one: she wanted to be married to Dr. Bernard Slip and not to Charlie Cain.

*I*t would be nice to say that Charlie now threw himself into his work, that he wrote like he'd never written before, day and night, living on coffee and pills, pounding out columns and fiction like a fucking literature machine.

It would be equally tempting to say that Charlie went on a bender, living on panther-piss liquor and pills, and forgetting about the shiny new job he'd been given at the newspaper.

The truth, like most half-measure truths, is a little of both versions. Charlie did write like he'd never written before. But he also drank a lot and took pills that were not prescribed for him. He was burning the candle at both ends but he was making ends meet. People are rarely one thing or another.

He continued to fuck his friend's wife. He didn't care. He never called her but he never told her not to come when she called him. They found a sexual rhythm together that was just this side of dangerous. Christine turned out to be a tigress when aroused and when comfortable with her mate. And Charlie, despite the disparate chemicals in his system, performed like the invisible man. He never said *I love you* back to Christine though she said it every time they got together. He was well-nigh operating without a conscience.

When Christine asked him one night if there was anything he'd never done sexually that she could do for him Charlie looked at her the way Bela Lugosi looked at David Manners' cut finger.

"Have you seen *Last Tango in Paris*?" Charlie asked. It seemed for a moment that a shadow passed over her features.

"I—I can't remember," Christine said.

"Get some margarine," Charlie said.

Christine looked at him to gauge his seriousness. Then she giggled and skipped, naked, into the kitchen. She came back with a tub of Blue Bonnet.

"Are you gonna spread this all over me?" Christine asked, with nervous sauciness.

"Lie on your stomach," Charlie said, taking the tub from her hand.

Christine giggled and turned over. In the half-light her round bottom looked plump and luxurious enough to eat. Charlie liked the extra weight she carried back there. He kissed one cheek.

"Oh, Charlie," Christine said. "I lo—"

"Shh," Charlie said.

Then he took two fingers of margarine out of the tub and set the tub aside. He took his ungreased hand and ran it over her bottom, as if inspecting it. He separated the cheeks and spread the oleo slowly down her crack and then greased her anus and crabwalk, making sure to get some inside with one finger.

"Oof," Christine said. "What are you cooking up?" She laughed uncertainly again.

"Christine," Charlie said, now suddenly tender. "You look like Spring to me. You stop my fucking heart."

"Oh, I love you," Christine said and flopped over to throw her arms around him.

"Christine, you are dear."

"Charlie, Charlie, Charlie," Christine said, kissing him all over his face the way she'd seen starlets do in the movies.

Charlie kissed her and held her and was about to send her back home.

She whispered, "What's the idea with the margarine though?"

Charlie smiled and whispered in her ear. Her eyes got wide.

"Really?" she asked.

Charlie said, "Really."

And so, after a pause as gravid as Rosemary right before her unholy birth, Christine threw herself on her belly and poked her round bottom toward the stars.

Charlie's column in the paper was a hit. They got more letters about it in the first week than about anything else in the paper.

His premise was a simple one: what do our novelists have to say about current or universal ethical dilemmas? He took any new literary novel as a jumping-off point. And it worked, for the most part, without him having to crowbar his premise into a study of the novelist's point of view. Fiction reflects, sometimes even more than the writer imagines.

Things were going passably well, though Charlie still drank too much and took too many pills. Any thought of Amber threw his little locomotive off the rails. He found, though, that he could write through the depression, as long as he didn't get too blotto. Some mornings he woke up on the couch with a head like a bee-hive and his laptop glowing in his lap. He would then vow to take a better measure of his alcohol.

While he was writing an essay based on a Salman Rushdie novel his phone rang. It was from an unknown number. Usually, he would let the voice mail take over, but, for some reason, this morning he answered.

"Charlie," a miniature voice peeped.

Charlie recognized Amber's voice even so reduced. He could not speak.

"I'm sure you're terribly mad at me. I can just hang up."

Still Charlie sat, his eyes making blurred, gleaming alphabeti-forms of his essay.

"I can explain if you'll let me," Amber said. "I know I said I'd wait for you."

Charlie almost answered. A hot anger bubbled in him.

"I was waiting, Charlie. I was grieving. I thought I'd never see you again but I was willing to wait years. You don't know what those mysterious nights in your bed were doing to me. I was so mad with love, with sex, with happiness. I could have lived with you in the dark for the rest of my life. That's what I told myself."

Amber waited. She tried to wait out the silence but could not.

"Then Bernard called and asked me to lunch. I hadn't talked to him in a long time. I really didn't want to talk to him or see him but he sounded so sweet and I needed someone to be sweet to me. You know?"

Charlie almost put the phone down.

"Charlie, that lunch turned into something I never saw coming. Bernard came bearing an engagement ring. Still, I resisted. I took the ring but told him I'd have to think about it. When he asked me if I were seeing someone else I said yes. I had to laugh a little, Charlie. I said, well, I'm not really seeing him. Then I had to explain. I told Bernard about our nights together. I know it was a betrayal of sorts, but I guess I wanted to see if it sounded insane. Charlie, it did. Bernard was initially angry, then perplexed, then, I don't know what. He insisted that I see you during the day and talk things out. He insisted I call you and tell you that I was thinking about marrying him. Charlie, the way he said it, it sounded so right, so sane. So, I left that restaurant with the determination to talk to you in the full light of day and see where we stood."

Charlie let a small sob out into the air.

"Oh, Charlie. I tried. I called and called. I got tired of calling. I'm sorry about where you were and why but I had my life to figure out, Charlie, and no one to help me do it. I still put Bernard off but he persisted. He told me I was the love of his life. And, though I could not say that back to him, Charlie, not honestly, I told him I loved him too and felt lucky to marry such a fine man. That's what I told him, Charlie. Go ahead and scoff. I don't think he's the love of my life. But he's there for me in the clear light of morning and every morning I am grateful for that. Charlie, if you're still listening, understand this: I love you. I love you but we're impossible together. I'm sorry but—"

Charlie hit 'end call.' Then he blocked her phone number

Then Charlie Cain shut his laptop and put it aside and he cried.

*T*hat night Charlie drank more than usual. He also chased down a couple Ambien, which he'd taken to chewing through the day as if they were Chocks Vitamins. He turned off his laptop and watched inane TV shows, his mind a blear, a cloud of inattention.

When his phone rang he heard it from a long way off. He discovered he was sitting on it. It took some spastic realignments to unearth it without standing. He managed to dislodge two sofa pillows first and, finally, the phone, which was still ringing

"Yep," Charlie said.

"Charlie." Christine's voice was breathy, like those actresses in those movies. Charlie had not even looked at who was calling.

"Sorry?" he said.

"Charlie, it's Christine," Christine said, with a bit more clarity to her enunciation.

"Christine!" Charlie boomed. "My goddess! More love monkey!"

"Well, Mr. Man, what's got into you?"

"You, Christine. I want you to get into me."

"I think I know what you mean. Why's I'm calling is that Ken's gone for the evening and I'm wearing only a scarf."

"Where is that scarf?" Charlie asked. He genuinely couldn't picture it.

"Around my fanny," Christine said.

"That fanny. Oh, Christine, that fanny."

"Yes, Charlie. You love it. Come get it. Come get me."

"Christine, I hope you know that my love for your fanny

is perfectly respectable. I respect that fanny scrupulously, unfeignedly, unboundedly. That fanny is as well respected as a church deacon."

"Charlie, you're in a merry mood. Hurry, please."

"Christine, I will be there quick like the simoom's desert wind. Winded. Desert. Wind dessert. I won't desert you, my dessert wind."

Charlie hung up. He stood up unsteadily, dropping the phone back into the couch cushions. He was wearing a sweaty t-shirt and boxers and, when he walked out the front door, he did not take his keys, nor did he lock the door. He walked straight—the term is relative—to Christine's front door and before he could slam his fist into the door Christine opened it. She was wearing a bathrobe, yellowed, with a dirty sash trailing it.

"Get in quick," she said.

Charlie bowed and almost fell over the threshold. Christine closed the door quickly.

"Charlie, when you say fast you mean fast. I assume you decided not to dress for the occasion." She giggled.

"I came to see your scarf. And to scarf you like a macaroon."

"Charlie, you're a nutty nut. I love you."

Christine opened the robe as if she were showing what was behind Door #1. The tiny, paisley scarf was tied around her waist with the flag part over her ass. Her pubic hair glistened in the low light.

"Ta da," she said.

Charlie tried to speak and when that failed he dropped to his knees and attacked Christine's crotch with his mouth. He made loud eating noises and his tongue flicked left and right, in and out.

"Oh God," Christine said. She held Charlie by the hair to steady herself.

Still, Charlie tipped over and Christine fell on top of him.

162

Charlie began to laugh like a buffoon.

"Charlie Cain, I do believe you're drunk."

Charlie tried to make his face a mask of seriousness.

"But, Christine, it's a test, don't you see?"

"What kind of test is that?" Christine said. There was an edge to her voice. Her fantasy evening was off to a peculiar start.

"Well, I wanted to see, if with a certain mix of compounds in me you could still get my dick hard."

Christine didn't know whether to be hurt or excited. Her face tried a mix of both.

"I think I can," she said, tentatively.

Charlie just lay on the floor and grinned.

"Do you want me to do something special? Do you want me to dance a striptease or something?"

"Knock me out," Charlie said. He laughed at his own joke.

Christine got off Charlie and stood over him. "Do you want to sit up to see better?"

"I've got a humdinger view," Charlie said. "Hum-dingler. Dingler, hum."

Christine smiled at him. She thought for a moment and then started to sway to unheard music. She gyrated around Charlie, and her movements did not go unappreciated. She could move those handsome hips. She let the robe fall and continued to dance around with only that ridiculous scarf.

"That's a great view, my pumpkin," Charlie said.

"Charlie, look at this," Christine said and she unknotted the scarf and dropped it over Charlie's face. For a moment Charlie left it there and it interrupted Christine's dance. When he took it off she smiled and turned around so he could watch her ass shimmy.

"Oh, honey," Charlie said in appreciation.

"You like that, lover," Christine said, adding a little more action to the rhumba.

Once again they found themselves on the floor just inside the door. This time neither suggested a move.

"Christine, sit on face," Charlie said. He spread out his arms and legs.

"Ooh, Charlie," Christine said. She lowered herself slowly, her powerful haunches supporting the awkward descent. She placed her pussy directly onto Charlie's mouth.

"Mmmm, mmmf," Charlie said. He began his work.

"Oh God, Charlie. Oh God. You sure can eat pussy."

Christine was getting worked up quickly. This evening was turning out okay after all. Her pleasure and her happiness combined and, had she the gift for introspection, she would have noticed that her life was good at that exact moment. She came hard, pressing herself downward so that Charlie could barely breathe. When she finished shaking she dropped onto her hands and knees, making a lovely bridge over Charlie Cain, while she caught her breath.

"That went well," Charlie said. He took two handfuls of ass and squeezed so hard Christine squealed.

"Ow," she said. "Hey, hey, Charlie. Guess what? The experiment was a success."

Charlie looked down the length of his body and saw, underneath Christine's umbrageous breasts, his erect cock sticking out of the opening in his boxers.

"The Flagship Cain!" he said.

Christine laughed. "Looks like old Christine passed the test."

"My dear," Charlie said. "For extra credit you must make poor, drunk Charlie come."

"Ooh, I can do that," Christine said.

She first wrapped her hand around the flagpole and enjoyed the feel of it. She was looking at the cock as if it were some numinous object.

"Charlie, you get so fucking hard," she said.

"Mm," Charlie answered.

"Now I'm going to suck you off," Christine said.

And just as her mouth surrounded him Ken opened the front door.

Back at home Charlie looked at his face in the bathroom mirror. He stood there for an inordinately long time. He was looking at a stranger, a stranger who'd been put through the wringer. His nose was flattened, caked with red/black blood in each nostril. One eye was swollen shut and one lip cut. He also had a sharp red line of blood on his forehead. He was trying to remember where that cut came from. Perhaps Ken still wears his college class ring. Charlie also had a painful ear; he distinctly remembered Ken slapping him there making his head buzz like a trumpet blown for battle. That might have been the first blow. Charlie did not hit back. Ken could probably best him anyway, but Charlie saw that it was meet and right to take his pummeling and go home.

Christine had just backed away and sat, naked and agog, watching while her husband hit Charlie again and again. When Ken had tired and he stood over Charlie panting, Charlie took the opportunity to stand up, gather his clothes and walk home. He did not bother to dress. Some neighbors were outside. He could hear the muttering like the sound of the galley at a murder trial. He did not turn left or right but walked in a straight line to his own front door and disappeared inside.

After this mirror gazing Charlie took a hot shower. Blood ran down the drain and Charlie watched it and tried to remember what it reminded him of. *Psycho*, that was it. He'd read some-where that they used chocolate syrup to imitate the blood in black and white movies. Charlie's face hurt, of course, but the pain seemed far away. It seemed like another man's pain and Charlie only a gongoozler to the brutality. Or like the pain of a character in a flick. His face looked like a face in a mob movie, the face of the rat, the squealer. Right before they wrapped his body in a rug and took it somewhere dark and lost.

The next few days Charlie drank more than usual, which means Charlie drank a lot. The morning after the beating Char-lie's face was stuck to his pillow. It was this pain that woke him and reminded him of what had happened the night before. It had actually happened. Charlie left the blood-stained pillow and went straight to the kitchen and finished off a bottle of red wine. By noon Charlie had mixed his alcohols and he was a mess.

Someone knocked on the door. Someone called on the phone. Charlie did not check either. He was no longer invisible. He was dead. That's what he imagined. He was dead and all his problems were gone and he didn't have to do anything. He didn't have to get dressed, or eat food, or go out. He could drink, take his meds, and stay floating in the ether.

Gone, gone.

And, worse, Charlie stopped writing. He stopped writing his novel and he stopped writing his column. Ellis called. Ellis visit-ed. Charlie did not move.

"I am dead," he whispered to the darkened living room. "I am an ex-Charlie."

Eventually, Ellis stopped calling and Charlie stopped being paid. He had very little money left but he was courting failure so his heart went toward the black. He bought food but mostly crap because it was cheaper. The house and yard, which he had only maintained sporadically, began to look like a derelict property. The lawn service ceased coming after Charlie chased them away with an old pitching wedge. Weeds replaced grass, paint dried and cracked on porch and walls, mail was left to yellow in the mailbox. Charlie lost weight, grew a beard, slept poorly except when the booze and pills gave him delirious blackouts.

Then his sister called. Charlie answered even though his head beat like Keith Moon on steroids.

"Charlie, what the hell?" Ruby began.

"Hello, shis," Charlie said.

"Are you drunk, Charlie? It's nine in the morning."

"I'm a not a drunk."

Ruby counted to ten. "Charlie, I came by last night. You wouldn't come to the door though I knew you were home. I heard the TV. So, you don't want to see me?"

"I do," Charlie said, though, of course, he didn't.

"Charlie the yard looks like shit. When was the last time you cut it?"

"Cut the yard?" Charlie asked as if they were talking about something outré.

"You had a yard service, didn't you? I am pretty damn sure a yard service was included in the will, along with the house. What happened to the yard service?"

"Yard service?" Charlie repeated, because the phrase sounded funny to him. Was it really called a yard service?

"Listen, Charlie. Grace and I have some news. I'd prefer not to talk about it on the phone. Can I take you to lunch, Charlie?"

"Lunch. Oh, not today, Ruby. I've got—stuff to do."

"Charlie, you can't keep putting me off."

"I wouldn't, Sish."

"Charlie, tomorrow then. I will come by around noon."

"Tomorrow then," Charlie said.

He hung up. His head told him poisonous things. He felt terrible. The thought of lunch, with or without his sister, made him nauseous. Charlie took four aspirins. Then he ate some Captain Crunch which had been in the cabinet for months. His milk was sour so he used milk powder, pouring it over the cereal and then dousing the bowl with tap water. It was terrible. He ate half the bowl and then urped.

That night, Charlie got antsy. He had to get out of the house. He was pretty sure the Volvo had no gas, so he set out on foot. He looked like an old dog shaved by a drunken barber but, for once, he was relatively sober. And he had showered.

Did he do this because he had loving on his mind? Only as clearly as he could form the thought. His mind was sunk in pink insulation, the prickly kind. His thoughts were prickly.

He walked toward Amber's apartment. Then he stopped and stood on a street corner, uncertainty further clouding his thinking. Amber had moved. Amber had married. Amber had married someone else.

A group of teenagers drove by in the buggy twilight, hanging out the windows of their Pontiac, and one of them threw a soft drink can at Charlie. It bounced harmlessly off his chest. One of the miscreants shouted, "Get a job, hobo!"

Charlie was hurt. Ridiculous how that hurt.

Charlie walked toward Patience Spent's house. Now he wanted comfort. Sexual or asexual, he wanted to lie with a woman and have her tell him sweet things.

As he neared her house he could see that the front door was open and Patience was outside, lit by the orangey sun in its last gleam of the day. She was as pretty as a candy shop. She was stooped, watching something in the grass, something small and pink. As Charlie got closer he was able to make it out: it was a small child, a baby as naked as Adam before the fall. It was a child so young it could not yet lift its head. It lay in the grass and Patience gently stroked its small Buddha belly as she sang. Her voice carried out into the slumber-stricken air and pierced Charlie like a lance. The song went on and on, sweet and fairylike, frothy and full of ancient sagacity. In its chubby little hand the baby held a small lotus wand.

Charlie ran in the other direction. He was a beast, a stricken thing. He fell onto someone's lawn and lay there while his heart went crazy and his breathing was erratic and painful. He began to cry. The sun went down.

Charlie met his sister at a midtown restaurant. He had shaved and dressed in a relatively clean shirt, and employed only a modicum of alcohol to grease the tracks. Just in case, he put some pills in his pocket. Lunch with his sister could prove stressful, though he did not know why he thought that. It was a premonition.

Ruby was already there when Charlie arrived. She was sipping from a sweet tea to which she had added Sweet and Low. She was dieting.

She rose when Charlie got close and gave him a perfunctory hug.

"Hello, Charlie," she said, without inflection. "You look hale."

"I feel like hale," Charlie tried.

Ruby neither smiled nor acknowledged the joke. "They do a good club sandwich here," she said.

"Club sandwich it is," Charlie said with false bonhomie.

"Don't order a drink," Ruby said, her eyes using her menu as a shield.

"I'm parched," Charlie said. Where was this phony jokiness coming from?

"Don't have any alcohol, ok?" Ruby clarified as if he were a child.

"Yes, ma'am," Charlie said. The thin mantle of cheeriness was slipping.

The waiter came. He was overly obsequious as if he were waiting on relatives he hadn't seen in years.

"Two club sandwiches," Ruby said.

Charlie nodded and turned in his menu.

"Charlie, I am not enjoying this," Ruby began.

"Wait for the club sandwiches," Charlie said. It was his last joke of the day.

"Grace and I need to move into Mom and Dad's house."

The way she said it Charlie, momentarily, thought Mom and Dad's house was a place he had never visited.

"B-but, I live there," Charlie said.

"Yes, I know. When you took the house Grace and I were doing well and had our own house and it seemed fair to let you live at Mom and Dad's. It was never a legal thing. There is no will giving you the house, and now we need it. Grace's business—and this is just between us—is bleeding money. We're having months where we barely make the mortgage. And we want to have a kid—eventually. Which means we need more room. I'm sorry, Charlie. This is just how it has to be."

"You can't have a kid," Charlie said, stupidly. "You're both women." His thinking got slow, then slower.

"We'll adopt, of course," Ruby said in her sober way.

"Where will I go?"

"Charlie, get an apartment. You obviously can't keep up a house and yard. The place is wrecked."

"I-I can't afford an apartment."

"Charlie, you've got the paper and I thought you and Amber were getting back together. She makes good money."

The waiter brought the sandwiches and before he could make a clubby joke about the club sandwiches he registered that the table was surrounded by ice like Superman's Fortress of Solitude. He set the sandwiches down and backed away with a smile.

Charlie could not speak. He could not eat.

"Charlie, we'll help you any way we can, of course."

Charlie looked at his sister. Had she always been this cold? She used to be so concerned about him, setting him up with her friends, checking on him when his heart had been broken, calling just to chat about inconsequential things. Apparently, she had lost that devotion. He was sure it was his fault.

"Amber married someone else," Charlie croaked, faintly.

Ruby had just taken a large bite of her sandwich and she put a finger up to signal that a response was on its way.

"Charlie, I'm so sorry. I didn't know that. Why didn't you call me?"

"What would you have done?"

"Offered support, Charlie. Offered love. These things seem unnecessary to you as if I am some lightweight new-agey friend. I'm your sister, Charlie. I love you."

"Ruby, this is not a good time for me to lose the house."

Ruby was quiet for a while. Charlie had hope that she was rethinking this plan and was finding it impossible after all.

"I'm sorry, Charlie. We've already sold our house."

"You've been working on this a long time."

"No, no we haven't. We put the house up for sale as a test. We didn't think about what we would do if it sold. We had no plan. We wanted to see what would happen. And, it sold within a week. Apparently, our neighborhood is an up-and-coming hotspot."

"Great, good for you."

"Listen, we'll help you find an apartment. Just tell us your price range and—"

"Zero. Zero to diddly-shit. That is my price range." Anger bubbled within.

"Charlie, ok, I didn't want to go into this. You're turning into a drunk, aren't you? That's the root of this. Amber married someone else because you're a drunk."

This was unexpectedly barbed. A cruelty entered in.

"I am not a drunk, my dear sister. I am not a drunk. And I'll find my own place to live. Don't worry about a thing. And give my love to Grace."

"Charlie, listen."

"You covering lunch?"

"What?"

"Can you pay for lunch?"

"Yes, but—"

And Charlie was gone. Ruby composed herself for a moment. Then she signaled to the waiter.

"Yes, ma'am?" he said. His obsequiousness was slightly hidden under a mask of uncertainty.

"Doggie bag, please," she said, waving her hand over Charlie's untouched sandwich.

*I*t was one thirty in the afternoon and Charlie started drinking. On the drive back home he took the pills he had secreted in his pocket. By sundown he was a gone goon. He didn't remember watching TV or eating dinner or going to bed. He woke the next day still in his clothes on top of the coverlet on his bed. He didn't have his shoes on and he never found them again.

He managed to get some scrambled eggs down though the eggs didn't look that great when he broke them. They were gluey. And they were gluey going down.

He showered and by eleven he was congratulating himself on not taking a drink or a pill. The lunch with his sister came flooding back. He replayed her unkindest remarks. It all stunk. He was wifeless, homeless, hopeless. Out of desperation he called Ellis.

"Hello, Charlie," Ellis said. His voice sounded as if he had taken the call reluctantly.

"Ellis, how are things?" Charlie tried. He could not even generate inauthentic affability.

"Fine. What can I do for you, Charlie?"

"I'm ready to get back to work," Charlie said.

The phone was full of silence. The silence was overflowing. On the floor around Charlie's feet silence pooled.

"I just don't think I have anything for you," Ellis said.

"Listen," Charlie began before he realized Ellis had hung up.

He called the editor of the town's weekly newspaper, a leftist paper which mixed arts, local coverage with political satire and thought pieces. Charlie did not know the editor but he had met her once at a party.

"Camila Thomas," she answered.

"Hi, Camila," Charlie said in what he imagined was the right mixture of lightheartedness and business. "You don't know me, but—"

"Charlie Cain. Of course, I know you. I used to love your column."

Charlie still was not used to phones ratting you out. "Yes, thank you. I have in mind a similar thing I'd like to pitch to you."

Camila's silence was not as protracted as Ellis's. "Hm, yes, well, thank you, Charlie. I don't have an opening right now. We're pretty well staffed."

"Well, perhaps you'll let me know if that changes," Charlie said.

"Of course," came back Camila's lie.

"Let me just give you my number."

"I have it here. Thank you for thinking of us, Charlie."

Where else? Charlie thought. Where else could my meager talents give me an in? There was a local magazine, but he thought their parent company was the same as the weekly paper's. Camila might actually be an editor there, also.

There was also a free magazine that covered news of Charlie's area of town. It was called Midtown Buzz. Charlie got out his laptop to get online and see if he could find a phone number. He was having trouble logging on. He got a message: No internet access.

Charlie had not paid his bill. The bill was here somewhere. Charlie didn't look for it. Instead he began to search for a copy of Midtown Buzz. It took a long time but he finally uncovered a copy underneath a stack of dishes next to his bed. He called the number of the editor.

"Editor," a cartoonish voice answered. It sounded like a child playing editor.

"Hi, my name is Charlie Cain."

"Yes, how can I help you? Did you get your copy this week?"

"Yes, thank you. I did. Very prompt. Thank you."

"Ok, good then."

"I'm wondering if you're hiring writers," Charlie said.

"Writers," the editor said.

"Yes, to write your articles." Did Charlie really have to explain what writers did? This was a bad start.

"I write the articles," the editor said.

"All of them?" Charlie asked. It came out with a condescending air.

"Every dang one of them."

"Huh."

"Anything else I can do for you? Want to take out an ad? We're having a special right now."

"No. No ad. Thank you."

Charlie brought out a bottle of plonk. He couldn't remember buying it. He had finished it by the time he started cooking his dinner, which was scrambled eggs again. He didn't want to waste the eggs now that he had reckoned they had not gone bad.

The next morning Charlie had a fresh idea. It wasn't genius. It was wretchedness. He was losing everything and, in some men that might have engendered a celebratory freedom; in Charlie it engendered terror and sorrow. He would have a yard sale. He had no idea how to do that. Then, a phrase floated into his sensorium: Estate sale. That's what people did when they sold everything.

They had estate sales. Charlie was ready to sell everything. He would scrape his old life down to the primer.

Charlie was drunk when the estate person arrived. She was about five foot two with black hair and eyebrows and a stout body that could have been a man's. Her name was Candace Something. Charlie didn't catch the last name and, in his head, she became for all time, Candace Something.

"So," Candace said, in preface. She only looked at Charlie from the edge of her vision. He must have been a disgusting sight. "Have you tagged what all you want to sell?"

"All. Sell it all," Charlie said, with a woeful pride. He was leaning on a golf club, making a near isosceles triangle with the ground. He grinned like a gommie.

"Ah, everything," Candace Something said. She cast her eyes around the living room. "Of course, we'll have to clean up a bit," she said.

"I'll wear a fresh shirt," Charlie said, still grinning, looking down at his bemired tee-shirt.

"Ha ha," Candace said, without mirth. "I mean the living room, of course."

Charlie looked around. Really the grin must hurt by now. His eyes made a mad, annular examination of the room and came back and rested on Candace. She was looking at him sideways. Charlie's eyes went up and down the estate seller, seemed disappointed at her height, and then met her eyes (what he could see of them). "I bet you clean up nice, too," Charlie said.

"I don't know," Candace said, in a small voice.

"You wanna shower with me?" Charlie asked. He would not take his eyes off the side of her face. But now her head started to rotate and she looked at Charlie full-on.

"Not if you were the last man on Earth," she said, through tight lips.

Charlie refused to drop the grin or his glance.

"Your loss," he said, and wandered out to the kitchen.

The rest of the afternoon went better. Charlie stayed out of her way as she walked around from item to item making notes. It took more than an hour.

"Ok, Mr. Cain. You wanted to do this on the third?"

"That time will work for me," Charlie said.

"We will see you then," Candace Something said. "I will have Mike Moore with me."

Charlie didn't understand what she was getting at.

"Mike!" he said. "It'll be great to see him."

On the third Candace and Mike arrived about 6 a.m. Charlie answered the door in his skivvies.

"Jesus, the sun's not even up yet," Charlie said.

Candace renewed her sideways glance.

"Mike Moore, Charlie Cain," she said. "We need to get started right away. Perhaps it would be best if you absented yourself. Some people get emotional over their things being sold."

Charlie looked at Mike Moore, who was wearing a cowboy hat. "Tex," Charlie said.

Mike Moore smiled an insurance salesman's smile, as false as dicers' oaths.

"I'm in your hands," Charlie said.

Candace turned her face away with a pursed-lip moue.

"Have you removed all the things you don't want sold?" she asked.

"I have," Charlie said. He nodded toward the door. Next to it sat a brown paper sack, slightly smaller than a grocery sack and not completely full.

"Ok," Candace said, and moved away.

"Charlie," Mike Moore said. "Why don't you shower and we'll get set up. And then, perhaps, you can go somewhere for the day. Catch a movie perhaps."

Charlie hated Mike.

"Whatever," Charlie mumbled and did indeed move into the bathroom and turn on the shower. Mike followed him so he could close the door.

Fifteen minutes later Charlie emerged showered and shaved and wearing only his towel.

"I guess I better find some clothes," he said. "I forgot to pack any."

Charlie went off to the bedroom.

"Jesus," Candace said.

When Charlie returned he almost looked presentable. His hair was slicked back and he wore a short-sleeve cabana shirt and a swimsuit. On his feet pink flip-flops. He found a lawn chair by the back door and took it and a cup of coffee, which Candace had brewed, out onto the lawn. He brought out a pair of pants and a shirt and put them into this bag of keepers.

"I think I'll just stay outside and welcome people," Charlie said.

He did not glance back to see how this was taken.

And that's what Charlie did. People arrived in droves. Some smiled and said hello to Charlie, who made a strange gatekeeper, and some would not meet his eye. Charlie began to assume that it was odd for the owners, who were soon to be non-owners, to sit in witness. And, as items were carried out past him, Charlie made comments. All quite genial but it provoked great embarrassment in the shoppers.

"Ah, did you get all the LPs?" he asked a long hair young

man, tall as a scarecrow, with a ponytail and an Adam's apple the size of a walnut.

"I think so," the young man said, quietly.

"Good buy," Charlie said.

"Goodbye," the fellow said. He didn't wait to hear Charlie expound on Led Zeppelin, Elton John and Booker T. and the MGs.

A young couple in a Honda van bought the bed and Mike Moore helped them carry it out.

"Lots of memories there," Charlie shouted. Though, in truth, not really. The last trysts with Amber, now so long ago, were the most fun that double bed had ever seen.

Charlie got hungry about one and started inside though he had no memory of anything munchable in the fridge.

"Is it really necessary that you come in?" Candace Something said, clutching Charlie's sleeve and hissing in his ear. "It puts off the buyers."

"I'm hungry," Charlie said.

"I'll bring you something," Candace said.

Charlie looked around at the strangers rifling through his things and weighed his options. They were not very interesting.

"Ok," Charlie said.

He returned to his lawn chair and Candace was as good as her word. She brought out a plate of various finger foods, cunning little cucumber sandwiches, and meatballs on toothpicks, and cakes the size of silver dollars.

"Whoa," Charlie said. "What fearsome hands crafted this repast?" He was smiling, trying his damnedest to get Candace to crack a grin.

"I always supply food for my sales. It's in my brochure."

"Brochure. Sure," Charlie said, biting a meatball off its stick. "Yummy."

Candace hurried back inside.

By the end of the long day Charlie's house had been all but gutted. All the stuff he thought of as junk found new homes. Candace was smiling at him as if she had performed a difficult piece of legerdemain. They were standing in the open doorway. Mike Moore carried out a barstool and put it in his own car. He gave a perfunctory wave and drove away.

"That's it, Mr. Cain. A very successful day. We'll be sending a check after it's all totted up and our cut taken."

"Candace, you're a darling," Charlie said. "This calls for a drink."

"None for me. I must be going."

"Candace, darling. One little drink."

Candace Something looked around Charlie's living room, bare except for a few oddments, some electrical cords, old magazines, and pieces of things which, obviously, were incomplete. These were sorrowful remains.

Charlie thought she was thinking it over. "A little drink and then, if you're up for it, we could get naked on the floor."

Candace Something now looked Charlie in the face. "Mr. Cain. I hope the rest of your life is happier than you are at this moment for you are a sad excuse for a man."

Charlie appeared dazed momentarily. Candace gathered up her few things and headed for the door.

"It doesn't have to be on the floor," Charlie said, half to himself.

Charlie made enough money from the sale of his possessions to put a down payment and the first two month's rent on an apartment in a rundown subdivision just east of downtown. It was a shithole. Ruby, out of guilt Charlie imagined, had put in a futon and one wooden chair, which looked like it came from a school supply warehouse. Plus, one janky lamp, as tall as a stork.

The empty refrigerator smelled bad. The cupboards were lined with peeling bug paper. There was a stain on the bathroom floor that looked like blood. And the plumbing sang when you turned on the hot water. It sang "Amazing Grace." It sang "Ruby, Don't Take Your Love to Town." It sang "Gitarzan."

Charlie spread out his few possessions on the futon. He kept his phone but sold his laptop. The phone didn't work but Charlie thought he might make a payment just so he could talk to—someone. He also kept a handful of paperback books which he had not read. A pad of paper. A few nice pens and a dozen pencils. A few bathroom items. A bottle of gin. And, the few items of clothing he had added at the last minute.

When Charlie was raking his medicine bottles into his bag he saw the small, dark vial fall among them. It was Dr. Raphael's elixir. Now, in his new place, Charlie picked up the vial and held it up to the light. It was almost full. Did this matter? Did he dare tempt fate twice? No, he put it aside. No.

For companionship he had one wee mouseketeer and an orchestra of roaches. At first, he forbade them enter his bed but, with the crumbs and orts Charlie left in the sheets, it was a losing battle. Charlie named the mouse Annette.

Charlie lay back on his futon, under the weak vitelline lamp, and began reading John Fowles' *The Magus*. Night came on and Charlie read. In the morning he woke on the futon, with the book splayed on his chest like a tattoo.

Charlie's landlord was a man named Snook who weighed 428 pounds. He rarely got out of his chair. His apartment, next to the laundromat, was his office. Tenants were expected to hand deliver their rent once a month, face to face with Snook, so that he could give them the current news regarding their tenancy. Some renters were given smiles and metaphorical pats on the head. These were tenants who paid regularly and who kept the outside area around their apartment free from trash. Often, these tenants were also of the female gender, lovely or not. Snook took great pride in having them before him as if he were a potentate deciding whether they should live or die. He made the women linger long and, sucking on a popsicle or a cigar, depending on time of day, he appraised them physically with his dark, piggy eyes, while ostensibly giving them all the recent changes to their rental agreement, or praising them for being such model tenants.

"You're a model tenant," Snook told one young woman whose husband was in the service and often deployed elsewhere. He took a particularly lengthy suck on his popsicle. "Perhaps you could model for me," And, while the poor woman wrinkled her face in disgust, mixed with fear, Snook let loose a series of coarse har, har, hars.

Charlie hated Snook from the get-go and the feeling seemed to be mutual. So, after one month, when Charlie was due to appear before him, Charlie had let his dislike fester and grow until it was a seething mix of alcoholic paranoia and simple, human distaste.

"Here ya go," Charlie said, tossing the envelope on the desk in front of the porcine Snook.

"Hold up there, Cain," Snook said, picking up the envelope and running his eyes over it as if it were a legal document with loopholes to be found.

Charlie leaned against the doorway. He was already tired of standing. He also had a hangover. It was ten a.m.

"I heard tell you had underage girls in your apartment," Snook said.

Charlie just stared at him. The charge was absurd and not worth an answer. Snook returned the stare and his expression was asking for a reply. Finally, Snook snuffled through his nose and spoke: "If you haven't, why haven't you?" And, of course, he laughed at his own joke.

"Can I go now?" Charlie said.

"I'm not the police," Snook said, relishing the concept that he seemed like the law.

"See you in a month," Charlie said, turning.

"You're not gay, are you?" Snook said, just to stop Charlie in his tracks. "I mean, it's ok if you are but I like to know a little about each of my tenants. It helps to keep things in order. I am a fool for order."

"You like your little kingdom, Snook. I understand. Power is power. Everyone wants some."

Snook looked Charlie over. Then he snorted as if he was in on the joke.

"Ok, Cain. Keep your nose clean," Snook said, and then began looking through a desk drawer for an imaginary necessity.

Charlie went home and had a beer.

*A*s time passed and his money dwindled and his flesh grew unhealthy Charlie thought that perhaps he would chance a date. He not only needed sex he needed the closeness of a woman. He wanted to breathe in perfume again. He wanted to believe that he was not yet deceased.

The problem was that Charlie had burned all his bridges. He had nowhere to turn. He had turned his phone back on, at least for 30 days, so he scrolled through his list of contacts. He was so desperate he considered calling Christine. If nothing else perhaps Ken could beat him up again.

In his list of numbers he saw the name: Lorraine. No last name. It took him a moment to remember her. She was the sexy neighbor who dismissed him with obvious disdain when he tried to present himself to her. He may have been drunk. Perhaps she'd like him better now. He dialed the number.

"Hello?" Lorraine answered, obviously not recognizing the caller ID.

"Lorraine, Charlie Cain. I don't know if you remember me."

"I remember you, Charlie."

"Oh, nice. Thank you. I have moved out of the neighbor-hood."

"Uh huh," Lorraine said. He was already losing her.

"I was wondering if you'd like to get together."

The silence went on for miles.

"Are you asking me for a date?"

It seemed absurd to Charlie, too. "Yes," he said.

More silence. Charlie was looking longingly at a bottle of gin.

"Lemme tell you something, Charlie."

There was a pause. Charlie thought perhaps he was expected to fill it. "Ok," he said.

"I need some sex."

Charlie was sure he had heard wrong.

"Uh huh," he said.

"I've just come out of a long relationship. It's none of your business. But I would love an anonymous screw. And then you'd have to leave."

"I can do that," Charlie said. He'd never been a boytoy before but he liked the idea.

"Can you get here by seven?"

"I can," Charlie said.

Lorraine hung up.

"Jesus," Charlie said to himself. Stuff like this didn't happen in the real world.

Was this the same real world where men were made invisible by a potion? Charlie had landed back in reality on his ass, and now he had to pick himself up and clean himself off and visit a woman, prettier than any woman he'd ever been with, for the sole purpose of having sex. Charlie showered and shaved. He went through his limited wardrobe. He had bought a shirt at Goodwill a few days earlier and he judged that it would have to do. His trousers had only one small stain. His one pair of socks he began washing in the sink.

As the evening approached Charlie's trepidation grew. He was no Lothario. He wasn't up for this. He thought about the gin. But, to his credit, he eschewed it and began to get dressed. His socks were still wet but he wore them anyway. They made a funny noise in his loafers. He looked at himself in the smoky mirror in his bathroom. His hair was as stiff as weeds. His eyes were not lively. His paunch, which seemed to come and go like Brigadoon, had returned. He sighed. This was as well as he could do.

Driving back it felt like he'd been gone years. The neighborhood looked the same. He was a trespasser.

The first doorbell he rang produced a heavy Greek man with a grin like a jester.

"Yes, sir? Yes. Yes, sir?" the Greek man said.

"Lorraine?" Charlie asked. He had a lump in his throat.

"Lorraine?" the man parroted.

"Does Lorraine live here?"

"Oh, no no. No Lorraine. She live next door. You want to come in?"

"No, thank you," Charlie said.

The fellow had nodded leftward so Charlie went to that house. Lorraine answered the bell after a few tense seconds. She looked at Charlie. Charlie knew what she was seeing. He had seen it himself recently.

"Charlie," she said. And walked away from the door.

Charlie followed her in. She was dressed in a caftan bathrobe that went all the way to the floor. It was made of a thick velveteen and shimmered when she walked. Charlie watched that walk and he remember why he had come.

"Do you want a drink?" Lorraine asked.

"Yes," Charlie said.

"Scotch ok?"

"Yes, Scotch," Charlie said.

Now, Lorraine turned and fully took Charlie in for the first time. Her face was like an abandoned birthday cake. She smirked. She shuddered.

Charlie grinned like a blister.

"Charlie, this was a bad idea. Sorry. Go home." She was still holding two drinks.

"Did I do something wrong?" Charlie asked. He felt near tears.

"Go home," she repeated softly.

Charlie turned and went out the door. He stood in the dark and heard Lorraine turn the lock. What could he do but go home?

Charlie drove home that night in a daze. He was literally dizzy and he could smell himself. He smelled of perspiration and despair. Once home he found he could not get to sleep right away. It was not loss that fed Charlie's insomnia. It was a terrible desuetude, a feeling that he wasn't there, that he didn't count. He was as sad as a null.

He drank.

Weeks went by and Charlie did not leave his apartment. He counted the money he had left. He tried to calculate how much time he had left, how much rent. He began to write down a budget but, after groceries, when he wrote 'Booze' as a column heading, he could not put a figure down. He tore up the piece of paper.

He sold the car to make his next month's rent. It just covered it.

Charlie's apartment was on the second floor of a two-story building. The two stoners who lived below him played their stereo as if they were alone on Yasgur's Farm. Charlie did not mind so much. It was the only music he had, even if their tastes ran to thrash metal bands and Charlie's to Leonard Cohen and Joni Mitchell. Sometimes the bass notes shook the thin floor and Charlie's guts bumped around and his head spun with drink and music and sometimes this is how he fell to sleep. The music often went into the wee hours, which made Charlie wonder about what his neighbors did for a living. As for Charlie, the hours of the day and night meant little to him. He had no schedule. And his curtailed life in this small, dingy apartment was smaller even than his aspirations.

He ran into one of his neighbors when he took the trash out.

The trash had gathered around the bin in his kitchen for weeks, so a critical point had been reached. When Charlie lifted the large garbage sacks the linoleum underneath was a disturbing dark brown and there seemed to be some kind of miniature life happening in the rotting floor. In flip-flops and boxers he stepped outside to find that it was sunny and hot. When did that happen?

He saw the neighbor—he thought her name was Candy, but it could have been Cindy or Tandy or Sandy—out of the corner of his eye. He hesitated. He thought if he could dash back inside she wouldn't have seen him. Could he make the bin and back without crossing her path? Fuck. He went forward. The black asphalt, glittering like gems afire, burned his feet through the worn flip-flops, his once toughened feet toughened no more. He tried to step quickly but the two bags slowed him down. The bin was too far from the sidewalk. It was a walk of shame through a bad part of town.

"Hey, neighbor," the neighbor called.

Charlie looked her way. He smiled. At least he thought he smiled. She was about 40, Charlie guessed, her face was di-colored from rosacea or gin blossoms. She looked rough but her voice was sweet.

Charlie had met her one night in the complex laundry room. It was around one a.m. and Charlie was as drunk as a boiled owl. Plus, he was wearing only a towel since all the clothes he owned were in the dryer. Charlie sat slumped in a faded plastic chair, shaped like a scoop, his chin on his chest. The woman came over to him anyway and introduced herself and asked Charlie if he were wearing only a towel. When Charlie admitted that such was the case her face wore a snaggle-toothed grin. What if I told you I needed a towel right now? she had said, her eyes wet with mischief. I imagine you'd see my enormous cock, cock-eyed Charlie said. As drunk as he was he thought he sounded sophisticatedly witty, the Noel Coward of the apartment laundry. I'll be right back, the woman had said. And, shortly after she left, the dryer stopped turning and Charlie gathered his clothes and went home.

Now Charlie felt as if he had to answer her. Some scraps of his manners remained. "Hey," Charlie said. "Hot."

The neighbor gave him a sly sideways smile. "Me or the parking lot?" she asked. She cocked her hip the way some women do. She laughed at her own joke.

"Ha, that's funny," Charlie said. He tossed the bags into the bin.

"My name's Bindy," she said and she stuck out her hand.

"Charlie," Charlie said. Bindy? He took the hand for the briefest of grasps—it was rough like a lumberjack's—and sprinted homeward.

"You wanna have dinner sometime?" Bindy called.

Charlie waved over his shoulder as if he hadn't heard her.

Once back inside he relished the darkness and the dank smell of his own space. So far Charlie had never opened the drapes. It was always cave-like, with the obscurity and the aroma of a bear's place of hibernation. Charlie looked around. He still only had a mattress, a chair, and a lamp. He basically lived in one room of the three-room apartment. He had not entered the bedroom proper. Once he opened the door and glanced in and it was dusty and smelled like old socks. The walls were poorly papered sheetrock. He had not been back.

Now, he fixed himself a vodka and orange juice and settled down to read Bellow's *Herzog*. It was his second time to read it. He'd run through all his books. Perhaps someday he should venture out and find the library. That would be a good day. Charlie vowed to do that.

A few nights later Charlie fell asleep with a glass of vodka in one hand, *Herzog* in the other, and a cigarette in his mouth. He set the mattress on fire. He woke to find one side of his bed afire, the flame beginning to lap at his elbow like a fiery puppy.

"Fuck," Charlie said.

He beat the fire out with Saul Bellow. He rolled over and went back to sleep.

In the morning the sight of the charred guts of his mattress was too depressing to think about. He drank.

*O*nce Charlie had put a pan of orangey bean and bacon soup in a small, thin-walled pot on top of the stove. He had bought the pot at Goodwill for 50 cents. It was well-used and blackened on the bottom and was so light Charlie wondered if it was metal at all. Charlie then lit up a joint—he had a small stash that he bought from the guys below him, though Charlie suspected that this was a poor grade of grass—and went back to his Bellow. The charred pages were chapters he'd already read.

About thirty minutes later Charlie looked up from where he was nodding over his book on his charred mattress on the floor and saw a plume of smoke coming from his stovetop. Charlie thought for a moment. He tried to gather his scattered wits.

Soup, Charlie said to himself.

In the kitchen the pot had burned through and the thickened beany goop had spread around the burner. There was now a large scorch mark on the top of the stove. One of his cheap, faded-blue dish towels had caught fire and burned leaving a small gloomy swirl on the countertop, the shape of a fox's shadow. Staring at that black circle Charlie thought he could enter it and disappear. He stood for a long time looking into it and—it looked back.

Charlie went moony.

Eventually, Charlie's reverie ended. He woke to witness his own disorder. The kitchen was a smelly mess. Charlie looked around and took it all in, the fly-specked window, the peeling ceiling, the babyshit yellow walls, the countertop now scorched, the floor now corroded, the stovetop stained and crusty. Charlie saw it all and he knew that he could do nothing. And he knew that he himself, Charlie Cain, was also nothing.

He left the apartment and started walking. His purported goal was to find out where the nearest library was, but he walked aimlessly. The flip-flops made his trudge awkward and somewhat painful. The sun beat down on his unprotected head, his bare arms. His food-stained t-shirt was cooking in the heat. An aroma arose from it that was not unlike campfire stew.

Charlie didn't even see the patrol car pull up to the curb and stop. He didn't see the black, female officer until she stepped in front of him.

"Hi," Charlie said. His mind shifted quickly: did they arrest you for being stoned? He'd heard of public drunkenness but, for once, he was not drunk. Because he had the joint.

"Good day," the officer said. Her voice was sweet like Aretha Franklin's, or so Charlie imagined. Did she look like Aretha Franklin? A little.

"What's up?" Charlie asked.

"Can I see some ID?" The officer was not smiling so Charlie stopped.

Charlie reached down to where there should be a pocket but he was wearing only boxers.

"Damn, I guess I left my wallet in my other pants."

"Sir, you're not wearing pants."

Charlie looked down once more to be sure. "Well, these are as good as shorts, right? Or a swimsuit. Right? You ever think that it's ok to be half-naked at the pool but if you…"

Charlie let his rhetorical question die because he sensed his audience's world-weariness.

"Name?" she asked.

"Charlie," Charlie said. "Charlie Cain."

"Where you going today, Charlie?"

"The library. Hey, I bet you can tell me the nearest library."

"Why the library, Charlie? Are you homeless?"

"Oh, no ma'am. I have a nice apartment back there." Charlie flung a hand over his shoulder. I must still be high, he thought. "I live back there. I was going to the library because I've read all my books twice."

"You got a library card, Charlie?"

Charlie thought hard about this. He calculated that if he answered this tough one right he might have passed the entire exam and he could go on his way.

"No," Charlie said. "Because I have no ID. I was gonna get me a card once I got there."

"That's gonna take some ID, Charlie. The library. They're gonna ask you for an ID."

Charlie thought about this. "You're right, officer. I am going to go back home and get my wallet which contains my driver's license and I'll put some pants on over this if you think that's best."

The officer stood with her arms akimbo and looked at Charlie. Then she looked away and made eye contact with her fellow officer, a white guy with pale skin and straw-like hair. She and he sent some kind of message to each other with their eyes.

"Charlie, I think that would be best. Why don't you go home and get yourself together and then walk to the library?"

"Yes," Charlie said. "Yes, that's exactly what I'll do." Charlie now used his smile again.

The officer, who didn't look a thing like Aretha Franklin, nodded and got back inside her car. They sat at the curb waiting for Charlie to move. So, he moved. He started back the way he came. After a few steps he heard the crunch of their tires as they pulled away from the curb.

"Oh, wait," Charlie called weakly backwards. "I forgot to ask you how to get to the library."

About a week later Charlie set his bed on fire again. This time the flames were on the wall side and a large pod-shaped piece of the wallpaper was burned away. And the hole in the mattress was larger this time. The stuffing had caught fire. It was a small blessing that Charlie had not set his own shirt on fire.

At 3 a.m., the witching hour, Charlie vowed to stop smoking weed and keep solely to the pleasures of the bottle. This seemed to Charlie a mature and intelligent decision. There would be no more fires.

As Charlie's alcoholism increased his appetite decreased. The booze was eating away at his stomach and denying his body the ability to process food into energy. Charlie lost weight and he could no longer look at himself in the mirror. His sinewy arms ached. His chest burned. His bony ass hurt when he sat on the toilet or on any hard chair.

Still, the body wants what the body wants. His wanted booze. But it also still wanted sex. Though his health had an adverse effect on his libido he still wanted a woman, if only in the abstract. Once, in the grocery store, he saw Patience and her son, walking the aisles like mortal humans. Charlie did not notice them until they were right up on him. As they passed Patience looked at Charlie and smiled a pitying smile. She did not recognize him. That hurt and her pity doubled the pain.

The towhead next to her also looked at Charlie. His bright blue eyes seemed to penetrate Charlie, to see through him, into him, to judge him and find him wanting. Son, Charlie thought. My son.

One night, the flesh grew frantic. Charlie walked out into the night and tried to remember the number of Bindy's apartment. He knew which block but he was unsure of the number. One of the bottom units. Ending in a three? Charlie had slicked back his hair and put on his cleanest t-shirt. His clothes hung on him as if he were a walking hanger. He had to cinch his belt tight to keep his trousers up.

He knocked on the door of 23. Bindy opened the door.

"Yes?' she said.

"Hey, Mindy. It's Charlie."

"Bindy," Bindy said.

"Bindy," Charlie said.

"Can I help you?"

"It's Charlie. From the laundry room."

Bindy stared at him. Unconsciously, she closed the door an inch, holding it in her hand.

"I was wearing a towel," Charlie said.

"Oh…oh, yeah. I remember now."

"What are you doing tonight?" Charlie asked. He tried not to judge her by her looks. He was sure she was generous and kind and probably great in bed.

"I'm busy," Bindy said.

"Oh," Charlie said.

"Well, anyway. Ok," Bindy said.

"Yep," Charlie said.

"See you around," Bindy said and closed the door.

"Yep," Charlie said to the door.

$\mathcal{R}$ebuffed by a woman he was not even attracted to Charlie felt as low as he could ever remember feeling.

He drank.

Days went by, weeks. Outside, autumn had come again. Charlie ran out of grub.

And now alcohol was almost his entire intake of nutrients. Food upset his ravaged stomach. In between bouts of booze— cheaper and cheaper booze—he swigged Pepto-Bismol. His was a liquid diet. He sought complete oblivescence.

He also stopped bathing and shaving. His skin showed bruises he didn't remember getting and he was often flushed and sweaty. He lost muscle tone. His side hurt and the pain that originally sent him to the doctor, now so long ago, had returned with renewed force. Charlie shuffled around his apartment like a man forty years older. He had no energy and he had no hope. He never thought about the future because he assumed he didn't have one. He was almost looking forward to the day they'd find his body in this ra-thole apartment. That's something he'd like to see.

But, even in this, he was thwarted.

One day two young punks knocked on Charlie's thin wooden door. They were hailing him before even giving him time to answer their knocking.

"Open up, Asshole," came their neighborly greeting. "Time to relocate."

And, contrapuntally, his sidekick: "Yeah, open up, Asshole."

Charlie opened the door and the young men there couldn't have been more than 20 years old. They were thin and wiry, tattooed and pierced.

"Snook says you're out," the taller one said.

"Yeah, you're out," his compatriot said.

"What the fuck?" Charlie said.

"Don't make this difficult, brother, cuz I'd sooner crack your head as look at you."

"I had no warning," Charlie said.

"This is your warning. Get out. Now."

"Where can I go?" Charlie said. His voice was as slow and weak as a winter fly.

The two hooligans thought that was as funny as a fart joke. They laughed, the smaller one leaning against the other. This was their craic. They enjoyed this. Charlie watched their nasty guffawing as if it was Death itself speaking his name.

"C'mon, Nogoodnik. We ain't got time to stand around."

"Ok, I guess," Charlie started but he didn't know what he guessed. "I'll get my stuff."

"Leave the furniture, Snook says, to pay for this month's rent."

"Furniture," Charlie said like a ghost.

The tall creep craned his head around the door jamb. "Jesus, Asswipe. You've fucked this up good. Snook ain't gonna like this one bit."

"Lemme get my clothes," Charlie said. He walked away and the two hooligans entered his apartment.

"Jesus, it stinks in here. You an addict or something. I've seen condemned houses look nicer."

Charlie was beyond their ridicule now. He put his clothes inside a brown bag and then emptied the medicine cabinet on top of the clothes. He walked straight past them as they jeered and disappeared out the door and down the stairs.

"Nice work, Charlie," the tall one yelled down to him. "You're a real artist of the flops."

"Yuh, a real artist," the other called out.

*W*here does a man go when he has nowhere to go? He goes nowhere.

All Charlie owned he was wearing or carrying in a brown paper sack, so worn it looked like another substance altogether. Charlie wandered the streets like a feral cat. He returned to his old neighborhood but could not go down Brock Way for fear of running into his sister. Or Ken, or Christine.

He walked to Sudie Nimm's house. It appeared she still lived there but Charlie did not have the courage to approach her door. He walked to what used to be Amber's house, a long damn hike. There was a strange car in the driveway and a Water Wiggle lying in the front yard like a colorful asp. He walked to Nocturna, the galley that sold Sudie Nimm's work. He stood outside its large glass windows and marveled at the well-lit space within. It all seemed so clean and bright and full of human potential. Charlie began to cry. He'd walked the entire day. He was hungry and beat and he wanted a drink.

To hide his tears he walked hurriedly down the sidewalk. He found an alley and stepped into its vegetative smell and cooler air and leaned against the wall. He let his tears fall until he had cried himself dry. Self-pity is a seductress and Charlie was without volition. He would follow anything now, even his own self-pity. Charlie reflected that, perhaps, he had always been a selfish man, one who listened only to his own heart. Then he decided he wasn't all bad. He had loved and had been spurned. His love for Amber was something pure and clear and clean. As he cried he thought about her and about their love, in which he had invested his whole being. Perhaps this is wrong. But, this Charlie knew:

he had given. He had given Amber the best part of himself and, for a while, she had responded and loved him back. Then—then, what? He couldn't even remember how he had lost her twice. His brainpan was awash in alcohol. And right now he needed a drink. He had a few dollars. He could buy a bottle. Tomorrow he would think about work, any kind of work.

Today he would get drunk.

And this is what Charlie did on the first day of his homeless-ness. He drank until he could not think or remember. He trekked to the southern part of the city, near the railroad tracks and industrial center. There was a large fenced acreage with a sign on the chain-link fence: Southern Cotton Oil. Beyond that a landfill. As the gloaming came on Charlie found himself sozzled as a stumbling beastie, and sad as a soul estranged.

He fell asleep on a pile of boxes next to a loading dock. It seemed, at the time, a private place.

*H*e awoke to frail sun. He was surrounded by men in overalls and work denim. Their smirks were not welcoming. Before they even spoke Charlie put his hand up.

"Thank you for the wake-up call," he said. "I would have been late at the office."

"Smartass," one of the men said.

"Oughta kick the shit out of him for camping here," came an-other.

"Fucking bum."

There seemed to be a consensus that Charlie was unhuman and, perhaps, needed reproving. He readied himself for a boot to the midsection but it never came. He rose slowly, part by part, like a malfunctioning mechanical horse. Once on his feet a moment of panic struck. His paper sack was missing. One of these bullies had absconded with all his worldly goods.

Then Charlie saw it wedged under one of the cardboard boxes. His bag and the boxes were the same shade of dun. Charlie scooped up his bag and walked away, feigning a dignity he didn't possess even before he was homeless.

Charlie did not know how to be homeless. All he knew to do was walk. A peripatetic lifestyle did not seem possible given that Charlie was so out of shape. What he really wanted to do was sit someplace and drink. Just drink all day.

But he walked.

This was a part of the city with which he was not familiar. There were factories and paved roads that seemed to have no name. On the side of a silo attached to one of the seemingly abandoned factories, in giant, faded letters, was written Redrider Industries. There were unkempt fields. There was a chalky, rancid smell. Charlie was thirsty and hungry. And he needed to defecate and pee. These were elemental needs, things one took for granted usually. For Charlie, they now became a damned difficult necessity.

He found a small stream after walking some distance through one of the fields. He stopped at the edge of the field, where the weeds became shoreline, and squatted like an animal. After this was achieved he felt a bit better. He covered his offal with some torn weeds and dirt. He felt ashamed. He began to walk along the shore of the dirty little stream. It was about five yards wide and was deep enough that, in places, Charlie could not see the bottom. It was also littered with castoff beer cans and fast food containers.

Suddenly there was a leprechaun in front of him. Charlie had been preoccupied with looking at the flowing water, wondering if it were drinkable and he almost ran into the short fellow; Charlie jumped.

"What's the cut, dickey?' the leprechaun said.

"Sorry," Charlie said. "What?"

"Who are ya? What do you want with Bertrand Russell?"

"What? The philosopher?"

"Who told you about the philosopher? I knew the philosopher. In hospice I met him. I been in hospice five times."

"I'm sorry. I'm not following you," Charlie said.

"Ok then. I thought you were my tail."

"No. I'm just. Never mind. I'm leaving now."

"You hungry?" the little man asked. He was not really a leprechaun of course, just a short man with red whiskers and a begrimed suit seemingly made out of green moss.

"I *am* hungry," Charlie said.

"I'm about to catch a fish."

Charlie now noticed the little man's fishing pole, a simple thin branch with string at the end. The string disappeared into the murky water. The pole lay on the ground by the water's edge.

"I—that is, I was really supposed to be—" Charlie was fumbling.

"Bertrand Russell," the little guy said, extending a small, grubby hand.

"Charlie. Charlie Cain." Charlie took the proffered hand in his, surrounding it with his larger human paw.

"Nice to have you for breakfast Charlie Charlie Cain. Fish should be coming up any moment now. Why don't you start a fire?"

"That your pole?" Charlie asked, just to say something.

Bertrand looked at the pole and back at Charlie, squinting one eye. "My pole. My pole. Course we could guddle a fish, early morning style, but I prefer the classic approach. String and bait. Right?"

Charlie started to ask what bait he was using and he bit his tongue. To talk to the insane as if they are sane could be proof you're insane.

"Fire, Charlie Charlie," Bertrand said, with strained patience.

Charlie looked around. There was a dry circle of earth at the edge of the weeds where a fire, conceivably could be built.

"I don't have any matches," Charlie said.

Bertrand looked Charlie up and down while giving his pole a gentle shake. "You ain't been on the bum long," he said.

"Um, no. I haven't," Charlie said.

Bertrand reached into the pocket of his jacket and tossed Charlie a half-full packet of matches. Charlie nodded and began to pile up some dry weeds and sticks. He didn't anticipate a very good fire from such humble beginnings. But, of course, he also didn't anticipate a fish coming from such rudimentary tackle.

But soon Charlie had a nice little blaze going. He went further into the field in search of more wood. He had gathered an armful when he heard a whoop from the stream.

"Hallelujah, ye ark angels and salt and pepper saints," Bertrand was hollering.

Charlie gathered a few more pieces of wood and hustled back. When he emerged from the field Bertrand greeted him with a grin and a fish the size of Charlie's forearm.

"I'll be damned," Charlie said. "What is it?"

"It's breakfast, sonny. It's a fish," Bertrand responded. He shut one eye and looked hard at Charlie. "I got a lot to teach ye," he said.

After they ate the bony fish, which tasted somewhat the way dogfood smells, and drank some coffee that Bertrand brewed from a small pack he kept secreted inside his shirt against his pocked chest and which they mixed with water from the stream, they both lay down and cast their eyes to the pale blue emporium.

"Tell me about yourself Charlie Charlie and, afterwards, I'll tell you about Bertrand Russell."

"You know you have the same name as a philosopher, right?"

"We did this scene already. It was a wrap. Let's move on to scene three which really packs a wallop."

Charlie thought Bertrand was joking but if he was he had the best deadpan in history. Charlie feared Bertrand meant what he said. Charlie further feared that Bertrand's sconce was twitterpated.

"I don't have much of a story," Charlie said. If you only knew the truth, he simultaneously thought. "I was ditched by the woman of my dreams and driven from my home by an unscrupulous sibling. I have not had gainful employment for a while but last night was the first night I slept rough."

"Slept rough," Bertrand echoed. He seemed to chew on that. "I guess you mean you slept outside like Natty Bumpo and that chick from *The Monroes*. Or was she with the Mormons?"

"I don't know who you mean," Charlie said.

"I don't know who you mean," Bertrand mimicked like a child. "I don't know who you mean. I don't know who you mean. I don't know who you mean."

Charlie was about to scream if he said it one more time.

"Grow up, Charlie Charlie," Bertrand finished. "What's in the brown sack? Your mum fix you a fried bologna sandwich to eat on the playground?"

"Listen, Bertrand. I thank you for the breakfast but I've got to be moving. I wish I could pay you in some way, but—"

"Now, Charlie. Don't be so sensitive. Don't leave old Bertrand. I'll show you around. You'll do better with Bertrand by your side. Believe that, ye gods and goddesses."

Charlie thought about it. Stumbling blind or lead by a mad-man. This was Hobson's choice.

"Ok, Bertrand, thank you," Charlie said.

Bertrand once again stuck out his little mitt. Charlie shook it one more time.

"Where first?" Charlie said.

"We need to see the preacher. Maybe get some day money. Sound good?"

Charlie had no idea what that meant, if indeed it meant any-thing. "Yes, perfect," Charlie said.

After Bertrand hid his rod in the weeds, they proceeded off together. From behind they looked like a hobo and his hobo son. While they walked Bertrand kept up a solid stream of non-se-quiturs and gibberish. Mostly Charlie just nodded and hummed to indicate he was listening. If asked a direct question it didn't appear necessary that Charlie answer seriously.

"What's her name, your wife-goddess, Charlie Charlie."

"Amber," Charlie said.

"Like the actress Amber Love," Bertrand said. "O Love! O Mother of God. Is this the end of Rico? You know what I mean?'

"I do," Charlie said.

"Women."

"Right."

"Charlie Charlie, I love them. Please don't speak disparag-ingly about the fairer sex. I love them unconditionally. Did you know my mother was a woman?"

Again Charlie thought there was a joke offered for a chuckle but Charlie swallowed it and just answered, "Hm."

"Listen, Charlie Charlie, a man's name is his castle, as the saying goes, and Bertrand respects another man's habiliments and armamentarium but lemme ask you this. Can I just call you by one Charlie? It's making my tongue tired saying it a second time."

Charlie doubted this little man's tongue was ever tired.

"Good by me," Charlie said.

"Goodbye you? Goodbye to you? Oh, good. By. You. You're aces, Charlie. I mean it. You're salt of the belly."

"Thank you, Bertrand. And you're a true gentleman."

Bertrand stopped and looked up into Charlie's face. Charlie thought Bertrand was about to cry. "Charlie, you're the kindest vagabond I've ever vagabonded with it. I mean that." He stuck out his hand again. And Charlie, having little choice, shook it once more.

Bertrand knew where the best soup kitchens were, and where the best place to find dry clothes, and where people were most generous with their handouts. Charlie didn't much like cadging money from strangers but, after thinking about it, he decided that the world had treated him unfairly and he didn't mind anything that might redress the imbalance.

That first day together they ate vegetable soup at a church in the hip center of the city, very near Nocturna Gallery. The soup was thick and flavorful, not just condensed out of a can. It was about the best meal Charlie'd eaten in a while. The bread they served with it was a little tough but dipped in the soup it was a filling supplement.

Throughout lunch Bertrand kept glancing at Charlie as if to say, Ain't I done right by you? Charlie smiled and nodded back at him. There was a fellow with a clerical collar walking among the lunchtime crowd and Charlie prepared himself for the usual sermon but this fellow was just a friendly presence there. He smiled a lot and patted the backs of a few regulars.

After eating Charlie and Bertrand stepped out into a day suddenly grown overcast. Above them the sky was the dark grey of rotting meat.

"Looks like a blower," Bertrand said. "We need an inside place right soon. Library's not too big a hike."

"There's an art gallery near here," Charlie said.

"Is there indeed? Charlie, you the arty type? You a painter in your former incarnation? I painted some, mostly houses and fences. You ever tried to paint a fence with a bull inside it?"

"Um, no," Charlie said. "To any of those questions."

"Ok, fair enough. Let's go to the gallery."

They reached the large glass windows and door of the gallery just as drops the size of grapes began to fall. They made audible plops on the sidewalk around them. The itinerants hustled inside. The receptionist looked up—a handsome man in his late 20s—and started to say something but he swallowed it. He smiled.

"Howdy," Bertrand said. Charlie blanched. This crazy leprechaun was going to embarrass him in this place made holy by the work of Sudie Nimm. "You mostly abstract art?"

"We have all kinds," the fellow said.

"Christian of you," Bertrand said. "We are all kinds and, friend, we're just looking. Need something for the den wall."

"Ok," the fellow said, and went back to reading a book.

Charlie walked on ahead and was standing in front of a large painting by Sudie, one he'd never seen, apparently recent. It was a wild tangle of color and fire and there was something sexual underneath the curved lines of its central figure, a face with a thousand red eyes. Charlie was drawn in and he suddenly thought of the days he'd spent watching Sudie and suddenly he wanted nothing more than to be back with her. He hoped she was happy though this painting didn't seem happy. It seemed—*ferocious*, almost cannibalistic.

"That's a hot one," Bertrand said. "Reminds me of something. A fight maybe. And of course there's fucking right there." Bertrand jabbed a finger at the center of the painting.

Charlie took a step back. "Really?" he said. It was as if Bertrand was seeing Charlie's interpretation of the painting.

"Sure, sure, lots of fucking. Art is full of it, don't you think? I like art. I guess I like it cuz I don't get to do much fucking anymore. It's all fucking, art is."

Now Charlie looked around. He was sure Bertrand's loud f-bombs would get them kicked out but the handsome gatekeeper never looked up from his book.

Charlie and Bertrand looked at every piece of art in the small gallery, even the ones not by Sudie Nimm. By the time they had made their slow circuit the rain had all but ceased. The asphalt outside was steaming.

"Shall we move along?" Charlie said.

"Lead the way," Bertrand said. And, on the way out the door, to the reader, "Thanks for all the fucking. My friend here's a virgin."

*T*hey wandered. They panhandled. They sat in a downtown park and rested. For dinner they had enough money for some Krystals and fries. After dinner Bertrand asked Charlie if he wanted to sleep outside again or would the mission be calling him.

"I don't mind sleeping outside," Charlie said. "It's nice enough."

"Right, Captain. Let's find a soft parking lot for our dreams."

Eventually they settled for a grassy area near the interstate. The sound of humming tires could be felt in their supine spines. The grass was still a bit damp from the storm so Bertrand found some newspaper underneath an overpass and laid it out as if it were fine bedclothes. Charlie was tired and his eyes were drooping.

"Goodnight, Mr. Charlie. Not meaning you're Caucasian though I assume you are. Just being funny. Goodnight Captain Charlie. Hope your dreams are full of tigers and waterfalls."

"Goodnight, Bertrand. Thank you for today. I'm not sure what I would have done without you."

"Probably been alone," Bertrand said. "Let a cloud be your pillow, as my mum used to say."

Charlie tucked his brown bag underneath one arm and fell asleep on his back. He woke an hour later when Bertrand tried to take the bag out from under him.

"Wh-what the hell?"

"Oh, eh, Captain. Just trying to make you comfortable. I'll move on over here now," Bertrand mumbled. "Just making you comfortable."

Charlie repositioned the bag inside his shirt and fatigue again washed over him. But, before he dropped off a second time, he thought he would have to ditch the loquacious Bertrand in the morning. He dreamt he was a fireman but his hose was too heavy. Burning children screamed his name.

He woke to find himself alone. He blinked a few times, then grabbed for his bag. It was still under his shirt. He looked around. This area seemed bleak and inhospitable and it smelled faintly of chemical burn. It was one of America's modern wastelands. Charlie walked.

After a few minutes of walking down the dusty road a car pulled up behind him and was idling as if in anticipation. Charlie looked but it was a stretch limousine with blackened windows. Charlie moved off the road and began to walk in the ditch. The enormous car moved along next to him. Then it stopped and a rear door opened.

"Charlie Charlie," a voice came out of the interior. Bertrand emerged as if from a black womb.

"You walking away? I told you to wait for the preacher."

"Bertrand, I—" Charlie began, when a female voice came from the car's interior.

"Bertrand," it said, sweet as honey, "It's ok. I can take it from here. Come here, Mr. Charlie."

Charlie edged toward the car. He looked around. They were as alone as Crusoe and Friday.

"Step in, please," the voice said.

Charlie stuck his head into the spacious back seats of the car. His eyes saw only dark shapes. He stopped. It smelled like new car and expensive perfume.

"Please," the feminine voice said again.

"Gwan, Charlie," Bertrand said. "It's the preacher, Charlie."

Charlie entered the air-conditioned interior of the car. The space seemed as large as Charlie's last apartment.

"Have a seat, Mr. Charlie."

Charlie sat on the edge of the seat. The woman reached above her head and turned on a light.

Charlie blinked. He was sure that he was in the wrong place. The woman sitting across from him was large and buxom and, in an artificial way, somewhat stunning. Her ample figure filled her black dress the way oranges fill a sack. The dress was short and tight and her plump but shapely legs were sheathed in shiny, black hose. She was holding out a hand, rimmed with small, bright red blades.

"Cassandra Preacher," she said.

"Charlie Cain," Charlie said, taking her hand.

"Ah," Cassandra Preacher said. "Mr. Cain." She held Charlie's hand and was softly rubbing it as if it were a lucky rabbit's foot.

"What—why am I here?"

"I told you, Charlie," Bertrand said, starting to enter the car.

"Bertrand, we won't need you today," Cassandra said. "Thank you."

"Oh, yes, I can see that. Yes. See that. Thank you. Thank you. Charlie—"

Someone outside took hold of Bertrand Russell and moved him gently backwards, and closed the door.

"Mr. Russell said you perhaps were looking for some quick money."

"Well, yes, I mean, I guess so," Charlie said.

Cassandra Preacher waited for Charlie to say the right thing. Her half-smile looked like a come-on. Everything she did looked like a come-on.

"Yes, I mean. I need some money," Charlie said.

"Good then. Would you come with us and do a little work for which you will be paid immediately?"

"Sure," Charlie said. "What kind of work is it? I have few skills, however—"

"Mr. Cain, it will be well within your capabilities and will only take a few hours. How does four hundred dollars sound?"

Charlie tried not to over-react. "I imagine I could go for that."

"Good then." Cassandra rapped on the darkened window between the front of the car and its spacious rear. The car began to move.

"What business were you last in, Mr. Cain?"

"Oh, well. The last thing I did was I was a writer. I wrote." Charlie was nervous in front of this formidable woman.

"A writer!" she said. "We could use you. Yes, in our business writers are revered." She smiled. It looked like a guillotine.

"What is your business, Ms. Preacher?"

"Cassandra," she said. "We make films, Mr. Cain."

"Movies?"

"Yes, movies. We make movies."

"I love movies," Charlie said.

"Most people do."

"Have I seen anything of yours?"

"It's possible," Cassandra Preacher said.

"Can you give me any names?"

Cassandra stared at Charlie. Then she stared out the window. Or it would have been out the window if the windows were not as black as her dress.

"We make adult films, Mr. Cain," she said at last.

"Ah," Charlie said.

"Does this interest you?"

"Well, I—I don't know," Charlie said. "I've never—"

Cassandra laughed. "You're not a virgin, Mr. Cain?"

"No, no." Charlie's mind was clouding quickly.

"Charlie, in a moment we will stop the car and hold a quick audition to put you at ease. How does that sound?"

"Yes, ok," Charlie said.

"And how do you feel about rough sex, Charlie?"

"Oh, well, ok I guess."

He thought it about the scariest proposition he'd ever had.

Cassandra knocked again on the window. And then she sat back and seemed to forget Charlie was there. The car rolled smoothly on and then stopped. It stopped so smoothly Charlie did not know it had stopped.

Now a panel between front and rear opened and the lens of a camera appeared there.

"Oh," Charlie said.

"Don't be nervous, Mr. Cain. I am sure you'll do just fine."

"I-I'm not too clean," Charlie said.

"Ok," Cassandra Preacher said. She sat forward on her seat and, with legs akimbo, motioned Charlie forward. "Undress," she said.

"Oh," Charlie said. He did not move.

"Mr. Cain, please. Undress. Or just lower your trousers. You'll like it. It will help you relax. And, we hope, get your dick hard."

"I'm sure—" Charlie began but realized that they did not want to hear him talk. Did he want to do this? Did he want the money?

He looked into her eyes. They were dark purple. Her red lips were thick and she put a nibble of tongue in the corner of them and smiled slightly.

Cassandra began to unbutton her blouse. The bra holding her sizable breasts was black and lacy and seemed to offer her breasts up like scoops of ice cream. She had small freckles across their mounded tops.

"Now, I want to see your manhood," she said.

Charlie unzipped as fast as he could. He took a brief moment to sniff his own armpits—they were pretty rank—and he was ashamed of the condition of his underwear. He feared his crotch smelled even worse but, at this point, he was all the way in.

Cassandra Preacher was looking at Charlie's erection.

"Yes," she said.

"Yes for me, too," Charlie said.

"I mean, yes, you have a nice dick. I think this is going to go fine."

"I think so, too, now," Charlie said.

Cassandra Preacher rebuttoned her shirt.

"What—what's wrong?" Charlie said.

"Nothing," she said. "You're perfect. You get hard fast and you look good."

"So—we don't finish here?"

"Mr. Cain, I'm sorry, I thought you understood. I am only the producer. Your scene will be played with someone else. First we'll get some wipes and clean you up a bit."

"Oh," Charlie said. "Well, ok. I sure do find you fucksome, though."

"Thank you, Mr. Cain."

"So, where do we do this?"

"Just outside here."

"We're at the studio?"

"No, this is a camping picture. We're in the woods."

"Oh, ok," Charlie said.

"Ready?" Cassandra Preacher was now fully dressed.

"Yes, I guess so."

Charlie followed her out of the car. They were indeed in the woods, on a small dirt track. Off to one side was a cleared space with a phony campfire. Charlie looked around. He hoped the young starlet was pretty. Not that it mattered. Charlie was ready to fuck and he was ready to make some money. Charlie, shirtless, was holding his pants up with one hand.

"Where is she?" Charlie said.

"Here," Cassandra Preacher said. "He." She gestured toward the car.

Out of the front seat stepped a burly guy in jeans and a checkered shirt.

"Mr. Cain, this is Mr. Lance Ramshorn."

Charlie blinked. Lance Ramshorn smiled and his teeth glittered like scarabs.

"Oh, no, wait," Charlie said.

"Right over here," Cassandra gestured. The driver of the car now emerged. He was about six and a half feet tall, built like an Olympic swimmer, and dressed, like his boss, entirely in black. In one hand he held a camera.

"No," Charlie said. And as he said it he felt the driver's hand, as large and hard as a frying pan, unfold like a hot pad along his spine. Charlie was shoved toward the makeshift campsite. He looked once toward Cassandra Preacher but, bored, she had her back turned and was talking into her cellphone. She put the phone against her shoulder and spoke to her star.

"Mr. Cain is ready, Lance. Charlie, this scene is the rough sex scene. We'll shoot it first and, if you're are still willing, we will shoot a more tender love scene. That's up to you. More money if we do. Thank you for your participation, Mr. Cain."

Lance Ramshorn took Charlie's arms and pushed him backwards. Charlie's pants were around his ankles. Which made it easier for Lance to turn him over. Charlie tumbled into the dirt. He turned and Lance was approaching. Lance was wearing chaps and no pants and his member was considerable. Charlie's mind clouded and then sharpened into steel-eyed focus. He made a dive for Lance's balls. He wished to stop this stud before he got started.

When Charlie awoke, they were gone. He was sore and he was naked, face-down in the dirt. He worked his jaw which felt out of line like a rockem-sockem robot's, and there was a foot-sized bruise in his ribs. He felt his privates and then his ass. He remembered vaguely what happened. He did not do the scene. He had not come and his bumhole had not been spiked. He did not get paid. Instead he was beaten up by Lance Ramshorn. Charlie thought: perhaps I will write my memoir and I will entitle it *I Was KO'd by Lance Ramshorn.*

He had also been left with no map and no money. Because he had had a dustup with the star they had not given him his dosh. Charlie vaguely remembered Cassandra Preacher saying something about not being able to use him because Charlie was too angry. "I can do better," Charlie said weakly to the wraiths around him. He was whispering to a loneliness dark as a shadow's shadow.

Charlie was not angry. He was, if anything, drained of emotion. The actor who was going to screw him was fairly nice and his member a handsome tool. In better circumstances he would have admired it. He was sorry now that he had fought, that he had struck the fellow. Had Charlie relaxed he would feel better now and he would be $400 richer.

Charlie stirred and every movement hurt. Slowly he got to his feet. There was a moment of panic when he thought he'd lost his paper bag but it was sitting next to the fake campfire. He looked inside and found small comfort there. A book, a razor, a sliver of soap, his phone, flip-flops, a playing card, a shirt, aspirin and his tincture. He found his clothes, piece by piece. His underwear was torn and filthy. He cast them aside. Once he was dressed, he sat up and looked around. In the half-light the woods seemed dangerous, predatory. Could he embosk there? No. He wanted to get far away. He wanted clear skies.

Once on his unsteady feet he looked around. There was the dirt road down which he had come. A mile or so, across soybean fields, in the distance he could see either a house or farm. He did not think knocking on a stranger's door would yield him anything encouraging. The dirt road was his only choice. And he walked it with shuffling steps; pain limited his movements.

After an hour he sat down on a squat, cracked concrete wall. He put his head in his hands. At his feet were the castoff items of a civilization winding down: McDonald's wrappers, juice boxes, a tangle of hair and wire, desiccated fruit rinds, a used condom. The sun was almost gone for the day. Soon he would be walking in darkness. This frightened him.

Then his phone rang. He had not thought there was anything left on his last card. He scrambled getting the phone out of the bag. Here was salvation.

He did not recognize the number.

"Hello?" Charlie said, holding his phone as if it were delicate.

"Charlie!" a hearty voice hailed him.

"Yes," Charlie said.

"It's Meyer!"

Joy first rushed into Charlie's chest. Then, just as quickly, Charlie's bile rose.

"Meyer," Charlie said, with venom. "Where the fuck have you been?"

"You mad at me, Charlie?"

"Meyer, I've been trying to get in touch with you for months."

"I know, I know. It's crazy. You won't believe me. Hey, Charlie, did you go to that doctor?"

"Yes," Charlie said. He was grinding his teeth.

"Oh. Oh. I see. Listen, Charlie, I went to the doc, too. I was having an issue with my wrist. The damnedest thing. Strange bird, Dr. Raphael."

"Yes."

"Well, he gave me these pills and I took one. Just one. And I went to sleep. Charlie…I woke up in 1864."

Charlie was quiet. Meyer was quiet.

"I don't know what to say to that," Charlie said.

"I know. It was a, you know, side effect."

"I understand," Charlie said, somberly.

"Hey, Charlie did you know that Quantrill was a right bastard?"

"Was he?" Charlie said.

"Well, anyway. I can't tell you what I've seen. It was harrowing. I hope the doc took better care of you."

"I?" Charlie said. "Oh, it was fine, Meyer, just great."

"What happened, Charlie? Did you go back in time, too?"

"No, Meyer, I was invisible."

The phone died.

Charlie looked at the phone. It was dead. He punched buttons. He shook it. He punched some more buttons. The phone was dead.

The phone was dead and it was dark and he was all alone in the country.

Charlie just sat. The night surrounded him as if burying him in wadding. He was sad, sad as a dream of lost love. Charlie hung his head between his knees. He was sore and sad and powerless and anxious.

Charlie was afraid of the night. It crept around him like the wings of sleep. He kept his head down.

Then Charlie heard a sound like wind through a field of poppies. Charlie looked up.

There in front of him were the woods, the trees dark as the Duke of Hell's black riding boots. These were the woods from which he had escaped and now they wanted him back. The woods were whispering, a psithurism like the music of rain sticks.

And from between the black columns of trees came diaphanous figures, rustling in the wind like spectral laundry. They were not exactly human-shaped though something about them seemed human. Perhaps there were faces. Charlie believed he was not seeing clearly. He blinked many times, until his eyes watered as if he were weeping.

He watched the figures, wafting and waving there for a good two, three minutes. Did he imagine that they had spoken? It might have only been the wind. But then one figure split off from the forest depths leaving behind its gossamer co-conspirators. Charlie was transfixed. The figure, now more clearly a ghostly woman, seemed to be coming straight at him.

When it was within twenty-five feet, standing clearly in front of him across the dirt road and in the middle of a small, cleared field, its face opened a black cavity in its center and it spoke.

It sang a soft soughing song: *"Go where you wanna wanna go, do what you wanna wanna do…"*

And then a battered pickup truck roared by, shuddering and shaking on the road right in front of Charlie, kicking up a dust storm so that the noise and the grit made Charlie stand and fist his sore eyes. When he lowered his hands all was as before. The night was all around, steel-grey, quiet, predictable and chill. No ghosts. No hope.

Had Charlie slept and dreamed? He did not feel as if he'd just woken. He looked down the road. He could see nothing. Charlie walked a bit. He did not know whether he was walking back toward town or going further into the unknown. He was absolutely quanked. Charlie muttered, "Now it is the time of night that the graves, all gaping wide…"

Off to his right Charlie spotted a derelict car parked in the cleft parking lot of a derelict building. It seemed as good a place as any to sleep. He stumbled toward it and when he had reached its rear door and touched its handle, something large and hairy and with the eyes of the dead jumped out through the window space. Charlie shrieked and fell backwards, hitting his head on a jagged piece of concrete. The beast landed on Charlie's chest, its sharp nails making tiny, bloody holes in Charlie's skin. Then it scampered off into the night.

Charlie felt the back of his head and there was blood there. There were also small stains starting in four places on the front of his shirt. Once he'd sat up and gathered what remained of his wits, he realized the creature was a possum.

Charlie crawled into the backseat of the car without further mishap. The seat was lumpy and smelly and Charlie didn't give a good damn. Before closing his eyes, he did an inventory of the items in his bag, the entire estate of Charlie Cain. Book, razor, soap, flip-flops, shirt, aspirin, dead telephone, the ace of diamonds, a phial. He picked up the phial.

He looked at it as closely as he could in the dark of the car. He opened it. Then Charlie said a short prayer and took a sip. He wanted, you see, to disappear.

When Charlie woke the sun was coming up over the forest. He blinked a few times. Where was he?

He was asleep in the putrescent backseat of a moldy car.

He slowly sat up. He looked at his sleeve. It ended at the cuff. Charlie had no hands.

Who can judge Charlie's state of mind? He was relieved to find himself not there. He exited the car and removed all his clothing except his shoes. The ground was strewn with a catalog of broken things. He put his shirt and trousers on the back seat of the car. He put his rotting socks in his bag and then, on second thought, he took them out and threw them on top of his other clothing. And, finally, with regret, he tossed this bag—his final possessions—into the dead car.

A pair of shoes left the rubble and found themselves on the same dusty road. What was he to do but proceed in the direction he had begun the night before? It was barely dawn and there was no one about. So, Charlie kept his shoes on for a while. After an hour or so a car rumbled by so Charlie stopped. A pair of shoes by the side of the road attracted no attention.

He hiked.

When the sun was well above the tree line the day warmed and the warmth felt good on Charlie's bare, invisible skin. He walked and walked and there was nothing and more nothing. If this used to be a better area there was no evidence of it now. Charlie was hungry but there was nothing in sight. He pulled a few green onions out of the ground but he spit out their acrid pieces instantly. If nothing else Charlie needed water soon.

When Charlie came to a crossroads—it was only a dusty X—he looked to the left and right and decided to keep going straight ahead. He had no idea how far he was from the city. This countryside was foreign to him.

Then the long road petered out. It neither ended nor kept going. Charlie was standing in dry grass up to his ankles. He still decided forward was the answer. He walked gingerly for he was stiff and sore from his encounter with the fly-by-night filmmakers. Soon he came to a small stream. Charlie knelt beside it and wet his entire body. He chanced swallowing some of the water which didn't seem particularly clean.

As he raised his head from dunking and drinking, he spotted a small boy about twenty yards ahead of him across the stream.

Charlie couldn't imagine what it looked like to see water flying about and the only thing there a pair of worn-out shoes. Charlie sat in the water and waited for the boy to move on. He was a curious lad, though, and did not leave quickly.

When he finally walked away Charlie slipped his shoes off and followed.

Across the stream, across another weedy field peppered with dandelions, Charlie crested a hill just in time to see the boy entering a small house. There was an old Studebaker out front and a windmill and a small garden and not much else. The road to the house was a road in name only. Charlie thought, not for the first time, that he had landed in a fairy tale.

Charlie approached the house. He was almost out of practice being invisible. But it was easy to slip inside because the door was standing open. And, just as Charlie entered he was confronted by a woman who shouted over her shoulder, "Sam, you left the door open again!" And Sam answered from somewhere within, "Sorry, Ma!"

The woman looked to be about thirty. She was heavy set with overly large breasts and brown, lank hair. She wore a colorless shift, covered by a worn apron. Her face was roundish with a wart beside her potatoey nose. She shut the door and looked around as if she sensed something was askew. She looked down at Charlie's muddy footprints.

The woman sighed, pulled a towel out of her apron and wiped up the mud. The furniture was old and scarred but the house was clean. She moved off into the kitchen and Charlie followed. On the table was a loaf of homemade bread covered by a tea towel beside a pitcher of iced tea. Charlie's mouth watered. He thought the best thing he could do would be to sit still and watch for his opportunities.

The woman stayed in the kitchen. She was preparing something else, chopping vegetables into a large bowl. It took a long time but eventually she left what she was doing and hollered at the boy again.

"Sam, I'm gonna take a bath. Don't touch that bread yet."

"Alright, Ma," Sam answered.

Charlie waited until he heard the water running and then he made for the bread and the tea. He tore a chunk off one end of the loaf and placed the towel back over it. He was sorry that Sam was going to get the blame but he was starved. He drank tea straight from the pitcher. He also sampled some of the chopped veggies, which were bland but felt good in his mouth.

Sated he began to look around. He found Sam's room where Sam was lying on his stomach playing a video game with head-phones on. He found the master bedroom and surmised that the woman and the boy were living alone. There was no sign of a male presence.

Charlie heard the sloshing water in the bathroom. Temptation took hold of him, though his balls and his side and his head ached. It had been a long time since he spied on naked women while in-visible. He had missed it.

Charlie looked through the crack in the door. The woman was lying still in the tub. Her body was layered in folds of fat and she had a heart surgery scar between her large breasts. The hair around her crotch was dark and thick. He gently pushed the door open some more. The woman sat up. "Wha—" she said. She looked down and Charlie realized he was still leaving footprints. She was stricken—afraid. Her face was a mask of unease. She was alone and vulnerable and she seemed about to cry.

Charlie felt horrible. He crept out.

"Sam!" the woman called.

Charlie went back to the kitchen and quickly went through the cabinets. He could hear the woman and Sam talking low. He took some crackers and cookies and a six-pack of Cokes in a plastic ring. He exited, back to his ambling.

Charlie felt like a wretched thing, a wraith that frightened women and children. The liberation he felt, being invisible and naked again, was souring quickly. He half-trotted down the narrow road, out of breath, clutching his pilfered groceries. He slowed as he put some distance between himself and the house.

There were no other houses around. There were fields of weeds and wildflowers. Where was he? North of the city? Had he gone so far astray that he had gone beyond society? He was unaware of areas this undeveloped. As the sun passed halfway on its recurrent arc Charlie came upon some large sewer pipes and a cleared area of dirt and half-finished ditches. One dirty, yellow earthmover sat like the bones of an extinct species. Charlie crawled into one of the pipes to eat some of his provisions. Out of the sun it was a little chilly and damp. Charlie ate some crackers and opened one of the tins which contained salty little fish things. Charlie had never had them before and the tin was unlabeled. Perhaps they were cat food. He put one on his tongue and its salinity nipped him. He found that he could enjoy them if he put a cracker in his mouth at the same time. When he'd eaten them, he washed it all down with warm soda. His head rang like peas in a bladder.

Afterward he was up and walking again. He was fatigued, worn out as an old shoe, and thought about sleeping in the culvert but decided he would do better if he found houses and people. He walked most of the afternoon, his feet sore and filthy, before he came upon another house. It seemed to be all by itself like the house he'd left

222

that morning. There was a fence around this one and as he snuck up to the gate a dog came from God knows where charging straight at him. A mongrel with a large head and spittle-flecked lips, it was built like a small bull and was the color of sin. The beast hit the gate with a crash and his jaws were slavering for a taste of Charlie. Could he see what humans could not? Or was it sense of smell? Charlie was certain he had a stronger musk than most people.

The door to the small house opened and a man stepped onto the porch. He was large and pot-bellied and his head was a couple sizes too small. He wore only soiled pajama bottoms.

"Slayer, what the hell, boy? There ain't nobody there," the fellow hollered.

Slayer looked back over his thick shoulders as if to say, fucking hell, can you not smell him? Then he looked back to Charlie, sniffed and turned for home.

Charlie returned to the road and hiked woefully on as the day slanted downward toward evenfall.

When the sun was setting over the trees it started to sprinkle. And, simultaneously, Charlie felt a kink in his gut like an animal talon. He put a hand to his side and began to trot again, looking for shelter. The only hope was the forest so he veered from the road and headed that way. The sky grew dark as Erebus and the rain began to pelt down in earnest. Charlie quickened his steps. He was so nauseated he was running bent over. A cloud the size and color of a battleship positioned itself over him.

In this way he did not see the hole until his right foot hit the side of it and he slid in. He fell far and landed in a small pool of water and sludge. He was doubled over in pain and began to chunder and shake. He managed to keep his face out of the water as the crackers and salty fish returned to the surface. Charlie's insides twisted and screamed and burned as if they were being clawed. Charlie rolled in muck. The rain thickened.

Then, as if to mock him, his body sent mast pouring from his nether end. Charlie was literally lying in a pool of his own puke and feculent flux. His battle was to keep his head up as the water grew deeper. He managed to slither upward enough, his cheek resting on something hard in the mud wall, a root or stone. In this way he stayed erect as the water came in and the food came out.

At some point Charlie blacked out because when he next opened his eyes the rain had stopped and a night sky shone above him, stars as bright as cat's eyes. Charlie got sick again and somehow went back to sleep.

In the morning the sun was a welcome sight. Charlie was able, for the first time, to see where he was. The hole was about twenty feet deep and long like a trench. Charlie had no strength. He tried slithering upward but, when he slipped down, he did not make any other effort. He was sick again but without product or relief. Again, he slept.

He woke again in darkness. As he lay in his own foulness Charlie thought he had reached low ebb. He was no longer a viable human and he asked for deliverance. He was a waste of harvestable organs. He called upon the dark gods and solicited them to allow him to enter the afterlife as soon as possible. He finally had, and was, nothing. He'd lost his food in the flood. All he was was flesh and not even definable flesh. He was flesh undetectable by his fellow man and woman. Charlie was nil. He was nullity. He was not worth spit.

Another dawn found Charlie still in the pit. He had not been whisked into the afterlife. He was still a revenant trapped in muck. The smell of himself and his warren was enough to make him sick again. His mouth was as dry as pith. He pulled himself up onto his knees. Then, slowly, he rose.

Charlie was weak. He was wabbly as a bled calf. He stood and rested his hands on his knees. When he straightened up he felt a little better. He surveyed the trap into which he had fallen. It was deep and it was wet. The walls were slippery with few handholds. Charlie walked unsteadily from one end to the other. He made one attempt to go straight up the wall. He managed to get about two feet off the ground before he found himself face down in his own filth. He cursed.

He tried calling for help but two factors worked against him. His voice was thin stuff. He meant to howl like a dervish but instead peeped like a chick. And it didn't matter much because no one was around for miles. If someone had heard—what then?

Charlie sat down in a different part of his hole. He used some of the muddy water to make a poor bath of his private parts. He had mud in every declivity of his body. He was thirsty but dared not drink the fecal rain water. While he sat he craned his neck to view the vast, empyrean blue. He had lost the earth so he had lost the heavens, too.

Then he spotted a good thick root sticking out of the wall about halfway up. He stood and moved under it. It would take a healthy leap but he might be able to reach it. His first attempt fell well short. He backed up against the opposite wall and tried again. His fingers brushed the bottom of the gnarled wood and he fell sharply on his side. He lay still for a while.

After he was sufficiently rested, he stood and leaned against the opposite wall. He took a deep breath and leapt upward. His hand caught the root. The root was solid. He was now dangling from it. What next? he asked himself. He began to scrabble against the muddy wall with every limb save the one holding the root. He would not let go of his root.

After a strenuous flailing he caught another handhold above him, which until he had grabbed it had been invisible. Now he had only to fling his legs upward, which he managed to do. He found himself lying on the edge of the hole. He was too knackered to celebrate.

After a while he stood. He looked around. He was in the middle of nowhere. He might as well be standing in a crater on the moon. What could he do but set out again? First, though, he had to rest. He sat on a tree trunk. Someone had scored a message in its rough surface: *I've walked and I've crawled on six crooked highways*. Charlie ran his finger along the little worm trail of letters. He was moribund, starved and thirsty. He was also visible, a substantial, ugly, brown smudge, vaguely human-shaped, on the edge of the wood.

He heard the boys before he looked up and spied them on the edge of the road. They were talking about him in excitable tones, which carried warbling over the muddy expanse between them.

"It's fucking Bigfoot," one of the lads said.

"Bigfoot?" the other said.

The one who spoke first raised a rifle to his shoulder. It was then that Charlie noticed both boys had rifles. The first shot hit Charlie in the biceps before he registered that there was no bang. They were hunting with pellet guns. The pellet pierced Charlie's skin and stuck there. It was easy enough to pull out. And, by that time, the boys were moving cautiously toward him.

Charlie turned and ran into the wood. It was rough going. There was no path and the brambles and roots tripped Charlie and whisked his ankles with stinging pain. Whip-thin branches battered his cock and balls. His face found a flurry of sharp leaves. Behind him Charlie heard the boys crash into the brush. They were younger and faster and Charlie could only pray that his half-muddied body was at least partly camouflaged. They shouted with glee; their blood was up for the hunt. Charlie was prey.

He ran serpentine for what seemed an hour and the woods only thickened and his body weakened. He heard his stalkers, off to the left, off to the right, but they seemed to stay on the trail. At one point Charlie ran smack into a branch because he was looking back over his shoulder. That sat him on his ass and he saw sparkles when he shut his eyes. He reluctantly got up and kept moving.

Another pellet went by but well to the left of him. Charlie figured they could not see him very well. And then he saw the stream. He made for it quickly but quietly. Another pellet hit the back of Charlie's shoulder and stung like a holy flame. Charlie slid quickly into the stream and went under. He swam underwater for as long as he could. He slowly rose to the surface, letting only his head crest the water. The boys were downstream looking where Charlie wasn't. He waited there for a minute, treading water to stay afloat, and they finally gave up the hunt and turned back. They hurried home with a story to tell.

Charlie got out of the stream on the opposite side. The water slid off him. He was clean again and again invisible.

Now Charlie was genuinely turned around. Not that it mattered. He couldn't get more lost than lost. He decided to walk the banks of the stream until he found more open land. The sun dried him and the small holes the pellets made were minor afflictions. At least the side of the streambed was soft and his feet felt better for it.

Eventually he reached an unwooded area, still unmarked by signs of civilization. Once again Charlie felt as if he had entered fairyland. It was country so unfamiliar to him he might as well have been in The Far East. Or Narnia, or Gormenghast. He set off across the fields. His depression returned with a vengeance. He thought about giving up, about lying down and letting the weather and the planet's natural rotting system slowly eat his body. But he did not give up. Charlie walked.

As he was climbing a gentle rise, he heard a sound that gladdened his heart, a heart which had been running on fumes. It was singing. And not just one voice but many. It was church singing, Charlie thought, though he had not been to church in decades. He was godless. But this sound was sweet as ambrosia and the stirring in Charlie was not just fellow-feeling. It was acknowledgment of the mystery of existence. Charlie's invisible heart expanded like a flower unto its sun. Charlie let his hope return, eking into him as if from a remedial bell jar.

As he crested the hill a valley straight out of an old western opened up before his eyes. The church sat in the center of that valley like a white shot glass in an emerald bowl. There were a few cars around the church and an asphalt road leading off to the north. The music carried up to him like a sweetened breeze. Charlie stopped and listened.

> *There were ninety and nine that safely lay*
> *In the shelter of the fold*
> *But one was out on the hills away*
> *Far off from the gates of gold*
> *Away on the mountains wild and bare*
> *Away from the tender shepherd's care*
> *Away from the tender shepherd's care...*

Charlie made for the church. The door was open. It was an invitation.

Charlie walked in and sat in a back pew. It was a simple church, white walls, a long nave with a painted concrete floor, a barely discernible transept, which made for a modest cross. He had found a choir rehearsal and he was the only audience. The female choir leader was gently swaying to the tune, using her thin arms subtly to move the tune forward. There were six choristers. They stood close together in the chancel as if for warmth. Only six singers making that empyreal sound. Charlie looked closely at the woman leading them. She looked familiar.

> *But none of the ransomed ever knew*
> *How deep were the waters crossed*
> *Nor how dark was the night that the Lord passed through*
> *Ere he found his sheep that was lost.*
> *Out in the desert he heard its cry*
> *Sick and helpless and ready to die*
> *Sick and helpless and ready to die....*

A tear ran down Charlie's cheek and it was then that he knew the choir leader.

After the last singer left the slim leader was tidying up, putting the hymnals away. A clergyman entered in stiff black and white.

"That sounded marvelous, Antonia," he said.

"I thought Jerry Ledbetter hit a sour note once or twice. And I think Lahna has been drinking again."

"And still you managed to make a dulcet sound. It is the Lord's work, Dear."

"Thank you, Clark."

The clergyman left. Charlie waited for a few minutes and then approached the front before Antonia could follow her husband out the door.

Charlie moved up next to her. "Antonia," he said, softly.

Antonia whirled around. Her face was a twist of fear. Then she held herself as still as a stone, straining her ears for another sound.

Charlie gently slipped his hand into hers.

She started, began to pull away, and then a strange light filled her face. She relaxed her hand into his. She stood there for a long minute, thinking, praying.

"It is you, isn't it?" she whispered.

"Yes," Charlie said softly into her ear.

"Oh, how I yearned for your return."

"I have traveled far to get here. I have wandered and been lost. I've wandered and wandered, wildered by my own absence. I've been lost for so long."

And Antonia said, "If you don't know where you're going how do you know you're not already there?"

Charlie tentatively put his mouth to hers. She spun into his arms and her mouth returned the kiss, hungrily, lovingly. Charlie pulled her close.

"Oh, oh," Antonia said. "I have thirsted."

"Oh, God, I'm so thirsty," Charlie said. "And starved."

Antonia pulled her head back but reached for his hand. "Come," she said.

She led him by the hand into the back of the church. There was, off the transept chapel, a small kitchen, all white wood, and as clean as a first snow. Antonia let go of Charlie's hand and motioned for him to sit on a small, brown folding chair. She bent to a small fridge and brought from it a plastic pitcher of water. She found a glass in a cabinet and filled it and held it out in front of the chair. The glass hung in the air like a magic trick and the water disappeared. She filled it again, and again the water was gone in a flash. Antonia smiled. She then found some thick brown bread and hand-churned butter. She fixed a few pieces of that and while Charlie ate it she found some cookies and placed them on the small, white table in the middle of the room.

Before she let Charlie eat she bent to him with water and a cloth and, under his directions, cleaned his wounds, where the brambles had scratched him and the pellets penetrated, and the small crusted patch on the back of his head. They were like faint red tracings in the air. She touched each spot gingerly and was surprised when the blood was red instead of indiscernible. She kissed him and moved away.

After Charlie had eaten, he sighed with contentment. Antonia moved toward him. She was dressed in a simple, mouse-brown dress and her hair was in a tight bun. She was as thin as a laughing flame and her face was plain and pleasant. She had a pronounced overbite, but when she smiled her face seemed lit from within. She put her hand out and Charlie pulled her into his lap. They kissed again.

After a while, with her head on Charlie's shoulder, she said, "What is your name?"

"Charlie," Charlie said. "Charlie Cain."

"Charlie Cain."

"Antonia."

"You remembered my name."

"Yes."

"It's funny. I've thought of you so often. I had persuaded my-self that I had dreamed you, that I had created you from my need."

"It was certainly an odd way to meet. On a crowded bus."

"Yes." Antonia's face looked serious and soft and wistful.

"I—I was a bit crazed back then."

"You were the first man to enter me in so long." She sighed. "And you were the last."

"I'm sorry," Charlie said and he massaged her thin thigh.

"Will you do it again?" Antonia asked.

"Oh, my dear," Charlie said. He kissed her passionately.

Antonia rose and again led Charlie by the hand. There was a cramped bedroom off the hall, next to the sacristy, and at the end of the hall the rectory began.

"It is my husband's place of refuge and prayer," Antonia said, opening the door.

"Should we?" Charlie said.

"It's where he sleeps because he doesn't want to be near me."

"I see. Where is he now?"

"Lie with me," Antonia answered, shutting the door quietly.

On the thin bed Charlie undressed Antonia. She was a radiant skelf: bareboned and youthful. They lay in each other's arms and they kissed slowly, shyly, but with passion. They were quiet for a long time, both relishing the comfort, both excited for whatever was to come next. Charlie lightly ran his fingers over her white body. Antonia sighed. Her small breasts were capped with dark buds and her pubic bush was as soft as cattail fluff. Charlie bent to her and kissed her between the legs. Antonia said. "Oh!" Charlie began to lick her in earnest. It didn't take long. Antonia had three orgasms. After the third she fell back into the world, exhausted and flushed. Charlie rejoined her on the bed and held her.

"Charlie. I've, I've never had that done before."

"Then I shall do it every day until you tire of it."

"I shall never tire of it."

They lay in each other's arms for a few minutes.

"I could try to reciprocate," Antonia said.

"It's not necessary."

"Oh, I know. I think I'd like to try."

And so she did. It was a rough first try—her slightly protuberant teeth scraped the sensitive head of his cock—but Charlie moaned and sighed and acted overwhelmed before pulling her upward and onto him. She straddled him like a gymnast on a pommel horse.

"Put it in," Charlie said.

And Antonia reached back and grabbed him. She stopped for a moment and seemed thoughtful, rolling Charlie's cock in her fingers. "I remember this," she whispered and then positioned herself over him. Slowly she sank down on him.

"Charlie," she said, with some intensity.

"Yes, my dear," Charlie said.

"Charlie Cain," Antonia said.

When the good pastor knocked on the door Antonia did not even flinch. The lovers were lying naked in each other's arms. Charlie started to sit up, but Antonia placed a soft palm on his invisible chest and held him down.

"Antonia," her husband said. "Are you alright?"

"Yes, Clark," she said, calmly.

The chaplain turned the glass knob and entered. Charlie again began to get up but Antonia said a soft shh. The chaplain's serious brow creased in opprobrium.

"I thought I heard you talking," Rev. Wilkins said.

"No, Dear," Antonia said.

"Why are you naked in the middle of the day, Antonia? It's indecent."

"I was hot and a little dizzy," she said.

"Cover yourself and then come help me with my reading."

"I'm not feeling up to it tonight."

The clergyman was pulled up short. He was tamping down some serious anger. "Antonia. Are you a child? We have work to do."

Antonia found Charlie's limp penis and began to pull it gently while she stared at her husband. Charlie placed one arm around her, a hand to her left breast.

Antonia closed her eyes and sighed.

"Antonia, what in the name of all that's good are you doing?"

"Nothing, Dear. Sleepy."

She had worked Charlie's cock up into a fine erection. She smiled. She found the little moist pearl on its tip and played with it, oiling the head so she could gently palpate it.

The preacher watched his wife's hands doing things in the air which seemed lewd. Perhaps she was touched, or possessed.

"What—what are you doing? Get up and get dressed."

He spun and was gone, shutting the door as if he could not stand to look upon his unclothed wife another instant. Antonia smiled beatifically and found Charlie's cheek with her palm. They kissed, spooning.

"Charlie, you're so hard again. Is that usual?"

"I left usual behind long ago, Dear Antonia."

"Here," Antonia said, working her ass up against Charlie and moving until he was inside her again.

"Oh, God," Charlie said. Then, "Sorry."

"Do not be sorry. God is here with us. And—Sweet Jesus!" Antonia was coming again.

Rev. Wilkins opened the door again just as Charlie was spilling his seed inside Antonia. Antonia's face was screwed up into a paroxysm of pleasure. She was about to come again, too.

Rev. Wilkins stood and watched his naked wife writhing on the bed in obvious ecstasy. He opened his mouth to speak but nothing came out. His wife's legs were wide open. In the middle of the day. On his bed. And she was—she was—he had no words for it. He left the small room, again closing the door.

After a while the lovers fell asleep in each other's arms.

One morning, Charlie, after using the bathroom, returned to the bedroom and found Antonia kneeling by the bed, praying, her hands tented like a child's. Charlie watched and waited until she opened her eyes and looked around.

"Charlie, are you here?" she asked.

"Do you often pray on your knees?" Charlie approached her and knelt beside her.

"I do, Charlie. Kneeling shows humility."

"I understand."

"Do you? You seem a spiritual man. Were you raised in the church?"

"No. Neither of my parents went but my sister was saved in high school."

"Did you believe her then?"

"I believed that she believed."

"Yes, that's how it is. That's how we understand each other. No one can touch another person's spirituality. It runs too deep. Its salvific effect is not to be underestimated."

Charlie thought about this for a while. Now the lovers were on the unmade bed in each other's arms.

"I think before my invisibility I was less spiritual. When something this—*paranormal*—happens, it tends to make one sensitive to what's unseen. Does that make sense?"

"Perfect sense, Charlie. Perhaps I sense your spirituality because you seem pure essence without your body."

"That's an interesting take. I'll have to chew on that."

"Tell me about how you became invisible."

"It's a long story, Antonia. I still have a hard time believing it myself."

"Tell me, Charlie. Tell me everything."

And Charlie did. Afterwards they made love again and then Antonia fixed them some eggs and toast. She could hear her husband in the yard chopping wood. The sound comforted her. There was a naturalness that surrounded her and made her peaceful. And she prayed some more while Charlie ate in bed.

"Reverend Clark Wilkins. Antonia Wilkins," Charlie said.

It was four days later and the lovers were in the master bedroom where they had both settled for the duration. It was shortly after dinner. Clark was in his room dealing with a parishioner who had been picked up by the police for having relations with one of his sheep. Reverend Wilkins rarely came into what used to be his bedroom. He kept finding Antonia naked on the bed and, rather than continue to be disconcerted by this new perverse strain in his wife, he decided to leave her alone. She still did her churchly duties, though with an abstracted air.

"Why are you saying our names, Charlie Cain?"

"I don't know. I still feel I must be dreaming."

"If this is a dream I shall never wake up."

"How long? How long can we go on like this?"

Charlie was walking a finger down the length of Antonia's bare side.

"I cannot divorce, Charlie. I'm sorry. Marriage is a sacrament. I stood in front of God and the congregation and vowed till death do us part. I still believe this binds me to him no matter how I feel about him personally. Do you understand?"

"No, that's not what I meant. I mean—well, we are deceiving your husband. Surely, he will, at some point, recognize another man's presence. I am eating his food…as well as his wife."

Antonia tittered. "Charlie Cain. I think until the day comes when he is sure of your presence I will love you as hard as I am able and I will keep my love for you true and holy and I will respect you and us and I will always, always want you."

Charlie was impressed by this speech.

"I cannot imagine you leaving," Antonia said. "Perhaps I am foolish and unworldly."

"I cannot imagine it either, Antonia. I love you."

"I love you, Charlie Cain. For always."

Once, on a temperate fall day, Charlie accompanied Antonia on her trip to town for groceries and other supplies. He sat close to her on the sofa-sized Buick front seat, resting his hand on her thigh. She reached her hand out and found his penis where it lay across his thigh like a sock fresh from the laundry.

"I like how that's always available," she tittered.

"You're changing my gears," Charlie said as he stiffened.

Antonia laughed so hard she had to let go of Charlie's pizzle.

In town they puttered around the Main Street, looking for nothing in particular, holding hands, as Antonia greeted parishioners, her husband's flock. They spent about an hour doing this when Antonia whispered, "I guess we should buy food now and get back. I have to cook Clark's dinner. And yours, of course."

Charlie kissed her cheek, stumbling slightly and almost stepping on a woman seated against the wall of the First National Bank. She was dressed in shabby but colorful raiment and she had a sign that said, *Astrological and Other Signs Read and Interpreted*. Next to her a small boy-child, three or four, danced with a tambourine. Gypsies, Charlie thought.

Antonia dug a few dollars out of her purse and put them in the tambourine.

"Thank you, bless you, do you want a reading?" the woman said.

"No, thank you," Antonia said. "That was for the dance." And she smiled sweetly at the child.

Charlie was standing stock still as if mesmerized. That voice. Now, he recognized the woman. It was Patience, his beloved Patience, now reduced to begging. And the boy—the boy—*was perhaps his son.*

"Please a little more," Charlie whispered to Antonia.

She looked queer for a moment and then put a ten-dollar bill in the child's percussion instrument. The child seemed to be looking at Charlie, as did his mother.

"You have a beautiful aura," Patience said to Antonia, her gaze taking in the slim parson's wife and her ethereal companion.

As they walked away Charlie's silence was like a vaporous cavity. There were demons there. Antonia, sensing some change in Charlie's emotional weather, put her arm around his back and held him closer.

And so, the past is never past. Charlie, though unseeable, still wore the chains he forged in life. Even if disappeared your life forms a tail. It was a small, hard seed, dark as sin, Charlie carried within him for the rest of his days. All he knew to do was keep loving, and this he vowed to do.

*T*he lovers stayed together enjoying what would become a life-long honeymoon. They learned to steer clear of Clark's attention, which was not hard. If the good clergyman was distant toward his wife before, he was now completely absent. He could not know that she had an invisible lover but he knew her newfound joy had nothing to do with him.

And Charlie stayed invisible for the rest of his life. Charlie told her everything, starting with his first visit to the mysterious Dr. Raphael. Sometimes the lovers showered together so Antonia could see a watery, wavering view of her paramour but, over time, she had memorized every inch of him the way the blind do. She liked making love with an invisible man. She loved his invisible hands and his invisible cock and invisible balls and the way his invisible buttocks tensed when he came. Sometimes she liked to suck him and jerk him off so she could see the clear gelatinous plume of his orgasm. She wanted to be by his side, and in bed with him, at all times. She still, however, performed all the duties of the church. It was safe and, for some reason, she felt less guilty about it because he was impalpable. She also thought it was as sexy as hell.

We can now sense the curtain is closing. Charlie's story, like many stories, doesn't end here. Perhaps it rebegins. We thank you for your attention. And the lovers, before turning out the light every night, spoke this way:

"I love you, Charlie Cain," Antonia said.

And Charlie Cain, the invisible man, always answered, "Antonia, I love you, too."

Photo: Cheryl Mesler

COREY MESLER has been published in numerous anthologies and journals including *Poetry, Gargoyle, Five Points, Good Poems American Places,* and *New Stories from the South.* He has published nine novels, four short story collections, six full-length poetry collections, and a dozen chapbooks. His novel, *Memphis Movie*, attracted kind words from Ann Beattie, Peter Coyote, and William Hjorstberg, among others. He's been nominated for the Pushcart many times, and three of his poems were chosen for Garrison Keillor's *Writer's Almanac.* He also wrote the screenplay for *We Go On*, which won The Memphis Film Prize in 2017. With his wife he runs a 146 year-old bookstore in Memphis. He can be found at https://coreymesler.wordpress.com.